To Dale,

Another
winter!

MW00909873

Norilsk

Norilsk

A TALE OF SUSPENSE
IN THE TIME OF THE OLIGARCHS

SUSAN GOLD

Full Court Press
Englewood Cliffs, New Jersey

First Edition

Copyright © 2013 by Susan Gold

Published in the United States of America
by Full Court Press, 601 Palisade Avenue
Englewood Cliffs, NJ 07632

This book is a work of fiction. Any reference to historical
events, real people, or real locales is to be understood in that
context. Any historical or geographical mistakes are the author's.

ISBN 978-1-938812-22-4
Library of Congress Control No. 2013950532

Editing and Book Design by Barry Sheinkopf for Bookshapers
(www.bookshapers.com)
Cover art from the author's collection
Author photo by Barry Sheinkopf
Colophon by Liz Sedlack

FOR LIZA AND JONATHAN
And their journeys

ACKNOWLEDGMENTS

Only robbers and gypsies believe that, as Søren Kierkegaard put it, one must never return to a place one has once been. I have, and I am indebted to many friends and colleagues who encouraged me to write about my time in Russia, where I worked for many years.

It does indeed fascinate and challenge; and my task here has been to craft a work of fiction out of a vast historical collage that has, for me, been infused with deep nostalgia for the time I spent there.

First and foremost among those friends and colleagues, I want to thank Barry Sheinkopf and Bookshapers.com for steadfast editorial assistance and guidance. My gratitude and appreciation also go to my dear friend and colleague Alex Motyl for his encouragement, invaluable editorial help, and perfect transliterations.

And last but not least, many thanks to Hildy Rubin for her editorial assistance and computer work to bring this endeavor to a conclusion.

"The dogs bark, but the caravan moves on."
—*Arab proverb*

The attempted coup was over, the summer heat was intense as Boris Yeltsin, with a heavy and uncomfortable bulletproof vest under his suit, climbed onto a tank in front of the Moscow White House—the Russian parliament building—and the empire fell.

The air smelled of cautious optimism. Days after the stand-off, Russian troops withdrew from the White House. Four tanks were left abandoned on the grounds, garlanded with flowers and Russian tricolor flags. In what seemed like another lifetime but had occurred only within a few days after the demonstration, armfuls of flowers had been laid on the street to cover a few dried bloodstains. The army was thrilled that the building, and Russia, had survived the chaos and violence. Seventy years of communism had been de facto de-legitimized by Yeltsin and two other leaders of big Slavic republics at a hunting lodge in Byelorussia in the fall of the same year.

What had caused the collapse? Not only the rigidity of the command economy, but something more prosaic—a cyclical downturn in global oil prices and an unsustainably large trade deficit in the Soviet Union driven by falling oil revenues from crude, its principal export commodity.

On Christmas Eve 1991, Mikhail Gorbachev had signed his resignation papers, and at midnight of the New Year the Soviet flag atop the Kremlin had been lowered for the last time and, in its stead, after an absence of seventy-four years, the Russian tricolor had been risen. The Union of Soviet Socialist Republics was no more. A bloodless revolution had taken place in Russia! Yeltsin, with the help of Western consultants, was ready for Russia's new democracy.

It was an indisputably defining moment of the twentieth cen-

tury, the end of a Utopian experiment of mind-boggling ambition that, in the name of creating a perfect society, had ended up butchering millions of people and repressing the rest—along with half of Europe.

I

MOSCOW

TWO YEARS LATER, ON JANUARY 10, 1993, Susanna Thompson was buckled in as the Delta 747 rapidly dropped altitude. She was happy to see snow-covered, dirty, gas-streaked Russia rolling beneath the airplane's wings. At fifty-three, she was still a strikingly attractive woman: pale skin, finely chiseled features, liquid green eyes, a charming figure. The black hair she usually allowed to fall loosely around her shoulders was casually gathered with a hair clip for comfort.

By the time the flight from New York touched down in Sheremetyevo, it was almost noon. She was happy to leave the crowded but silent shuttle, set foot in the dingy airport, and trudge to the passport check arrivals line.

Sheremetyevo the airport, always grim, was shrouded in semi-darkness, as if someone had forgotten to turn the light switches to full power. After a lengthy, arduous, and predictable wait that the regulars somehow saw as the price for setting foot in Mother Russia, a young, beefy, very serious official stared at her, glared at her multiple-entry visa and passport through the computer, and as she smiled, his eyes x-rayed her face; he grunted and shoved the documents back across without a word.

Susanna entered Russia proper. Her legs felt shaky as she headed to the baggage carousel to wait for her suitcases. As always, there was a shortage of carts, and arriving passengers moved like penguins with luggage dangling from both hands. The airport was crowded. At another carousel stood *chelnoki*, Russian cargo mules, smart members of the proletariat miraculously transformed into capitalist entrepreneurs—traders who made shopping trips regularly, buying goods abroad with all the savings they could muster, and returning after a few days in the hope of selling long-coveted items from distant lands of plenty. These professional smugglers, with a passport to new riches, were almost invisible under mountains of boxes containing children's bicycles, Japanese stereos, video recorders, and discount computers, confident the right bribe, to the correct pair of hands, would persuade bored customs officials that these goods were for personal use only.

Efficiency and productivity are not Russian concepts. Two hours later, Susanna had finally made it to the long queue of baggage control where, if she strained and stood on tiptoe, she could see groups of Russians with signs and flowers waving to the passengers on the other side of the opaque glass partition. She immediately spotted Volodya, a former law student who had dropped his classes soon after Russia's new market revolution. With the right connections, a little bit of luck, and elbow grease, he could make his own fortune. He was also Susanna's driver and gofer, and she noticed him clutching a bouquet of wilted flowers, though, as much as she craned her neck, she could not see Boris, who was always at the airport to greet her.

Finally, the customs inspector grimaced and handed back her documents, and she hurried through the exit.

She and Volodya had already exchanged three warm kisses on both cheeks, and cautious hugs, when she recognized Vera, Boris's ex-wife, shuffling nervously nearby. Startled and disarmed, Susanna greeted her cautiously, with a reserved gaze. Something was wrong. After many long hours of travel, her spine had straightened. "What's she doing here?" she whispered, "and where is Boris? He telephoned a few days ago, saying he was in St. Petersburg on business, but that he'd be waiting here when I arrived."

Volodya shrugged. "I don't know . . . today, the flight arrives much later than normal. Perhaps he is detained on other business. Don't worry, welcome! Here, all is *normalno*."

Vera, eyes wet, began sniffing. "The less you know," she said without looking at Susanna, "the longer you live." Volodya began guiding the baggage cart toward the parking lot, where the office Lada was parked.

Vera was in a hurry to leave. She glanced around and whispered to Susanna, "I must go now, but very soon, you must visit us in Polina's dacha. Uncle Fima will be there as well. He cannot wait to see you, especially now, Susanna. Peredelkino is beautiful in winter. Remember how you used to go, how you say, cross-country with Boris. We can do the same," she whispered, looking away. "We have good heat, and the roads are cleared after every snow." Her voice was controlled, halting; Susanna was beginning to understand that something had happened to Boris, and she was beginning to feel anxious.

A frozen, quiet day was ending in Moscow. A light snow

was falling, and even the chemical haze, and the steam rising from coal-fired central heating furnaces, seemed agreeable as shapeless neighborhoods with gray apartment buildings suddenly erupted from ill-kempt, snowy lots.

The blocks of flats continued for at least another ten minutes, interrupted only by an overused power station or an Orwellian skyline of factory smokestacks barely visible within the billowing clouds of their own emissions.

Outside, snow was still falling, now damp, unrelenting, whirling in all directions at once.

The highway into town was wide and rough: four lanes in each direction, more treacherously pitted with dips and potholes than she remembered.

The car passed the World War II monument celebrating the victorious Russian battle for the capital and, a little further down the road, the arch commemorating Napoleon's entrance into the burned-out city a century earlier.

It was already dusk in the great *stolitsa*. Moscow defies measurement and loathes explanation or definition.

The city hangs suspended in all its contradictions—halfway between day and night, east and west, past and future, picturesque and squalid, sane and mad, good and evil.

Regardless of how often she had made the trip from New York, she was very tired, jet-lagged, and increasingly frantic as the heavy door of the apartment house shut with a muted bang and they were pushed into the lobby. The concierge, busily knitting, barely looked up from her table, greeted Susanna, and peered at the suitcases. In the distance, the iron door of the elevator rumbled.

Susanna and Volodya were barely out on the third floor when the calm ex-Bolshoi ballerina Natalya, already waiting in the hall, cheerfully opened the well-padded door and welcomed her with enthusiastic kisses. The apartment had everything Susanna needed. A bedroom with a small annex that Susanna could use as a study, a large living room, a kitchen, and a lilac bathroom hung with fresh orange towels.

Natalya directed Volodya to the bedroom with the luggage and dramatically seized Susanna for yet another tour of the place. "*Evromont* here," Natalya said. "All appliances, Western material and Turkish labor," she added, as they entered the spic-and-span kitchen where three blue-enamel Polish pots shone on the counter and a new Siemens refrigerator stood in a corner, and passed the vestibule of glassed-in book cabinets and bibelots before turning to the airy bedroom, furnished in ersatz Italian provincial 1930s—a large half-emptied armoire, a comfortable bed covered by a slippery rose satin embroidered bedspread and pillows, night stands with small, languorous cherub statues, and light bulbs pinched by raspberry glass globes. In fact the bedroom was decorated in two tones—rich mahogany, and the luscious natural colors of summer berries. The ballerina sketches on the wall were all poses of Natalia— in a true Petipa-like ballet wonderland set; alas, a large television on an industrial chrome stand seemed to confront the beautiful bedroom like an alien creature.

In the large living room lay a raspberry divan and an imposing armchair; another small brown velvet settee and smaller chairs surrounded a dining room table where the exhausted and disoriented traveler finally settled. She was looking at the burled-wood German cuckoo clock on the wall, ticking in rhythm with her migraine.

"You like the clock? Maybe it ticks too loud. Very antique, you know. My father brought from Germany after Great Patriotic War."

Susanna nodded. The noisy clock set off her internal alarm about Boris's absence at the airport—and no calls or messages. Besides, as always, it would take her six days to get over the jet lag, a day for each hour of time change, and she was in no mood for Natalya's stories. They sat down for evening tea and still another briefing on the apartment, politics, and gossip of the Bolshoi. Although Susanna loved the ballet, she could barely focus on her landlady's excitement over local gossip and the fifteen hundred cash, in dollars, for the monthly rent.

Natalya, at last realizing the timing for small talk was bad, quickly gathered the money into the narrow purse strung like a talisman around her neck, carried the used tea service into the kitchen, checked the bathroom again, started the bath water, returned to the table, and officially complained in a whining voice, "I've waited for you for you such a long time, *moya sladkaya*. I want to tell you the latest ballet gossip and see ballet performances with you. As you know, I still get the best parterre seats—and I hope you are happy in apartment. It is the best one in building. But you don't look well, *lastochka*. What's the matter? A headache? The barometric pressure in Moscow has dropped today and is responsible for migraines and bad moods."

She dragged Susanna to the door and proceeded to drill her again in the kinks and peculiarities of the five locks before handing her the keys. She also managed to sneer at the next-door neighbor, who had been waiting jealously for Susanna in order to get in on the welcoming action and perhaps also find another expatriate tenant for her apartment. "Volodya and I will leave now. We see you tomorrow. Welcome to Moscow! Please rest and sleep. Remember, the most important thing for a beautiful woman is good sleep!"

Susanna was at loose ends. She felt sick, perspiring as she was from the aggressive heat in the apartment and still very disturbed over Boris's disappearance. The building was a prodigy of Moscow central heating. She opened the little square *fortochka* in the tall double-glass panel for air, dragged her pajamas from the suitcase, and got into bed.

But even with bones and muscles aching, Susanna tossed and turned, and sleep wouldn't come. Where were Boris and Tyotya Polina? Old anxieties about people disappearing in *Aktions* began to emerge, evoking horrors of the "war against the Jews."

Susanna lost her childhood from the age of five, when Nazi boots, German shepherds, Ukrainian collaborators and *Einsatztruppen* stormed towns and villages to make the country *Judenrein*—forcing Jews to dig their own graves before killing them. Her brother and her entire extended family were murdered in the killing fields and gas chambers of Eastern Poland. Only the kindnesses of strangers, *sudba*, and destiny helped Susanna and her parents survive in a bunker under a barn for two years.

She forced herself to stop thinking about her past by picturing Boris's apartment on Tverskaya clearly: Five large rooms, one of the most spacious places in Moscow, and her favorite flat—a harp and grand piano, cabinets in dark wood displaying Meissen china, fine bronze statuary, porcelains and paintings, all inherited by Boris and Polina from his famous father, a former deputy minister of trade during the NEP period. Boris often joked about how his father's friendship and business deals with Armand Hammer had produced one of the best private art collections of the avant-garde in Moscow. Like father, like son—Boris was a doctor, but Russian art was his foremost interest.

Susanna had often spent time relaxing there, listening to the silence of the old paintings, in love with Aivazovsky's *Sunset*, and especially coveting the modernist Boris Dmitrievich Grigoriev's *Sailors at a Café*: both paintings supposedly Boris's ticket out of Russia.

It was after midnight when she finally decided to telephone Boris's apartment. The line wasn't working. As was her executive style in Moscow, telephone numbers of the building's office were written next to personal information. She rang Agafya, the housekeeper, married to the caretaker, a brother of the concierge of the apartment house, all living somewhere in the building's nether regions. Every Soviet leader since Stalin had used janitors as secret police informers. Sly old women denounced their neighbors or pointed out apartments that housed enemies of the people.

Susanna was circumspect and apologetic about the late-night phone call. "Oh, it's you, Miss Susanna. The American is back in Moscow. It's very late! Why are you calling when we are all asleep?" Agafya was trying to seem indignant but managed only to sound nervous. In an annoyed monotone and sleepy voice she told Susanna that lately there had been a lot of explosions and fires in Moscow. "Newspapers report that guerrillas from Chechnya are blowing up our buildings! But there aren't any here." Only some faulty wiring had caused a small electrical fire in Boris's apartment, and she hadn't seen him for a few days either. Tyotya Polina had left with her sister for arthritis treatments in the Tall Pines Sanitarium. "You know the one. The special local sanitarium where all the rooms have German china in imported cabinets with crystal glasses and refrigerators. Where they have armed guards! It was one of Stalin's favorites. I think you have been there." Awake enough to describe all details of the sanitarium, she barked, "Don't worry yourself. I am sure all is *normalno.*"

Senseless to go to the apartment. Agafya had a Soviet brain, programmed not to disclose information—and maybe she really didn't know.

A painful ripple ran down Susanna's spine, and she shivered. What business in St.Petersburg? Why the fire? Where is everybody? I must try to get to the bottom of this. She dialed Lyova Kartsev's number—her longtime KGB friend, good-looking, attractive, and her facilitator when dealing with local bureaucratic hassles. His wife picked up the phone, perfunctorily announced that he was on a *komandirovka* for his new security business, would only return the following week, and hung up, annoyed.

Two a.m. was a world to itself, an hour both early and late. Fear was beginning to clutch Susanna. Afraid of losing Boris, she stuffed her head under the pillow and tried to rest.

Near dawn, she fell into a deep sleep, but awoke abruptly when the alarm rang. What's happening here? she asked herself again. She needed his smile and reassuring voice, his stroking hand in the car, a quiet dinner and warm conversation with him in the Dom Kino club, and his self-assured lovemaking.

A bloodless revolution. History was changing before her eyes, and in a land of icons, Boris Yeltsin was the newest. But on a cold winter day, despite the "democratic coup," all was supposed to be *normalno* and stable in Moscow. On the plane, she had seen herself bundled in her Chinese quilted coat, happily walking through the cleared paths of the park, with new glistening snow festooning the winding branches, and inhaling the brisk, clean winter air. She had been less ambivalent, happier than usual, almost enthusiastic about returning to Moscow in such politically heady times. The exotic life of the expatriate—like the new apartment she had rented just outside Moscow's Garden Ring on her last trip, a Stalin-Gothic skyscraper that expressed not architectural style, but a form of worship of Stalin. There were seven of them—one for each part of town—the gray, brooding skyscrapers, built for his *nomenclatura* and constructed by German World War II prisoners, with lofty and ominous balconied windows, elegant ceilings, and lustrous parquet floors. The apartment Susanna had rented in the Kiyvskaya District had become a commodity asset in the new market economy for ballerina Natalya Zorina, who had moved in with her parents. The place was west of the river, part of the Hotel Ukraina complex, and faced a thick green park near posh Kalininsky Prospekt, a few blocks from the White House, the Russian parliament building, where Yeltsin had dissolved the legislature after the siege and the fighting between his supporters and those of and the Supreme Soviet had taken place.

Just a short walk across the park, near the Kiev Station and outdoor market, stood the Radisson-Slavyanskaya Hotel: the company's new offices on the twelfth floor shared space with other multinational firms. Because of the international cachet, the hotel was swell and tony. Two drinks at the bar robbed a customer of twenty-four dollars; pizza and beer in the lobby café cost seventy-five for two; and the lower-floor mezzanine was a heady mix of boutiques—Versace, Galliano, Gucci, Prada, Pink, and Cerrutti—a shopping mall for the fashion-conscious new Russians.

She had personally arranged, vetted, and engineered the new office, apartment, and staff just a few weeks before being promoted to Vice President, Non-Ferrous Metal Operations for Russia by her multinational, Global Metals Group, GMG—the newest office of the world's second largest trading house in global commodities. Valya, a young teacher of English, trained at the Institute for Foreign Languages at MGU (Philology Department, Moscow State University), had been thrilled to be hired as secretary with a salary of two hundred dollars a month, and Sasha, a wizard Moscow *komputershchik*, a new success in the new Russia, had been delighted to work for a foreign firm for the salary of one hundred and fifty dollars a month. The pair were the information technology staff for GMG while Susanna de facto headed their Moscow trading house in global commodities. GMG's operating income of US$ 2.55 billion equaled the GNP of Guatemala, and it had, as its annual report proclaimed, "Ninety thousand people, exploring and identifying new distribution avenues for industrial metals, constructing energy lifelines in thirty-five countries around the world, intensifying the company's global market presence, and stretching gold bullion and platinum group metals products and service across geographic lines."

But where was Boris? As Susanna's psychiatrist sometimes said, shit happened—frightful shit again, for Susanna and Boris this time. Can lightning strike three times?

She called Valya in the morning and told her not to expect her, as she had to leave town immediately for an important business project waiting for her in Kalinin. She would call soon with her new schedule. No question asked, no explanations necessary: in Russia nothing is precise, so she had time. She couldn't be bothered figuring out the new electric coffee pot Natalya had bought for the kitchen, boiled some water for tea, added sugar for energy, and called Volodya to drive her quickly to Tyotya Polina and Boris's dacha.

2

PEREDELKINO

FALLING SNOW, BRILLIANT SKY, AND A wide but rough
highway out of the city, two lanes in each direction,
treacherously pitted with dips and potholes: Volodya
swayed to the left, glided between the hollows, turned off
abruptly at an outdoor market to buy a bunch of pirated CDs,
and continued to Peredelkino.

Once the congested heart of Moscow had released them,
he drove recklessly, cutting across lanes, passing grimy boulevards, peeling mansions, huge apartment complexes, Brezh-
nev-era concrete tenements with laundry hanging stiff on
cheerless, unkempt balconies, many dotted with satellite
dishes—the marker of new wealth.

Moscow slid back faster, and the spaces between buildings
widened. Birch forests flickered past the window as the car

raced along. A cold wind drove a mosaic of gunmetal clouds before it. Volodya took many turns on unpaved roads, passing dilapidated wooden houses with old tin roofs, eaves laden with combs of icicles, crooked fangs five feet long, chimneys with plumes of smoke, and whimsical old hand-carved wooden window frames with shorter icicles firmly attached.

"Susanna, were you able to find out why Boris didn't show up at Sheremetyevo yesterday?"

"He might have been detained in *Piter* on his art business. I'm sure Vera will know."

"Yes." Volodya shrugged. "Normal business there."

"Tell me, Volodya, what have you been up to since I left, and how are your law studies? Did you register again in the university?"

Volodya grunted then laughed. "This is not the time for education. I will have plenty of time for university and law school after I make money. But I am taking one correspondence course in business management. All of Russia is in wholesale plunder. Business, and the almighty dollar, are now my career."

She wanted to interrupt but realized that he needed to go on. "So how are you spending your time?"

"Everywhere you turn, there is money to be made. I now have my own *business*—how you say?—*partner* in car transportation and delivery. It's really my father's, but I am a full partner. You know, before Yeltsin, he was an important man in government, a deputy minister of transportation. He has the old connections and is important again. The company has been privatized. We have thirty people working for us in our offices in Sheremetyevo. My father has a young new wife, and maybe a younger mistress, two small children, a new dog, a dacha in Dimitrievo where the family lives, a smaller house for his domestic and security staff. I work with him, of course.

My father gets registration and customs documents for cars from Poland and Europe. Since you left, I have already made five trips to Lviv, and drive great cars across border to Russia. I have partners in a garage for mechanical work, and our firm sells Mercedeses, Citroens, Cadillacs, and anything else important people want to buy. We also sell some Benzes to Uncle Fima, who is well connected to members of the Siberian Duma. He is always in need for good cars for his political friends—a *very* long wait for new Benzes in Moscow now. A great contact, Uncle Fima is! *Bozhe moy!* Nobody remembers the first man who walked on the moon," Volodya explained, "but everybody knows Uncle Fima—we have a thousand schemes, and a million connections!"

"But, Volodya, don't you understand this is all terribly *illegal*?" Susanna exclaimed. "You cannot work for GMG and do mafia business at the same time! Racketeering is against American compliance laws!"

Volodya suddenly became sullen, irritable; his mouth twisted into a tight sneer. He took a deep breath, zooming ahead with his typical ferocity. "But this is *Russia*. Political power goes together with economic advantage. Everything has changed, but the law has remained the same. All business is legal now. That is why I will return to studying law—everything is up for grabs: cars, weapons, trucking, prostitution, gambling, banking, currency speculation, arbitrage, everything. This is a bad investment climate for foreigners, but it offers great business deals for *us*!" Susanna liked Volodya, and suddenly felt fearful that she would have to dismiss him. Her losses in Russia were mounting.

"The country is changing day by day. Cash is the key. Remember Karl Marx: We have the 'primitive accumulation of capital.' Now is the time to strike!"

"Oh, for God's sake, Volodya—perestroika, or how the

Russians say, *perestrelka*, and democracy, have ruined my business here. The financial system has also collapsed. Yeltsin is just another corrupt, good-natured drunk."

"That suits us fine. No more Soviet barbaric rule. Yeltsin climbed onto a tank, and now we have our flag back and are building our 'dermokratia' with cradle-to-grave corruption! Corruption for the sake of democracy. We steal and think nothing of stealing, because everyone is stealing. Soon we will have Paradise on Earth." He chuckled.

"*Crapokratia* as you call it—but I believe that, after the stealing, Russians will own property and become landlords and administrators, the country will have a real market economy, and democracy will follow."

"Susanna, you are a true romantic and very naïve. Any projects here are a dangerous mistake."

"What are you saying? You know that now I've been *promoted* I must be *productive* for GMG. Corruption is rampant. I must find a way to be successful *without* 'baksheesh,' especially now."

Volodya smirked. He shook his head, hands stiff on the wheel.

"I've spent many years," Susanna explained, "working with Almazyuvelirexport and the nonferrous metals ministry in Moscow. You simply have no understanding of American governance laws."

Volodya smiled sarcastically. "We are creating a real sovereign democracy here *our* way."

"Remember, GMG is one of the top Fortune 500, respected globally. If you remember, last year I was invited to dinner at the Kremlin."

"Of course, I drove you there. When *you* were telling *me* how great Russia is. But times have changed. Fathers and children of 'Arbat' are controlling their own country, *kruto!*

Cool for Russia, don't you think?"

"Volodya. We *can't* do business the Russian way. Our multinational requires collateral, contracts, banking supervision, government guarantees. I have to make *that* work here."

She wanted to discuss Yeltsin, and politics, but he discouraged her. Gorbachev's ideals were in the past.

"There's not much you can do now. You are a goddess from the promised land of the almighty dollar, but our people will outmaneuver you at every step. No room for independent business, and a foreign business *cannot* survive here. To do business, you need a powerful Russian partner—or support of state authorities. One man's profit is another man's loss. Susanna, don't forget—we have *never* trusted foreigners."

"Then how can I survive? My colleagues from Almaz have no business for us. They've opened their own marketing office in Connecticut. Norilskmetal must have many tenders from the Finns, Belgians, and the English."

"Well Susanna, you know that Kulichkov is back in Norilsk, his native land—a son of a political prisoner in the gulag. Remember his stories about the Arctic?"

"How can I forget? I learned my *dirty* Russian *slang* from him. I wined and dined all of Almaz with performances, drinks, dinners, discussions, and I'm still sitting on a very thick file of business memoranda filled with letters of intent, proposals, protocol agreements for further business development with Norilsk." She was out of breath. "I am in a straitjacket now!—not permitted to work with Almaz! Imagine, after all these years!

"I am sure Kulichkov is sitting on a thick *papka* from our company filled with letters of intent, proposals, annual reports . . . I have become a writer of memoranda! All this winding and dining—and nothing came of it."

"You know your friend Kulichkov has been demoted to

commercial director. Make friends with the new boss from Georgia, George Bablidze—now very important chief in Norilsk."

"What you are saying is not helping me."

"It's only going to get worse. Moral myopia is bad for you and other investors—a dangerous mistake. But you have some choices. Enjoy the cultural events, buy more antiques—and get out. Or go to bed with your Russian friends to sort out your business agenda. If the ice is thin, you must walk fast. Try to get to Bablidze as quickly as you can."

"Yes, I know." An awkward silence followed.

"What about Uncle Fima, Boris's well connected relative?" Volodya suggested. "He can help. We just shipped a Swedish Volvo from Ukraine to Krasnoyarsk—almost brand new, a gift from uncle Fima to Mr. Borisov, member of the lower Duma from Siberia. Fima travels there and overseas, you know, under the *krysha* of friendly politicians. His protection, you know. My father dines in elegant Moscow restaurants and has seen him with very important people."

For a winter day the weather was colder than usual, and Volodya drove with the heater rattling and blasting. Susanna looked sadly at the passing countryside. The horizon opened up like a fan where the land was flat and the road stretched along meadows and bogs. A dirt road branched off to a handful of cottages and a tilted Easter cake of a church framed by birches. She asked. "How is my friend, Alexander Zhukov?"

"A very rich man now. President of Omega Bank. He calls it a pocket bank, but Omega has many branches in *off shornaya zonas*. Not many foreign investors now—Zhukov will be happy to move dollars from the east. Uncle Fima also works with Omega Bank for money transfers to charities and cultural institutions he supports. But I would be careful there—Fima may be a dangerous mistake." Volodya joked salaciously.

She looked away from Volodya. "I'm not sure I under-stand. What do you know about this?"

"He is new to the field of *prichvatizatzia* . . . but very ex-perienced in business—part of the criminal underworld."

Susanna nodded, and again, there was silence. She tried to stay focused on the Russian countryside—beautiful and comfortably familiar, dotted with pine trees and gleaming bare white birch trunks. The snow had become heavy on the groined branches of the firs, brilliant with the sunshine. Oc-casionally a breeze lifted the snow from the trees and blew it sparkling into the air.

"So you have some choices. *Kruto*! 'Go to bed' with your associates and friends, active in our new Russia, and have your company's investments go down a black hole, or have a good time. Enjoy the cultural events, buy more antiques—and get out."

Susanna was not discouraged. "I'll try to involve Zhukov and his bank, the American State Department, and GMG's Russian-American bank in Moscow. You know my friend, Mr. Philip Dunlop? Cooperation with Russia is part of for-eign policy. Our State Department is encouraging the devel-opment of democratic principles here, and he'll help."

"*Kruto*," Volodya agreed. "Business continues *normalno*. We Russians love your academics, especially from Harvard! American consultants do their own stealing while advising on privatization!"

Soon they reached a gated cluster of well-appointed houses belonging to the privileged and drove through a lovely birch forest to Polina's dacha. The sun beamed brilliantly in the deep unbroken blue of the northern sky. Some of the country houses in the neighborhood, now smothered by deep snow, were being morphed into fortified English *kottedzhes*, and barricaded with wooden planks and coiled razor wire.

A neighbor's dog started barking furiously at the car. "The same ugly, vicious creature is still here. I promise I will poison him one day," Volodya sneered maliciously.

"Thanks for the trip, Volodya. I'll call you tomorrow about my Moscow schedule, and when I need to get back. *Poka!*" In a moment, Susanna was out of the car.

She was already walking down the winding path when she heard Vera and Polina's voices on the other side of the enclosure. They were pushing open the tall wooden fence gate as Susanna made her way in. Polina Isakovna waddled toward her, crying, her two gold front teeth glinting in the sun.

"Susanna, my wise and golden one, it's finally you. We have been waiting for you all night. We knew you would come right away. We are gifted by God with an angel from heaven. You are a holy person," she exclaimed.

They hung their heavy coats in the vestibule and exchanged boots for slippers.

"Welcome! Please come in. It's very warm here now. Boris installed a new heating system last fall." Susanna stood between the door of the hallway and the long and narrow living room, cluttered with furniture. She felt like an intruder. Her eyes explored everything anew. The old Biedermeier furniture, the piano, always out of tune, a grandfather clock that never worked, the pictures, the glassed book cabinets. Images of Boris resting on the old gray sofa stored away in her mind reminded Susanna that the room was only a walkway to the veranda overgrown with honeysuckle in summer. She stopped at the narrow windows and looked out at the sky which had turned slate gray. Vera turned on a floor lamp, and pushed Susanna gently forward, holding her by the shoulder. "You won't recognize the place. Besides the heat, a new European kitchen!"

"Please, Vera Sergeyevna, open Boris's good Armenian cognac for our angel guest. For lunch, I prepared your favorite dumplings, and the fish soup you love, *ukha*, my dear and wise Susanna." Despair, death, and terror radiated from the older woman's clouded eyes. Savory and wonderfully subtle aromas wafted as Polina shuffled unsteadily back to the kitchen, while Vera rummaged around in a dusty cupboard for the cognac bottle and glasses. Finally finding them, she wiped them carefully with a cloth. Susanna saw them shining in the glow of the lamp as Vera filled the glasses. Then she pushed herself up against the back overstuffed sofa, closed her eyes, and patted for a spot for Susanna.

"We are happy to see you here, finally! Good things happen together! Uncle Fima is in Peredelkino today, and will join us for lunch. He has become a well-known philanthropist, supporting the arts, especially the ballet school in the culture palace in Norilsk and one in Krasnoyarsk."

"Krasnoyarsk, Taymir peninsula? How can that be, Vera?"

"Well, I am surprised as well. I never trusted his reputation. A man with no education, criminal records with the Soviets, a known thief. He sells foreign cars to Duma members at big discounts, and they support projects Fima bankrolls in Siberia and above the Arctic. Be careful, Susanna!"

"How can you be certain?"

"Huge endowments and bribes for their Ministry of Culture to support the Norilsk Ballet School. Many of their best dancers are chosen by the Bolshoi, you know. Rivers of cash flowing through crooked hands."

"Boris's uncle Fima? With family in Odessa? A sentimental and ingenious man. Always the jester and protective of women. Impossible!" Susanna replied.

"Hardly a ladies' man, Susanna! Bent on proving his mettle, he moved to Moscow, and joined a gang specializing in extortion. Well, he is here collecting money from generous friends who owe him favors, dacha owners in Peredelkino—and can't wait to see you and pay his respects."

Susanna felt her lip curl and shook her head. She sank down on the sofa beside Vera, and could feel Vera's sigh through the sofa frame.

Without pause, Vera began. "Boris left by train for a meeting in St. Petersburg with his business partners, Zhora and Sosa. You know them—his old Georgian friends from the chess club at Dom Kino.

They were negotiating important art business in St. Petersburg for their gallery in New York. Also, as you know, Susanna, Boris was the doctor for the Moscow hockey team. Since *perestroika* there is no money for sports or sports medicine, and no state money for athletes, or trips. The team cannot travel to Europe or America; no money for athletes, visas, or plane tickets. The players are abandoning Moscow and leaving for Canada, Minnesota, New Jersey. Even an executive from the NHL was here negotiating with Moscow's hockey manager and Boris to recruit our players."

"I understand." Susanna sighed. "Our Boris was a child of Soviet privilege. He was permitted to travel when Russians were prisoners in their own country. He would tell me that in days of shortages, his family had fresh veal and caviar." She sipped her cognac, crying, and Vera continued.

"Now he needs an income and was always looking for other opportunities—with hockey players, with Zhora and Sosa in the art business for their gallery in New York, as well as with you and GMG metals, and our second revolution *privatizatzia*, voucher privatization."

"This is madness! Boris was a medical doctor, not a businessman or industrialist."

"You know, Gaidar, Nemtsov, Chubais, Kovalyov—the young intellectuals have faith in capitalism and new democracy coming here."

"What do all these people have to do with *Boris*? He was a doctor!"

"Well, Boris loved any opportunity to make money. And you know, doctors know how to keep secrets. He goes to the MICEX, the Russian commodities Bourse, every day. He had a lot of important friends. They trade commodities and raw materials. Bablidze wants to control the majority of shares of Norilsk, and Boris buys vouchers for him and also trades for himself—maybe, how you say, price manipulation?"

Susanna, jarred by Vera's account, suddenly understood that Boris might have died for other reasons.

"Uncle Fima is also active in the Bourse, and your company is known to have big success here." She took another sip and closed her eyes.

"Well, what about St. Petersburg?" Susanna interrupted, already under the quick influence of cognac. "I knew Boris was a man of many interests, and that he knew his art very well, and was active in the art business. He was going to introduce our company to Bablidze but never divulged his own business interests."

"You know poor Boris was a man of many talents and many interests, what you call a Renaissance Man."

Susanna was impatient and anxious. "Vera, please—what exactly *happened* in St. Petersburg?"

"We don't know. He telephoned Polina Isakovna from St. Petersburg to say that, somehow, he'd lost his apartment keys, and to be sure she stayed home and unlocked the doors for him. Tyotya Polina said he was happy as usual, went to the Bourse, then sports clinic to check patients, attended to errands, and made another set of keys. His mood was very good, his appetite for his favorite dishes excellent, and he waited for your arrival from America."

Vera paused for a big gulp and continued in a lower, more unsettled tone, in English, "Then Polina left for few days with sister Bella for arthritis treatments at the sanitarium. When she returned she found a nightmare—*koshmar* in apartment! The beautiful apartment gutted, the satin drapes burnt, Grigoriev and Aivazovsky paintings gone, wallpaper singed and torn, telephone lines cut. Polina's bedroom, how you say, trashed, loose pillows everywhere! An electrical fire in Boris's bedroom!"

"Vera, please—why was he murdered?" Susanna was terrified and wanted the information now.

"Our Boris is no more, and the police are proceeding with the investigation, an inquiry about theft and arson. Boris dead from smoke inhalation, arson, or heart attack. How you say, surely, 'foul play.'"

Susanna rose impatiently. What could be her sense of purpose now? Her body was frozen with fear. She put her hands to her temples and wiped her forehead, covered in beads of cold sweat. "Has anyone been in touch with the police? How is the murder being investigated?"

"Captain Kalugin, from Petrovka, is in charge. But what can we do? How can we go to police? Nothing good ever comes from getting mixed up with the police. We are afraid to speak with Kalugin, afraid of misunderstandings with the precinct. The police do what they always do: nothing. Even Uncle Fima hadn't called them."

"Understood," answered Susanna, remembering this instinctive Russians' fear.

"Many days now, and no news," Vera continued haltingly. "Boris's body has been cremated, but we knew you were coming and waited for you to have a Jewish burial—one Boris would like. Polina Isakovna wants to bury him next to her husband and parents in the Jewish cemetery."

Susanna placed her hand on the sofa arm, as if to steady herself, as a faint breathlessness came over her. Her head spinning, she again sat down heavily. She felt glued to the spot. Already disoriented by the events since Sheremetyevo, she was in a state of complete bewilderment, shock too immediate for grief. Terror raced through her thoughts. With growing panic, a cold wave settled over her shoulders. She was shivering again. Paralyzed, with a look of agonized recognition, she gazed at Vera. Her fairy-tale world in Russia now disintegrated, the specter of life without Boris as her anchor in Moscow had stunned her. No other choice—she had to deal with the Moscow police precinct.

Vera coughed and dramatically wiped her small nose. Polina Isakovna sat heavily on a chair near the kitchen and began to cry quietly. "My poor Boris, gone. Why did they do this to me? I want to die for him. I need valerian right away." Susanna stood, put her arm around Polina, and squeezed her hand gently without speaking. She turned, leaning forward, and embraced her. "Nothing else in the world is worse for a mother than losing her son—I know how you suffer, Tyotya Polina."

Polina sighed again, and shuffled back to the kitchen to continue preparing lunch. Close to the kitchen, a table covered with a stiffly starched linen cloth awaited the guests. Setting the table is a separate ceremony in Russia—Polina, the hostess, tidied herself, laid out the proper plates, silverware, and glasses, and called Susanna and Vera.

Uncle Fima arrived just in time for the meal, and with a deep sense of caring, hugged Susanna, whispering condolences and sympathies. They sat very still in the small dining room nibbling on the appetizers: salads and fish soup served by

Vera. In no time, a heap of dumplings was placed before them, with a dollop of sour cream sliding slowly down the rim of the bowl. The *ukha* was aromatic, thick and tasty, as was the *zharkoye* with cabbage, and the rhubarb *pirog* as light as French pastry. Fima ate slowly, savoring lunch, and especially praised Polina's *ukha*.

The meal was grim with many muted toasts to Boris, and a subdued welcome to Susanna's arrival. Uncle Fima's tone for this occasion was priestly. "I'm so sorry about Boris," he whispered. "Such *gore* for me, the family, and you, Susanna. So tragic." A short, balding, and round-faced man with soft eyes and an impish grin, he was the least intimidating Russian Susanna knew. He had always been a street-smart hustler, "the spoon that stirred the pot" now impossible to imagine as a *bolshaya shishka*, a respected business tycoon, supporting cultural institutions in Siberia while selling expensive cars to legislators in the "new" Russia. He seemed broken hearted and melancholy but eager to ask Susanna about her plans and immediate company business, reassuring her that he was there, as always, to help open doors in Moscow. She congratulated him on his new work and briefly described the GMG project with Norilsk. "You are family! I need your help to discover the circumstances of his death! Why meetings in Piter? How did the keys disappear? You know the Moscow Mafia and must pitch in. His murderers must be brought to justice."

Fima appeared baffled. "Goddamn if I know," he muttered. "If I discuss this, they are going to clam right up—the only art I know is beautiful plump, naked women—hah, hah! And don't know if I can pursue this level of cover-up with bandits."

"But Uncle Fima, I must stay here to be productive for our project. Boris is no more," she added softly, "and you must help."

Fima ignored her discomfort, and changed the conversation. "Our new democracy is fragile; our boys and your consultants are stealing absolutely everything, and it is impossible to stop them. We need more foreign investment, companies with capital to work with us in mining, production, and processing. Nonferrous metals can make GMG rich here."

Susanna was dumbfounded. Her adrenaline was going. How would the new politics and the mystery of Boris's death play out? While speaking with Fima, it had become clear that she, as an American, was expected to handle the investigation with the police. It was also her duty to inform Boris's relatives in Brighton Beach, including another Dr. Rozenbaum, and the doctor's son Dima, now an American lawyer.

Uncomfortable with Susanna's comments, Fima changed the subject. "Have you visited Pasternak's dacha, dear Susanochka? The place is being restored as a cultural house for writers. Very interesting and not far from here, a healthy walk in the morning."

Vera smiled. "Good idea. I will take Susanna there tomorrow." A serious Russian lunch ended in the late afternoon: It was already dark. The scene was melancholy, buffeted by feelings, impossible to resolve. Fima endlessly complimented Polina's cooking, excused himself, kissed everyone, and departed. Vera and Polina, their hearts and stomachs heavy, were dozing in their chairs. Susanna's thoughts returned to the winter the year before. They were cross-country skiing through the woods when Boris again told her how beautiful she was, how he always wanted to make love to her, how much he respected her, and how he wanted to spend his life making her happy. Shocked and mystified, still jet-lagged, her reflexes slow from cognac and lack of sleep, Susanna needed to breathe the sharp pure winter air and catch the end of the day. She pulled on her warm boots, a heavy ski hat, and, balancing carefully in the snow, trudged up the path to push open the gate and take in the scent of the forest, the silent snowflakes, and the almost-full moon over the birches.

But even there, in that deep gray winter splendor, she felt vulnerable and overwhelmed. Again, thoughts of Boris, in Peredelkino early the previous summer, just last year when they were lying on divans on the wooden veranda in the country house. She smiled as memories flitted past. The place smelled of jasmine, hyacinth, and honeysuckle. A wave of feathery blossoms sailed over her head in the hot wind. She was catching up on news from the *International Herald Tribune* while Boris, simply enjoying the comforts of home, gazed at the apple and peach trees thick with creamy petals: at first glance, an absolutely convincing scene of domestic contentment, each absorbed in their separate worlds yet so completely aware of each other's presence. Effusive warmth, a sense of familial intimacy and well-being. Glances between them almost lasted too long. Eyes locked together, they lapsed into silences that spoke more intimately than words. She had lost all sense of place and time. He had been her comfort, her friend, her consolation. He'd made her forget herself for many years and at last begin to live in the luscious invincible present—which was no more.

The silence outside was complete, peaceful, the air special, but even surrounded by serenity, she was enraged. Sosa and Zhora? He had discussed some art business in St. Petersburg, but how, why? They were his childhood friends. Blood throbbed in her temples. Like fiction taking place in reality: Difficult to believe. She cast an anxious look around and tried to put some distance between herself and events, as if she had just read Vera's story of Boris's murder and notice for the funeral in a newspaper. Trying to dissociate herself from pain, she was afraid to speculate, yet she had to rethink *everything*.

She shuddered again and shook her head in despair.

She must go to Moscow and speak with Captain Kalugin about a criminal investigation, and call Lev Kartsev, a retired colonel in the KGB and a friend. She mis-dialed his number twice. Another phone call to Lev's wife. "Hello, Zhanna. So sorry to bother you again, but I have alarming problems here, and I must get in touch with Lyova. Can you help?" Her hands trembled as she dialed, and finally Lev's mellow and re-laxed voice answered. "Lev, Zhanna gave me your number. I'm in Peredelkino. I am trying to discover very personal is-sues, and hope you are returning to Moscow soon."

"Welcome back, Susanna. Good to have you back." His voice was quiet and caring. "So you are already resting, in Peredelkino," he quipped, trying to calm her with humor.

"Yes, of course, I am aware, *vkurse* about Boris. So sorry."

She began to tremble again at Lev's mention of Boris's name, and he sensed panic in her voice. "I've been away for a long time—important business with clients—but I'll be back as soon as I can."

Susanna was momentarily taken aback by the intimate and reassuring tone of his words. She had always sensed that he liked her and would have tried to seduce her if it wasn't for Boris, but always remained a trusted friend. It was better that way, especially now. Moscow was like a small village rife with endless gossip. She knew of Lev's reputation as a serial *"bab-nik."* He was tall, lean, and as handsome as a Russian movie idol, not without personal vanity. Women were intrigued by him. His dark eyes gleamed and he radiated a fierce and un-compromising intelligence, while the stubborn set of his jaw revealed that he was a dangerous man to cross.

"How much did Vera tell you?"

"Enough for me to ask you to investigate, and provide some answers here."

"Yes, yes. I'll do all I possibly can, and give you whatever help you need. I am returning very soon and will call. We can meet at the Metropol, in our usual place."

Thanks, Lev, I don't know what I would do without you."

3

FUNERAL AND POMINKI

BUTTING A SUBURBAN METRO STATION in the
wretched southeastern part of Moscow, two black
Mercedeses, one belonging to Uncle Fima, the other
to the rabbi, were blocking the arched wooden gates of the Jewish cemetery. Tightly packed graves had been defaced and
neglected, with names impossible to read, many of them van-
dalized with cunning precision. Even the gold engravings
around the photographs staring out ghostlike from portraits
engraved in headstones, a Russian custom, were gone. Gone
too of course was the golden harp that Boris's father had added
to his mother's headstone, a reference to her background as a
harpist at the Moscow Philharmonic.

Polina Isakovna Rozenbaum was a wreck—someone had
shoved several white roses into her hands, which she had trou-

ble holding. The woman's matted hair, as much as her eyes, suggested distress. The collar of the loose black sweater under her jacket was torn in the traditional Jewish sign of mourning. From time to time, she threw her arms up to the heavens, as if begging the Lord to take her as well. She often fell limp into the arms of fellow mourners; she howled to Boris how he dared leave her, how no one in the world could love her like her son.

It was a kind of a *shtetl* funeral in Moscow, each small overcrowded plot, crammed with many family members and relatives, going back generations. Vera Sergeyevna, with roses pressed to her heart, stood despondent by the grave. Although the couple had long been divorced, now she was his faithful and mourning wife clutching flowers of innocence. Neighbors, friends, many sportsmen, and colleagues came to the cemetery. Although in the 1930s and 1940s Stalin had killed off the better half of Boris's family, the surviving Rozenbaums were there—lots of cousins, aunts and uncles, some wailing, feigning heart problems, many praising Boris's moral rectitude and generosity to the old Jewish community in Moscow. Younger people were pressing their faces to old bosoms, while some enterprising ones, spotting the foreigner Susanna in the crowd—a well-connected American friend to Boris—pressed business cards into her hands.

The cemetery crew was also on hand—old men with shaky hands, moist eyes, and big bellies standing around the grave, awaiting the burial. "Comfort, Polina Isakovna!" an excited relative shouted in her direction.

"May you be comforted among the mourners of Zion and Jerusalem, amen," a thin, wilted aunt cried out.

Vera and Uncle Fima had earlier decided to ignore the wishes of the synagogue, and several angered relatives, and had Boris cremated.

Soon it was time to bury the ashes, and a path respectfully opened for the Moscow Lubavicher Rebbe. The procession of mourners grew silent as a sign of deference to the rabbi, and Hebrew prayers were recited. Vera Sergeyevna took in a lungful of air, paused, and made the sign of the cross. Two elderly relatives came toward the grave, carrying a cellophane-wrapped jar full of dried flowers, and placed it near Boris's remains. The ashes were lowered in the casket, and he was buried beside his ancestors in the family plot. Relatives stood in line to drop shovelfuls of earth on the grave, pausing and looking up between each effort as heaps of flowers were laid on the fresh clay, and the rabbi, standing tall, extended his hand to the male relatives surrounding him.

Vera suddenly spotted Sosa and Zhora, Boris's old Georgian friends, among the mourners. "Murderers! Animals! *Swine!*" she shrieked from where she stood by the grave. "You took my Boris! You took my prince!" Uncle Fima rushed to Vera, putting his arms around her. She pushed him away, shouting, "Help me, *help* me, Uncle Misha, to strangle them with my very own hands!" Faces turned in Vera's direction, while Susanna, in anger, broke several stems of red roses and flung them into the grave, intentionally allowing thorns to pierce her fingers and draw blood. Two cousins, holding Polina firmly under each arm, led the procession to the cemetery gates. Other relatives followed slowly. With twilight rapidly approaching, another gray day was ending in Moscow. A light snow was falling; gusts of wind pushed strips of paper and plastic around the graves.

THE NINTH DAY AFTER BURIAL is a special Russian day of commemoration for the dead. According to Russian folklore, the soul leaves the body and is guided by angels to its next destination. Uncle Fima, Boris's relative, an important apparatchik and a "new Russian" who had made millions in his recently opened General Motors Moscow car dealership next to Revolution Square and traded many other commodities, as well as cars, was in charge of the special day, the *pominki*, the funeral repast.

People attending a Russian funeral are usually invited back to the house for a meal, nostalgic remembrances, and well-phrased toasts to the deceased. But since the apartment had been burnt and gutted, Uncle Fima had arranged the party at the Hotel Rossiya, inviting only very significant others from the cemetery.

Right next door to Red Square, the Rossiya is perhaps the quintessential example of Soviet architecture. The building, with two hollowed-out inner courtyards covering almost a kilometer in circumference, is a graying monolith, its size matched only by the sameness of its design. It is a ten-acre eyesore; expatriates call it a shithole. The Russians joke that the best thing about staying in the Rossiya is that, from the inside, you cannot see its ugliness.

Inside, the clientèle was unchanged. Men in black turtle-necks with lumps under their blazers patrolled the lobby. Leggy, desperate Russian *femmes fatales*, many stunning blondes featuring pouty lips, large, limpid eyes outlined with heavy eyeliner, tight bodies in minidresses, small, perky breasts, and nothing else under clingy Italian sweaters and tight leather, strolled through the hotel stores and lobbies. Besides oil, many of the women were Russia's main national product, and could be ordered long distance from Kansas City or Minneapolis. Susanna especially noted a redhead in snake-skin pants and impossibly high heels joining the parade of curious, aloof beauties always ready to fall into a new adventure, to trade up and, if lucky, to escape to Italy, Germany or America.

Uncle Fima had reserved a private room. Bottles of vodka and special Georgian wine sat on three elegantly set oblong tables. With an uncomfortable and icy stare, Fima scrutinized the arrangements and décor, nodded, and pulled out several hundred-dollar bills for the waiters. They stood erect, bowing to the guests in military fashion, and one officially announced the set menu: black caviar, blackened sturgeon kebabs, an assortment of smoked fish, bouillon, dumplings stuffed with shrimp, breast of duck, fillet of beef in red wine, and, because it was a funeral ritual, no dessert, nothing sweet, just cognac, tea, and coffee.

It was Susanna's first time at a *pominki* ritual. She sat next to Polina and Vera, and felt miserable realizing again the reason for this commemoration and quietly began to cry.

After many private vodkas and *zakuski* (appetizers), toasts to the deceased began. Although viewed as *ne-kulturno*—revealing a lack of refinement and education—many of Boris's older relatives began to cry as they remembered what a great person he had been, always helping them with medicines and doctors who saved their lives, finding the right mechanic and garage for their cars, sending able electricians, plumbers, and carpenters to make repairs that saved their dachas from ruin.

Polina's sister began the lament. "Unhappy that we are! Misfortune will be upon us evermore!"

Polina Isakovna began to whimper. "Borka, Borka, my only son, my little sun, why did you die, why did you do this to me?"

It was time for the formal ritual to begin. Swallowing a spoonful of black caviar and downing a tall glass of vodka, Uncle Fima stood up, waving still another glass. "Since my son Vitya left for New York, Columbia University School of International Relations and Law," he enunciated precisely, "and my daughter Sonia is in Florida studying multicultural history, Boris was my helper, a healer, an educated, cultured, and saintly person. We drink to Boris and Jewish heaven! *Amin, Ura!*"

Uncle Misha had risen to his feet, and was standing silently at his chair: "*Yiskadal veyiskadash!* May His great name grow exalted and sanctified."

An oppressive, grim silence followed, broken only by Vera, crying and pointing at Sosa and Zhora. Guests stole mournful glances at each other and at Fima as the waiters poured wine. More gloom and fancy food followed. Zhora, his chin oily with sturgeon, a little off-balance, sprang up and crossed himself. "Now we begin our Georgian service. First, a toast. The best bottles of Georgian wine are on the tables! Saneravi, Tzinandali! Waiters, pour the wine!"

The waiters, bowing with one hand behind and with the other swishing a napkin, began to pour as Zhora continued, a gun bulging from his left armpit, "To Boris, my dearest and oldest friend, my heart is filled with sorrow. I loved him very much. He is going directly to martyr's paradise and he is looking down on us tenderly."

"*Amin, amin!*" relatives and friends murmured.

"Nine toasts for nine-day journey to paradise, for his soul to greet his respected ancestors." He crossed himself again and continued.

Bella was a bag of nerves. Panic-stricken, she turned to her sister and muttered, "This is sacrilege. This boy isn't even *Jewish!*"

"Tyotya Polina knows that I am half or at least a quarter Jewish. My great-grandfather was a Romanian Jew." Zhora whispered something tender to her and continued, "I was in the same class with him in first grade, in School 253, before we moved to Tbilisi. Every year, we lived in the same pioneer camp in Yalta, slept in the same tent, swam in the Black Sea, smoked cigarettes and looked at magazines I brought from home with pictures of beautiful German girls. Boris was a great intellect, an expert in history, art, philosophy. He loved Russia, and he was always asking: 'What is our country? Who are our heroes? What is our past? What do we believe?' Also a special Russian talent for chess—he was always a champion. Let's drink to Boris's journey! Ura!" Zhora whistled for his friend Sosa to join him while his face, wet from tears, alcohol, and excitement, tried to ignore Fima and Vera's scornful glares.

Suddenly, a tipsy cousin in a black turtleneck and Tommy Hilfiger leather parka jumped to his feet and jolted Zhora sideways. "Yes, Boris cannot play chess anymore. If it wasn't for you and the other Georgian, he would still be alive to sit with us! You should be *dead, you riff-raff, you scum! svolochi!* I'll kill you for this, Zhora, wait and see. *Your pominki* are coming soon! Drink to the bottom! *Truth* is on bottom! *Istina na dne!*" and punched him in the face.

"Please, order, for our cherished friend's journey," shouted Fima. A rustle of hands locating holsters followed under one table as Sosa jumped up to defend his friend, and suddenly five men were in the melee, cursing as only the Russian language allows, spitting and punching away. Fima, sitting next to Polina, grabbed her hand and stared Sosa into submission. Other relatives were paralyzed with fear. Uncle Misha reached for his nitroglycerin, swallowed some pills, and jumped to the front, followed by his son, Filka. They tried to break up the fight. "*Rebyata!* Kids, these are Jewish pominki. No signs of the cross here, no Georgian blessings, no fights with our Georgian friends."

Unexpectedly, a new figure, not seen at the cemetery, raised his head, glared at Fima, and hauled himself out of his chair.

George Bablidze was paunchy, dark, handsome, and cool.

He was perfectly groomed in a handmade Italian suit, Hermès tie, and tasseled alligator shoes that emphasized the fact he never set foot on Moscow's dirty streets. He slowly approached the group at the front table, hugged and kissed Uncle Misha, Fima, Zhora, and Sosa, hushed the commotion, and raised another glass.

"My name is Ghiya, I have been Boris's good friend since university days. I live in Tbilisi and the arctic."

The breakup of the Soviet Union had thrust Georgia, where Bablidze worked as a captive of Soviet industry, an *apparatchik*, into civil war and desperate poverty. Since he was trained as an expert on metals and geology, his university buddy, Boris, a Moscow doctor, had helped him find work, and Bablidze had hustled his way to the top of the trench warfare in Norilskmetal. Now he was on his way to becoming one of the most powerful men in the new order.

Bablidze smiled sadly, baring his white teeth enough to suggest German dentistry. "Boris was a great young man, who became a righteous doctor, a leader. He loved his people, his mother, his friends. Made fatherless by the Great Patriotic War, now his soul is traveling to see him again. I make Jewish toast, '*mazel tov*,' for happy journey for Boris's soul."

The rabbi interjected, "You only use '*mazel tov*' for weddings and bar mitzvahs, not sad occasions."

Bablidze remained unruffled. "Well, to Boris's saintly journey and to our new Russian NEP; our market economy. For the chosen people, for the Jewish rabbi from America—director of Jewish church and *Chabad*, I donate five *shtukas*, badly needed for the new ark and *remont*." A *shtuka*, Susanna knew, was a thousand-dollar bill. "In Tbilisi, we begin new Judaica Fund for Polina Isakovna, holy mother of holy man, Boris."

Zhora again pushed his way to the head table and began another toast. "The Jewish people, except for the anarchists and Reds who killed our tsars, have a long and peaceful history in Russia. They are our brothers, and whoever is their enemy is our enemy also."

Uncle Fima bellowed, "To the Jewish people and Israel! They have their own state, the best soldiers, the best military. *Amin.*"

A Georgian hockey player jumped up. "Our friends here are welcome in Tbilisi, always! When you come, my mother will be your mother, my wife your sister, and you will always find water in my well to drink. To Boris, my best friend, my doctor, *ura!*"

Zhora and Sosa staggered to Polina's table and loudly kissed her on both cheeks. "Polina Isakovna, for your Judaica fund, and a *kapitalnyi remont* for apartment, we give another five shtukas."

The scene was like something out of *The Godfather*. Susanna, silent and sullen, frightened and confused, kept watching the commotion. She might have been hallucinating, but she saw Boris standing near Sosa. Apprehension lay like a dead weight on her chest. A betrayal and death at home, a murder in Moscow. Questions began to form unobtrusively, gradually, in her mind.

Destiny demanded that she live on the edge now. Peter died of an aneurysm—medical doctors and family utterly helpless. Now, challenged by Boris's death, perhaps she could somehow resolve this mystery, understand who he really was, embrace the Russian bear and dance with it.

"What am I doing here, she wondered. Who are these friends, criminals, gangsters, hit men? Boris did talk about a Georgian friend, the new director of Norilskmetal, but in Norilsk, not Georgia. I feel like Prince Myshkin, a holy fool, an innocent surrounded by schemers—a puppy in the den of wolves, a silent bystander. Lightning, like death, has struck again!" She began putting the puzzle

together. Zhora and Sosa in St. Petersburg with Boris on business? The lost apartment keys, Boris "not delivering," revenge and hit men, an art deal gone bad? Boris owed money and didn't deliver. Arson, disappearance of paintings in the apartment? Sosa and Zhora and their Russian art gallery in New York? Boris, an informer for the KGB? Dinners I was never invited to when Boris was entertaining Russian UN "diplomats" in Moscow? His use of their diplomatic pouches which facilitated the transfer of "art on order" for the gallery? Boris and Bablidze, and money made at the Bourse? How was Boris involved in business with Bablidze and Norilsk? His deceptions caused her great anguish. She had loved this good man who had kept her calm and grounded, shielding her from brutal loneliness, five thousand miles away from home. Now, for the first time since her return, she was grieving the loss of her son at home, and Boris, and hot tears flowed. She had woken with it, eaten with it, tried to work with it, but now the combat, the suspicions, the losses, plunged her into real despair.

The overcast Moscow day ended at four o'clock, and it was already night when Volodya escorted her to the overheated apartment house lobby. A *babushka* with a distinct aroma of pot roast and onions about her, some relative of the concierge assigned to vetting the guests, looked up from her knitting, scrutinized her, examined her clothes, and grunted. Susanna was weary and drained as she tried to remember the sequence of keys that unlocked the apartment. First key to the right, second to the left, turn twice to open the padded steel door, and then the long key for the inner door. She repeated this intricate process once inside. Locking all four chains, she dropped her coat and boots in the vestibule. Opening the door to the living room, she began pacing and breathing slowly. Finally subdued, she felt less agitated—but never so abandoned.

Fatigue overcame her as she collapsed on the bed and slept

and dreamed she was swimming downward through black water in smooth, powerful strokes. Just as she thought of returning to shore, she was joined by a mysterious man and a child. They touched her hand and swam away.

4

SLAVYANSKAYA HOTEL

THINGS ALWAYS LOOK BETTER IN THE morning. Cheerful red geraniums, their elongated stems outstretched to high kitchen windows in search of northern light, were reassuring and comforting. After another fitful night, she dressed, drank strong coffee, and prepared to meet Volodya outside.

Two men, wrapped in padded orange jackets and hats against the grim freeze, armed with snow shovels and twig-and-straw brooms, were clearing the fresh snow in the street around her building. She was out early, bundled in her Chinese coat and fur *ushanka*, walking briskly through the courtyard.

"Privet, Susanna, too cold to walk this morning. The motor is idling, the car is warm, jump in."

"Thanks, Volodya. But snow fell last night—the first big snow since I'm back, and the temperature hovering only at freezing, in sympathy with my grief. The world is quiet, and I want to walk."

"Well, then, I'll keep you company through the park."

The day had indeed dawned deep blue and rich gold, but the stillness and splendor of the light turned her mind in the opposite direction.

For the first time since the funeral she truly grieved for Boris, and for herself, and shuddered, allowing herself to process the fact of murder, and the struggle and violence Boris might have suffered.

"Volodya, can you imagine Boris's shock and terror when the suspects entered the apartment, the *razborka*, confrontation, arguments, settling of accounts not settled, talk of revenge, reprisals, violence?"

"Why, I'm sure Boris was armed! Why couldn't he fight them off, or use his gun?" replied Volodya.

"Yes, he was well built and muscular, a swimmer and soccer player in his university days, you know. He must have known the assailants, and was either overwhelmed or confident he could settle the *razborka*," Susanna noted. "Death seldom comes as assault, and few resist it with violence, as he must have. The ordeal of strangulation must have come in stages. First, disbelief and a wild thrashing of resistance. Then, dawning recognition of dwindling resources, the chemical smell of an electric fire."

She described the scene forensically, as she had imagined it, her mouth and jaw set. Volodya was startled. As their muffled footsteps slowly crunched on the narrow walking paths, he realized she was trembling, losing her confidence.

"Dear God, dear Boris!" Looking up at the trees hushed in snow, she continued, "Can you imagine? The weight and pressure of pillows stifling his mouth and nose, excruciating pain, a broken nose, a collapsed rib cage, spasms, limpness, death." She had to say all of it out loud.

Crime, extortion, and violent endings had always been a part of Russia. Stories about vengeance go back centuries, and revenge is a recurrent theme in social history: serfs slitting their masters' throats in rebellions, tsars staging mass executions of insurgents, revolutionaries plotting to execute tsars, Stalin's elimination of a whole stratum of society as enemies of the people.

She was obsessed, and helpless. She knew she had to wait for Lev and his contacts in 38 Petrovka, the central police station. There was no other help in sight.

Confronting the fog of suspicion, anxiety, and pressure that Boris's death had generated, there was no going home— she needed to stay in Russia and produce results for GMG for the Norilskmetal project.

Thoughts of Peter's sudden death were unrelenting, too: The only child, twelve, just on the brink of ceasing to be a little boy, struck by a brain aneurysm; in ten days, he was brain dead. The death of a child is like burying your fondest hopes. It remained an incomparable loss, a bullet in the heart. The pain never abates. After months of grieving with an analyst in New York and the eruption of acute inflammatory shingles and high fever, she had come no closer to healing.

The boy's death had destroyed his father, a doctor who couldn't save his own child. He had been hospitalized with a nervous breakdown and hadn't been the same since.

Their marriage, always dispassionate, broken long before, had made the pain too overwhelming to share.

Matrimonial fidelity came into question for both—rumors and innuendos about affairs: Susanna's many trips to Russia, Fred's medical conferences and business negotiations, and a social life with overnights in his apartment in Manhattan. Peter had kept them together, provided her with tenderness and emotional fulfillment absent from her marriage. Susanna, always furious, in need of Boris's love, had finally sued for divorce and, to escape pain at home, run away to Moscow, where another bullet had struck her.

SHE FELT IMPOSSIBLE EMPTINESS EVERYWHERE. As she wound her way to the hotel, she shuddered and her head began to pound. She craved solitude and contemplation. Always distracted, her gaze remote, she couldn't focus on huge business challenges ahead, or even the day's agenda.

It was her first week back in Moscow, and Boris lived in her head, always. The red flag had not fluttered over the Kremlin for two years. The "October events" had ushered in a political and economic disaster, the regime lay in ruins, the empire in dissolution. All the talk of democracy and a free market had simply meant wholesale plunder—the last lingering dream of socialism turned into inflation, unemployment, and economic shock.

Her multinational had become redundant. Russians were suddenly their own entrepreneurs, with personal guards who drove private 600 S Mercedeses with tinted windows and limousines with armor plating.

The CEO of GMG, meanwhile, was a new-breed executive, a genius with an attention deficit disorder who demanded immediate gratification, an oxymoron in Russia. His economic horizon was short, and Susanna's Moscow satellite stood in sharp focus with the board of directors. She was relieved to be away from the corporate culture of GMG, where Jack Hanken took the pulse of the company by simply wandering around asking questions. An eerie sixth sense made him smell money being lost. Opening the door, unannounced, he would invariably surprise her. This was fun for him but not for her. She was between a rock and a hard place, relieved to be away from Wall Street, where Hanken's endless refrain was: "What have you done for me lately?" She knew that, in Moscow, business moved at a glacial pace. In order to solve Boris's murder, she would have to obfuscate, fudge telexes every day, and produce a litany of smoke and mirrors for Wall Street.

THE RADISSON SLAVYANSKAYA HOTEL, AN OASIS in the center of Moscow, Russia's first deluxe Western-style hotel and business complex, felt welcoming and familiar. In the elevator on her way up, a businessman who also had an office in the hotel greeted her with more dark news. "Welcome back, Susanna, have you heard that our friend, Ed Mashall, the American partner of the hotel's new joint venture, had just been shot seven times?"

Stunned, she could only whisper, "Why Ed, why Ed?"

"Russian security services were 'protecting' him. The cops had been hit men. He had been murdered outside the hotel by people who knew he was wearing a bulletproof vest and therefore aimed for the head."

"Why in the world would anyone want to shoot Ed, for God's sake? He loved this country, and was a big investor here."

Valya was already in the office, preparing coffee in the new Siemens pot, and Sasha was busy reading the Interfax news and studying a book, *Advanced Computer English for Dummies*, for the newly purchased computer. Rather than expressing excitement and anticipation that normally preceded her first day back, the pair were glumly silent. No doubt news of her son's death and Boris's had traveled quickly. The Russian way was silence, distraction, denial, and secretiveness. A deep sense of empathy is never verbalized. There is, on the other hand, no *schadenfreude*: The greetings were quiet and cheerless. Dismayed, glancing at Valya, Susanna suddenly remembered their souvenirs, which lay forgotten in her suitcase.

She rocked back very slightly on her heels and instinctively raised her arms at the elbow in a gesture of determination and defense. She was gazing out of the office window at the Kiev train station, wrapped in a morning haze of snow and aqueous mist. When the station was built in the early years of the twentieth century, it had been a magical addition to the Moscow skyline. Now the clock tower and soaring, fairytale roof looked forlorn against the bustle and grime. Beneath her window Muscovites padded silently across the snowy streets leading to the station. Only the echoing calls of the loudspeakers announcing the trains reached her. A sea of makeshift kiosks surrounded the station, the signs of the wrenching transition that Russia was making to the market economy. Vendors there sold everything from apples to cotton panties to kitchen faucets to cable wires. She might as well have been watching a silent movie about Russia, or in a fishbowl looking out. Without Boris the place remained an exhibit, the only comfort that her American passport and multiple-entry visa allowed her to leave at any time.

Her expatriate position shielded her from the grit of the land and created a distance between her and the people, whose monthly salary would not have covered an evening of drinks at the hotel bar. She realized at that moment that on her own, without Boris, she would have to get her hands dirty to discover his Russia. She dreaded the office briefing she had to send every day and the early-evening follow-up telephone call from New York. "Valya, please let me see the proposal *Metody Upravlenya Zapasom Palladiya* we sent to Kulichkov last year? I will rewrite and edit the material for the Central Bank, and we can telex the stuff to Hanken tonight. Meanwhile you can begin reviewing the Russian translation. I will make the changes where necessary."

Valya, in a perpetual state of envy, was learning to appreciate Susanna's long-windedness. It gave her time to look for the old proposal, push fingers through her hair, and steady herself, adjusting to her boss's distracted pace. Wasting time is a very Russian trait; it's how Russians remind themselves that life is more than just a series of goals, results, and numbers.

Flinging her Hermès scarf on the desk, Susanna returned to her chair, corrected the *computershchik*'s report for New York, took a deep breath, decided not to wait for Lev, and telephoned Uncle Fima.

"Fima Abramovich, please. Susanna from GMG is calling."

A gasp at the other end of the line, and an endearing, "One moment, please." "Good morning, my wise Susanna. So good to see you in Peredelkino, and so terrible about Boris. He was like my son here. How I'd like to get my hands on those miserable Georgians!" Hearing the man's reassuring and comforting everyday voice, she choked back tears. He sensed this pain and went on lightheartedly, "You looked great at the *pominki*, altogether like a young girl. How are you feeling?"

"As you can imagine, Uncle Fima. But trying to work. GMG is only interested in results, and I am in the limelight here." With your help, we can do important business for Russia, for Europe, and America."

"Moscow has been very difficult for you since you arrived, and for both of us, a tragedy and a mystery." He coughed. "An arson-and-robbery case about the apartment has been opened by the police precinct on Tverskaya. We don't know—they are still investigating."

"But Uncle Fima, how can that be? A theft-and-arson case

when Boris must have been murdered? His death was not a heart attack! But anyway, I am focusing on business, pushing away tragedy."

"Allegedly murdered—the police investigation is inconclusive. But great that you are working! Really a *molodchina!*" On the telephone, she could not see his smile.

"No alternative for me. I was surprised to see Mr. Bablidze at the *pominki* as well. I must to stay here to find out the circumstances of Boris's death—how and why? You must know, Uncle Fima, my firm has been working on a business project with Norilskmetal for a long time. I am rewriting and updating strategy for meetings with the Central Bank and the Ministry of Non-Ferrous Metals."

Fima's voice was comforting, but he sounded confused. "Of course, Boris was associated with Aleksandr Kulichkov, but was also good friends with Bablidze. Yes, Kulichkov was the old boss—now only industrial manager—a useful *apparatchik.* I am sure your proposals all went to, how Americans say, 'the circular file' hah, hah."

"Possibly, Uncle Fima. Many projects addressed to me end up in the wastebasket as well. *Bozhe moi,* I've had many telephone conversations with Kulichkov when he was chief, and sent proposals detailing GMG's interest in upgrading Norilskmetal's infrastructure, in return for metals, specifically palladium."

"Well, Boris's old-time buddy, Mr. Bablidze, is the new president now, and Boris was waiting for your return for introductions, and discussions about the Norilskmetal project with the new chief."

"Uncle Fima, you are the only one to help me now! There is no one else except you."

"Of course, yes. . .you must trust me like you did Boris, God be with him, and provide me with your company's business plans."

Suddenly Susanna's mind drifted away again. She had difficulty and she could no longer focus on work.

"Hello, Susanna, are you still there?"

Oh God, Susanna thought. "Yes, of course, Uncle Fima. He must have been murdered. Why? I loved him. He was my dearest friend and my advisor, and he was instrumental in pushing GMG's business forward. Now you are my only help. I must get this project done! I have no one else to turn to, and I will be forever grateful."

"Understood, Suzanochka!" said Fima with confidence and sympathy, and she was reassured. "I feel *so* sorry for you, and I will help. Rely on me to consult."

"I am grateful." She caught her breath, swallowed, and glanced at Tanya. "We can have another approach, Uncle Fima. You must know I have been in business with your car dealership for many years."

"How so, my dear?"

"Indirectly, of course. For many years, I traveled to Detroit to negotiate industrial supply contracts with Almazyuvelirexport for rhodium, platinum, and of course, palladium for catalytic converters for cars in your showroom! Now, you and *tyotya* Polina are my only family friends here . . ." Her unfocused mind was racing in all directions. "Is Bablidze still in Moscow?"

"Of course, Susanna. Still resting from the *pominki*, and other functions and meetings—escaping both arctic wastes of Siberia and his warm family in Georgia. Well, you know our joke, a Russian can legally have two wives, one in Tbilisi, and one in Moscow. Hah, hah! Why do you ask?"

Susanna was agitated, fumbling for words. Taken aback by so much direct information, Uncle Fima's voice had grown thoughtful and again retreated to Russian humor. "Yes," he went on, "I've read the dealership files, and studied your former contracts with Almaz. I am honored to be in same business bed with your company, Susanna, hah, hah! Like with my wife, I am always ready to go where she goes, and the same for you! Any good excuse to help, *zolotaya*, and a *muzhik* always will. Compromise and assistance are important to women."

She bit her chapped lips again. "Please ask Mr. Bablidze for discussions in my office about mutual cooperation with GMG, your projects, and Norilskmetal. I will ask our friend Alexander Zhukov, the president of Omega Bank. He is interested in project financing for foreign investments, and Philip Dunlop, from the State Department, to join us. We have a cash-flow model ready for financing business in Norilsk. Our legal department has drawn up all the waivers and indemnities including government regulations to protect investors' rights. We are seeking guarantees and cooperation from the governor of the region, and we can have foreign policy support from our State Department. We just need Mr. Bablidze's and Norilskmetal's interest to move forward." She blurted all this out as rapidly as if she were checking off a shopping list.

"Suzanochka," Fima said after a longish pause, "I understand, but I'm not clear about your firm's idea for investment for Norilsk. Capital for infrastructure and modernization? I need to see your business plan and carefully study your entire proposal and GMG's figures for subsidizing refining, smelting, assaying, and transportation. I must have all the financial details."

"I'll have Valya deliver the copies of documents to your offices immediately. You will have the information before the end of the day."

"I'm very good at listening to your problems, *dorogaya*, but you know Russian anecdote: patience, go slow, you cannot jump over time! One cannot sit on a cock and eat herring at the same time. Your head must be straight when you negotiate. Ghiya must relax few days here, must see good friends, relatives."

"But you don't know GMG, Uncle Fima. I get paid to produce. Not like in your old Soviet five-year plans."

"Relax, my sweet one, you will feel better tomorrow. I will take care of you! Offices are bad for introductions. We will invite Bablidze and your important associates for Georgian dinner very soon. Maybe next week, we make arrangements."

STILL UNEASY, SHE WAS STARING AT HER phone, hoping to wrap up the day, when it rang.

"A telephone call from Mr. Hanken," Valya announced. Feeling a sense of panic, Susanna, half rising from her chair, lifted the receiver.

"What's up, Susanna? What's happening in the Russian market, our new frontier?"

"Well, I'm revising our proposal for the management of palladium reserves to the Central Bank, and our legal department, for review. I'm eager to hear their comments so I can schedule a meeting for discussions with Mr. Kuzmenko, the Central Bank's Deputy Chief of the Commercial Department."

Silence on the telephone, and then outrage: "Just some more bureaucratic flimflam! The old communists are only wearing new hats! Only lunch and dinner for the Russkies! No Bolshoi Ballet or opera? *Another waste of time!* Look, Susanna, we don't know where we stand with the Central Bank or the Arctic, and I'm waiting for a *strategic plan* from you! I'm ready to tell them to go to hell."

"Yes, Mr. Hanken, I'm hammering out the details for a strategy, and I will be ready with a plan next week. It hasn't been two weeks since I'm back in Moscow. We have to keep our powder dry."

"The whole thing's a load of hocus-pocus," Hanken declared. "We're the Mount Everest of the metal multinationals, and you have to be the first and the best and put GMG over the top, Susanna. Because if you're not, we'll find someone who will. Someone younger, Susanna, right? Someone with more drive and class, with more creativity, committed to innovation."

"You must give me time, Mr. Hanken. Russian bureaucracy moves in mysterious ways. Now, with the perestroika reforms, there's greater urgency for foreign investment. Yeltsin has an aggressive approach to economic reform. But no need for details over the telephone. You will see the telexed document tomorrow." All she could do was listen to herself in amazement. She was too weak to talk any more when she wished him a productive day and he brusquely hung up. She had fought the fear of failure all day, when suddenly the possibility hit her with a gale force—Hanken's disturbing message had sprung at her when she was least expecting it. She thought of Peredelkino and Fima's reassuring telephone conversation and decided to call Philip Dunlop, a friend at the U.S. embassy to let him know she was back. She was certain he'd heard about Boris and needed his company for comfort.

The all-pervasive sense of death slowed her pace as she took the elevator to the lounge, which was beginning to fill with smoke and loud chatter from the bar. She peremptorily greeted a couple of Swedish neighbors as they made their way in after a day's work, and continued staring into space. She waited uneasily at a small round table, resting on dolphin-tails, with comfortable art deco chairs for Philip. Along the wall stood a Biedermeier *secretaire*, its top section a miniature Greek temple, and a matching sofa with more dolphins carved on the arm-rests, heraldic emblems—architecturally a mixture of styles impossible to describe. Looking around, she focused on the heavy green velvet drapes in intricate patterns, held back with heavily tasseled ropes shutting off treacherous Moscow. There are so many ways of escaping from that which one fears, not the least of these is hatred. The table was away from the bar, a comfortable place to drink straight scotches late in the afternoon.

Susanna's eyes were apparently following her cigarette smoke as Philip hurried in and embraced her. "I've missed you, Susanna! Welcome back to our revolutionary excitement and the euphoria of privatization and criminality—second gold rush." He looked uncomfortable. "Haven't been in this place since you went home, and I've forgotten how cozy and *gemutlich* it is here."

"It's the Deco furniture, velvet curtains, and cigarette smoke—something like Vienna."

Philip moved his chair, took a sip of scotch, looked away, and pressed her hand. "I am so sorry about your son, and Boris, of course."

"It's incredible. I've been grieving for both. Peter remains a blur of joyful energy. Not post-traumatic stress, just pain and shock. I came here because I knew Boris would help me heal, and now this—why Boris, Philip? I must get to the bottom of this. My ideas are pure speculation, and this project may be the end of my career here."

"Why, Susanna?"

"How can an expatriate woman get sucked into a Byzantine detective investigation about a Russian citizen? Can you imagine?"

Philip shrugged and reached for her hand again. "It's been a violent winter for you, and here as well." To avoid more discomfort, he began with their American friend Marshall. "The natives muscled him out. A clash with his Russian joint-venture partners."

Susanna swallowed hard. "Sadly, this criminality is getting too close to home."

"Welcome back to Russia!"

She motioned to the waiter to order more drinks and bring her favorite snack—a silver tray of open small sandwiches—black bread, butter, and red caviar.

"How can I lend a hand, Susanna?"

"Good to see you here again, Philip. I am alone here and you are a trusted friend. I must remain working here to solve the circumstances of Boris's death, and also produce a protocol agreement with Norilsk, and need all the help I can get."

Philip, agitated, now swallowed some scotch. "Yes, many of our big companies are investigating the new gold rush. The American Chamber of Commerce has signed up many of The Fortune 500 firms. 'Enormous opportunities for foreign companies,' they say. Our State Department, as always, is not effective, and the IMF just relies on funds from the United States."

Susanna hesitated for a moment, then nodded. "Yeah, right. I've been commuting for twenty years, doing productive business with Almazyuvelirexport. Our contracts were as solid as Russia's sovereignty. Since perestroika and the great sell-off, I haven't been able to do *anything* here. All I get are telephone calls from shady characters offering us deals in export licenses for cash deposited in some unknown offshore pocket bank."

"You mean like the old Nigeria proposals."

"Yes, Philip, and worse. Last night I had a call in my apartment from a metal engineer, followed by another call from a sexy-voiced geologist. Everywhere in the government—in the Kremlin, in parliament, the ministries—ministers have been selling licenses to anyone willing to pay the price! My KGB friends are using their connections and becoming the biggest property owners in Russia. I know that's certainly the case with Norilsk."

"Yes, I know," Philip remarked empathetically. "Russian business is now big bang and gangster capitalism. Shock therapy and instant privatization! Gobbling up the most lucrative assets and factories, currency speculation. Dollars are finding their way to secret bank accounts in Switzerland, the Seychelles, or Cyprus."

Susanna was relishing her favorite *zakuski* and not paying attention. "The only way I appreciate this stuff more is black with a spoon."

"The new Russian capitalists are wheeling and dealing on their own—retooling factories, importing Benzes, jeans, computers, rock albums. . . ."

"And also hiring English-speaking nannies, I hear."

The large room had a serenity to it. The waiters, delivering drinks, floated, eyes attentive to customers. It felt strange to be back, and she shook her head in silence and looked around the lounge, recognizing many expatriates she knew quietly smoking and drinking—a time to decompress from the day's bureaucratic frustrations. "It's impossible here now," she whispered.

"You, like hundreds of other strategic investors, are paying high rents, wining, dining, writing business plans, targeting markets, and waiting for some return on your financial capital, while criminals are cashing in on business opportunities. State has reported twenty-three bankers were murdered this year in gangster assaults," Philip uttered grimly. "Yeltsin's democracy is sinking into a quagmire of violence and lawlessness."

"You can say that again." Philip nodded encouragingly and reached for his cigarette. "Winter is a season for deaths here.

An English engineer was found burned to death in his own apartment. A young Californian who came to do good, stabbed to death. German chef beaten to death on a central street, his face torn."

"Yes, Philip, they can shoot, they can kill, and they can strangle." She was back to square one. "Boris's family is afraid of the police. Can you imagine? Discovering Boris's killers has become my impossible responsibility."

Philip saw confusion and despair in Susanna's eyes, as tears welled up and began to roll down her cheeks. He was pleased to see Susanna again but worried about how vulnerable and upset she appeared. Mixed emotions were racing through his mind when Susanna interrupted again. She was pale, her hands shaking. "The Herculean challenge of producing for the Norilsk project—I'm under serious pressure to sign a general protocol agreement with Norilsk, and I must get to the bottom of the Boris mystery. You must help me, Philip!"

She burst out crying in self-pity and couldn't continue for a few minutes. He reached for her hand again, observed her face, smiled tentatively, and, feeling helpless, whispered, "So sorry. You need lots of time to heal, Susanna."

"But some trauma is chronic and never heals."

Philip was uncomfortable. He fingered his glass, moved his chair, and glanced at his watch. "Communism produced a sea of blood here, and more terror. More brutal than the czars." He paused, rubbing a finger across his lip. "But, Susanna, if anyone can, you can cope with pressures. You can push forward. Explain your project to me. What are your ideas about Norilsk?"

She leaned forward on her elbows.

"Okay. Metals, like oil, are Russia's strategic resources, its sovereign wealth. We are a strategic investor, with equity capital of thirteen billion dollars and a market capitalization in excess of twenty-three billion, assets exceeding ninety billion, and a net income of more than one point eight billion. Our Russian-American Bank here is anxious to invest and not worried about Russia defaulting. We are proposing a bankable project with Norilskmetal. GMG is willing to finance Norilskmetal's modernization and refurbishment by installing more efficient, automated, higher capacity equipment. Our tender also includes another flash smelter, and consultancies for in-house training management. All state-of-the-art stuff."

Philip put his hands on the table and laced them together. "Understood. That's the carrot. What's the stick?"

"Platinum-group metals prices are volatile. They fluctuate rapidly. We must lock in collateral for three separate tranches, with agreed-upon prices, shipped to Amsterdam, and confirmed by KLM and Credit Suisse."

"Is that everything?"

"If they deliver. This project may work because it reinforces Washington's policy here. It's good for State and the IMF, and your Harvard consultants. We are the only superpower left."

Philip smiled cynically and lit another cigarette. "The numbers are so huge, I can't really get my head around them. But good luck! The rules of the game are the same. You will have to plow your way through corruption and the same Soviet red tape, now called 'privatization' and 'criminality.'"

Susanna sighed and raised her glass, saluting his observations. She moved her chair close to his, and, in a hushed tone, said, "Also, we have letters from the regional governor, confirming support for the project. But there has been no history whatsoever of private property here. Until Yeltsin, the state owned everything, absolutely everything: diamonds and metals, food stores, shoe factories, oil fields, and barber shops. Now you have *perestroika* and democracy. And you must take off your diplomat's hat and commit State in our discussions with Bablidze, the new director of Norilsk."

"We are old friends, Susanna. I'll do what I can."

She needed him to be more sharply focused. "We need to strategize a business agenda, Philip. I have solid contacts with the EBRD in London; the State Department and the IMF are now major players in Russian economic policy." She looked at him to be sure he was alert.

Finally he caught on to her business plans. He understood. Then carefully examining her face and bosom, Philip was content. Suddenly he seemed indispensable. Again clasping his hands, he countered, "Well, why don't you buy export licenses until you get something going that's bigger?"

Susanna realized that he still didn't understand that she needed State support with Bablidze. She reached for her glass and hesitantly adjusted her sweater. "Cut the bullshit, Philip. You're in the State Department, perks and lifetime pension, posts around the world. You're also IMF here, technically employed by the UN where Washington calls all the shots. But we are a respected multinational, subject to American racketeering laws, and my work hangs on productivity!"

He cleared his throat. "Remember Nikolai Gogol," he said with a hesitant smile. "'Russia, speeding like a fiery troika, where are you flying? Everything on earth is flying past, other peoples and states move aside, and make way.'"

"Well, Philip, I'm a passenger in that troika now, and flying nowhere. You must focus on my CEO's very short horizon, and my . . . uh, own catastrophes."

Suddenly, looking into her eyes, his diplomatic body language became more genuine. He took a deep breath, and raising both hands, snapped, "Who knows more about privatizing command economies than you? Who can write a better strategic business plan? You were the first woman to work in

GMG's commodity-trading madhouse in New York. I under-stand the payback from raw materials is pretty fast. Very good for your CEO's need for immediate gratification! You've spent the last two years advising the Poles on privatizing busi-ness—and what about your work with Hungary and Czecho-slovakia? After the dismantling of the Berlin Wall, you spent more time shuttling between Budapest, Warsaw, and Prague than any other businessperson I know. Thanks to *perestroika* and *glasnost*, Russia is ready. Gorbachev was unwilling to kill his own people or people in other countries. We know that if one shot had been fired in the main square of Prague, there would have been no Velvet Revolution. All that's been a re-hearsal for the big one—Mother Russia herself!"

"Never mind all that intellectual crap. We cannot lose *time*, Philip! We *must* get something going while Bablidze is in Moscow."

"Hang on! Being part of history is never easy! We will be in touch tomorrow. But I must get back to Spasskaya before the end of the day." He hugged and kissed her again, and rushed out of the lounge.

Maybe it was the scotch, but Susanna's mood also light-ened. She now had a lobby of three—Volodya, Uncle Fima, and Philip—to support her. Perhaps she had more friends than her anxieties had allowed her to believe. From the darkest night came a tiny ray of hope: a triple-win situation. Susanna believed she could compartmentalize her thoughts by focusing on the challenging Norilskmetal project, keeping her boss and the multinational's board of directors at bay, and the legal de-partment content with proposals. When not working, she would be distracted by attending embassy receptions, impor-tant cultural events, and antique art auctions with Philip. One hand washes the other. Good for Philip's reputation in Moscow to be entertaining a sexy and interesting American

businesswoman from one of the largest multinationals. For-
eign-policy decisions regarding Russia would be validated in
America's newest frontier of democracy. All this, plus
Zhukov's interest in providing partial financing, more liquid-
ity from Omega Bank. And Lyova Kartsev would be back
soon. A win-win for all.

5

VERNISSAGE

LEXANDER ZHUKOV WAS BETTER KNOWN AS an art
expert than banker; an art historian and connoisseur,
he was now the model of a Private Citizen Giving
of Himself to Public Service. Zhukov had none of the hustler
in him: aristocratic investment banker, quintessential Russian,
only healthier and in better shape, with pink skin, pug nose,
blue eyes, and sandy hair, he was the son of a senior foreign
trade official, and had spent his childhood following his father
to overseas postings, including New Zealand and Australia,
an unheard-of privilege in the USSR. Realizing early that real
money was to be made in banking, he jumped straight from a
promising diplomatic career to a $300 million business, which
he liked to call a "pocket bank." He felt privileged to have been
asked to invest by GMG to participate in lending capital to

Norilskmetal.

Omega Bank had delivered a hand-written invitation to Susanna's office while she was away, inviting her to an important Soviet art show in the Manège, which might be of special interest. The exhibition, titled "The Russian Land and Its People," would display socialist art from private collections. Socialist Realism had become hot with collectors, an exciting, on-the-edge-item, and had moneymaking potential for the art world.

Philip had the flu and was not enthusiastic about the invitation or about attending. "I have a bad cold. This is not government business, my driver is on holiday, and I am not eager to be tossed around by Volodya, who travels at the speed of sound, ready to mash any Lada or Volga on the road. Valiant Soviet women, nationalism, and heroism. I'm sick of that."

But she was eager: her first time at an official event without Boris. "Philip, you *must* come and be there, for me and the State Department! This show is by invitation only. They're showing Soviet artists unknown in the West. Moscow's political elite will come—important government officials, interesting types. There'll be good food, and plenty of cognac for your cold, and more insight into the ideology and the history of proletarian culture representing peasants, workers, and soldiers."

"Oh God. I've been at this game for fifteen years.

I saw enough Soviet propaganda in the old days to last me a lifetime."

"But Philip, you don't know many Socialist Realist artists, the artistic credo of the 1930s. Some of them were very talented, won international and state prizes. The joyous paradise of happy and diligent farmers! Soviet family life, children filled with love, warmth, and discipline, giddy festivals of workers on farms and factories!"

WILD-EYED VOLODYA DID INDEED DRIVE impatiently and recklessly as always, cutting across three lanes on wide Moscow boulevards, swaying to the right and left on side streets where the Lada glided between hollows, and jumping over potholes. Philip tossed uncomfortably in his seat, clutching the car's safety handles.

It was early Saturday evening, and shops were closing. In the gathering darkness, the city was starting to grow quiet. Late February snow was still falling, damp, cold, and unrelenting, whirling in all directions. A wide sweep of their headlights brought into sudden sharp relief the vague shapes of pedestrians, a couple passionately embracing, a young person recklessly crossing the boulevard, an old man shuffling by with a crumpled newspaper under his arm, and several ageless, heavy-faced, unkempt women weighted down by bloated plastic and canvas bags, making their way home. In smaller streets, white trees quivered in the cold, wet dark of late winter, and lamps glowed in the soft haze, their light reflecting the façades of nineteenth-century mansions, crumbling former residences of the pre-revolutionary merchant class, old beauty made by people, not the state, now ornate offices of new millionaires and billionaires. The scene was like a dramatic and familiar stage set of some stately, uninteresting play.

"Wait for us, Volodya. "We expect to be here for some time." She and Philip sprinted briskly through the white, deserted square to the Manège, where Zhukov was waiting.

"Just a minute," a man in a hussar uniform, with an insolent face, called out in a bored tone. "This is by invitation only!" Susanna scowled and was rummaging in her purse when Zhukov spotted the pair and stared at the doorman, who dove forward with his whole body, releasing the doors.

"Welcome! I am so honored to see you here, Susanna," said Zhukov as he dramatically kissed her hand and took their fur coats to the coat room. She excused herself to the ladies' room to inspect her appearance, tidy her hair, put on lipstick, and, after tiny pats of makeup, drop everything back into her purse. It was the only time she had paid any attention to herself or felt attractive since losing Boris. She shrugged and quickened her step to the corridor where the men waited.

THE WHITEWASHED HALL WAS WELCOMINGLY warm, the hum of conversation pleasant. At first Philip surveyed the place over Susanna's shoulders, bobbing quickly up and down—his way of discharging unease—and nodded mechanically to the countless dignitaries, many of them familiar, drifting about. The ubiquitous narrow red carpet, unrolled for every official state occasion, reminded him of the last time he had been there, about two years before, when Russia was still the Soviet Union.

He exhaled, finally relaxing after Volodya's ride, smiled as he spotted the long tables generously laid with *zakuski*, caviar, bits of herring impaled on toothpicks, and bottles of wine, vodka, and cognac, good for his cold. Conscious of being Susanna's escort, he drifted in her direction.

The crowd was befittingly festive, the *nomenclatura* of old Soviet cultural bureaucracy gathering, the ladies in their beehive hairstyles and fancy frocks designed for slenderer frames, the gentlemen slimmed by the shiny French-tailored suits that signified access to special clothing stores. Susanna looked attractive and sexy, and Philip followed her silken legs, shook many hands, and even though he was not completely recovered, was delighted to have come.

"Congratulations, a thousand congratulations! What a gem!" She was chatting up the minister of culture and smiling speculatively at something he had said. Susanna, in her pale dress, was the incarnation of harmony and proportion, Philip thought as he considered plans for future challenges to his masculinity. Grabbing a small cognac, he had turned to join her again when his progress was suddenly halted by an exceptionally bejeweled matron whom he recognized as the minister of culture's wife. Her breasts and face bounced with mirth, and her meaty earlobes flashed sapphires the size of walnuts.

"Oh, Mr. Philip Dunlop the Second! What a great pleasure to meet you here! We last meet at embassy party two years past."

"Why, it's you, Sofia Alexeevna! Delighted! What an honor to see you again—such captivating company! You look glamorous as always," remarked Philip and, with a gesture of hyperbole, carried her hand to his lips.

"Yes, I happy you come to see great art of Mother Russia. Socialism with human face, our heritage! Many important people. Moscow's artistic, how you say, *crème de la crème* also here." She immediately excused herself and, with a burst of laughter and a flirtatious wink, flitted off to another group. Philip smiled and headed back to Susanna.

Enlightened and curious, they made their way past long walls of spotlit paintings: tides of workers and peasants; the Great Leader, larger than life, surrounded by wide-eyed, mesmerized children with half-opened mouths; grim, militant soldiers and peasants with pointed guns, clenched fists, and ripped clothes, heroically battling in the Great Patriotic War; hydroelectric stations, smoking factories. Production of useful objects for the revolutionary masses! Revolutionary transformation of everyday life!

Susanna was drawn to a large painting, a remarkable scene of birch trees bathed in sunlight, a blue river along an emerald shore dotted with cows, and sturdy girls beaming as they strode through fields, proudly carrying sacks of potatoes. "I actually love this one. This painting transcends all ideology,

Philip. I will have to ask Zhukov about the artist—perhaps he can get a price for me." She was again missing Boris. His smile of long ago came into her mind, and her stomach tightened with sadness. Boris was an encyclopedia of Russian culture and history for her, and she missed the personal history of the artist, the artist's place in Stalin's cultural order, his present residence, and a dinner invitation to negotiate the purchase.

Alexander Zhukov was right behind them, beaming.

"Very famous artist, Soviet Academy of Arts first prize in 1950! Loved by Stalin. Name is Malinin. What a pity—last month he was still alive, but now dead. Bad infarct."

Suddenly, as they turned the corner, they almost bumped into a startled Uncle Fima decked out in a gray Zegna suit and Hermès tie, with a "fortyish" cosmopolitan ingénue in a slinky white gown, definitely not his daughter but someone Susanna vaguely remembered from the art world. George Bablidze was one step behind them.

"Oh, Fima Abramovich, and Mr. Bablidze! What a surprise!" Susanna bubbled. "I haven't seen you since the sad tribute to our friend Boris. So nice to find you in a happier place. I did not know of your interest in art and art history. Let me introduce you to my American friend, another art history buff, Philip Dunlop II. Of course, you must know our local 'art tzar' Alexander Zhukov, responsible for this great event."

"Yes, of course," Fima replied, leaning forward. "Last month, we were lucky to find a Benz 550 for him. Green, the color of American dollars! Hah hah! Honored to see you again, Mr. Zhukov."

The lugubrious eyes of Fima's slinky friend eluded the company as the woman waltzed away. Susanna and the group, nonchalant, continued the conversation. "And allow me,"

Fima declared, "to introduce your American friend formally to Mr. Bablidze, a good comrade and director of Norilskmetal. Of course, Susanna, you remember him from our unhappy day at the Rossiya. He is still escaping from frigid Norilsk for Moscow fun! Hah hah!" His clever eyes flickered business opportunities and money-laundering schemes. He studied Susanna and continued. "Important for us to be here with serious people tonight, for my General Motors dealership in Moscow, for privatization and foreign investment in Russia's future, and for people like you and Mr. Dunlop, of course! We rename this show 'Russia, the Land of Privatization and Foreign Investment!' and I am soaring on the muse of commerce, hah hah!"

Susanna's eyes lit up immediately upon hearing the words "investment" and "privatization" imagining Norilsk. She sauntered closer to Uncle Fima and his friend, as if walking on air, paying special attention to Bablidze, more handsome than all the others milling around the exhibit. Bablidze took special pleasure in being unspectacular. Philip had spotted it in the nerveless immobility of his courteous body as Fima introduced him.

"Mr. Bablidze is a well-known geologist and metallurgist. His experience in separating metals goes back a long way, like these paintings," he quipped. "I am honored to be working with true professional and scholar."

"I am indeed impressed." Susanna smiled and nodded convincingly.

"Together, George—Ghiya, that is—and I work on a new refinery project for Russia. No more shipping metal scrap and chips and computers and spent catalysts to Germany, Belgium, or Indian refining companies in New Jersey!" Fima continued.

"Why, Fima Abramovich! You are a titan of trade and industry!" Susanna exclaimed.

In the midst of the social chatter, she heard the familiar voice of Sveta Khaykin, an investigative reporter from the *Kommersant* and a good friend:

"Why, Sveta, great to see you! What are you doing here? No human rights problems in the Manège for Amnesty International or the Memorial Group? No surveillance for you this evening," Susanna teased.

"Hi, Susanna. So good to have you back and enjoying our art! So terribly sorry about your tragedies." The mention of losses saddened her friend, and Sveta, instantly regretting the allusion to them, abruptly changed the subject. "We were just children with red neckerchiefs when these paintings were created, so I came to take a closer look. Our teachers explained the miracles of heroic labor—central to the iconography of Socialist Realism. The artist Arkady Plastov—the painting right behind us—won the Stalin Prize in 1938. A time of terror . . . "Some very fine artists here, though, Soviet masterpieces now going for very high prices. What are you working on now, Susanna? These are exciting times for foreign companies."

"A financing project above the Arctic," Susanna said quietly.

"Well," Sveta murmured. "I've been trying to get there myself—striking workers, disturbances and grievances—some commercial flights canceled. Protesting workers at the smelting complex are venting their rage at management's failure to solve wage disputes, and the State is involved . . . "

Susanna was unaware but uneasy with the information. She raised her eyes.

"We must get together very soon in a quieter place."

"Yes, after I return from the Arctic. Look after yourself, Susanna. *Poka!*"

Distracted, Susanna returned to the conversation with

Bablidze, wanting to impress him as a member of the American meritocracy with her knowledge of Russian history. "As you know, Alexander III appointed Count Witte minister of the economy—a man who wanted to make Russia a great capitalist power. But Witte couldn't succeed. Russia was two hundred years behind the West. Now the country continues where Witte stopped. Russia is on the road to open markets and democracy—free markets, not only in art, but in mining and industry."

"*Ura* for new times, and our success in Norilsk!" Fima smiled heartily, reaching for his glass. "Exactly, I agree with you Susanna. We, like all Americans, finally believe in capitalism and private property!"

"Imagine," Philip remarked, "Moscow—a minor feudal principality, followed by the Mongol raids, czarism, the all-powerful central state, and now a free market *Rus'*." He sounded as if he were reading a history text at the wrong time, the wrong place.

Mr. Bablidze was silent, his face almost blushing: He squinted, admiring Susanna. "Yes, of course, we met at the Rossiya. Very sad time! Boris's *pominki*. He was my good friend, and also interested in Georgian artists and hockey players. A surprise and great pleasure to see you here."

Susanna, astonished by her good fortune and Bablidze's attention, pressed on. "Yes, Count Witte was a great Russian statesman, responsible for Siberian colonization, you know—and indirectly for your success in Norilsk."

"You are very well informed," he remarked, studying Susanna.

Fima relaxed into an easier posture as he gently rubbed the sleeve of Philip's cashmere jacket and explained, "We now have the most lucrative market in the world for foreign investors and industrialists. *Property* is the way to democracy.

I think it is wonderful thing. Everyone should have some of it! Our Russia should stop being the *kormushka*, a feeding trough for the world's metals! We must refine metals and ship the bullion from Russia in our own planes."

"I think the poor man has had too much champagne," Susanna murmured to Philip.

"We price metals at Russian prices at home and export bars and bullion at world prices on free market. Metal flies to Zurich, Amsterdam, London, New York. We have many friends and very smart people in Norilsk. We just need financing to upgrade technology, and our export potential will make South Africa look like, how you say, crumbs!"

There was no stopping him. "Yes, of course." Susanna nodded. Fima was writing his own economic plan for the Kremlin. She sighed, dug her heels into the red carpet, and listened. Boris should have been there! She felt alone and insecure. She depended on him, trusted his Russian business instincts more than her own. He would have known precisely how to interpret body language and handle Bablidze and Fima Abramovich. He continued, "This is not how we say 'potato patch business'! But how you say, 'arbitrage business'! Money goes to the Central Bank of Russia, not Lichtenstein or Cyprus!"

"Of course, Fima Abramovich, you will become Russia's celebrated arbitrageur!" Excited by her discussion with Bablidze and flattered by his attention, she again had an epiphany, an Adam Smith moment! Uncle Fima's network of connections and microeconomics, Bablidze's position of authority, and her work for GMG! Natural resources in Norilsk fused to the international commodity business, headed by one of America's most powerful companies! With Boris gone, Fima will become the facilitator for the project, between Norilsk chiefs and the Ministry for Nonferrous Metals in

Moscow, now in central focus to the CEO and her board of directors. Susanna, Fima, and Alexander Zhukov with his bank's "hot money" pursuing the Norilskmetal project with the international agencies and the State Department. Susanna would make *fortunes* for herself and GMG. Philip Dunlop and Zhukov found her sexy and interesting. She was determined to compartmentalize her life—and hide the grief by socializing at embassy receptions, cultural events, antique and art auctions, while Philip advised her on foreign policy decisions in America's newest frontier for democracy!

Her eyes glittered for the first time since her arrival in Moscow. With a tense smile she approached the subject tangentially. "You know, gentlemen, the world of art and commerce is always the same. Like the Medicis in fifteenth-century Italy —money and power wear the same hat, have the same interests. Now the art market here is also international business, and your interest in art is very useful for the New Russia."

Zhukov continued Susanna's commentary. "During communism, only the party dictated art. The good artists were forced to interpret aesthetics only as socialist objects, not possessions. Art was a weapon for socialism, while capitalism translated into bad aesthetics. Unfortunately, communist ideas translated not only into low-grade production, inferior commerce, but also interesting art. Just look around!"

Uncle Fima and Bablidze carefully scrutinized Zhukov and nodded tentatively. Zhukov's eyes sparkled as he lit another Rothman cigarette, twirled his flute of champagne, and looked at Susanna and Philip. "Red propaganda. Red backgrounds, red flags, red stars. Parades of red banners, red pioneers marching. Shining eyes of children understand joy and happiness of communism. Just look at Boris Vladimirsky's masterpiece, *Roses for Stalin.* Brilliant red roses reflected in smiles of children and red pioneer scarves, children mesmerized by

Stalin's kindly face! Almost quaint."

Bablidze replied seriously, "Don't forget! This art belonged to the people and was displayed in hospitals, public buildings, schools, offices, factories, and museums in the country."

"A most challenging effort for curators to mount this exhibition," Susanna added excitedly. "You are a true Renaissance man."

Fima ventured his expertise as well. "Here, look at the paintings of how you say, *narod*, the people of mother Russia, very poor people—mostly seamstresses, soldiers, sailors, and peasants."

Uncle Fima wanted to continue, but Philip Dunlop cut him short. "Look at what the *narod* is wearing—tattered clothes—such poverty—no Versace or Fendi here." He helped himself to another glass of champagne. "Very good champagne. Russian, I see," he murmured, just as a waiter offered a small linen napkin.

"Soviet sparkling," Zhukov declared, looking up with a face full of childish pride. "We're going to be exporting the stuff very soon."

Philip put his glass down, and, all tongue-in-cheek, remarked authoritatively but somewhat sarcastically, "A wonderful show! We are happy Russian nationalism prevails again."

Finally, in happy recognition, Fima grabbed the sleeve of Philip's jacket again. "You know, Mr. De-de-Dunlop—oh! Now I remember you! We meet last two years in U.S.-Russian Business Council conference at the American Embassy on Spasskaya. Susanna and GMG are your perfect business partners for Russia! Of course, you are Mr. Philip Dunlop, how you say, a diplomatist!"

Suddenly interested in engaging Philip, Zhukov smiled,

pulled more deeply on his Rothman, and continued like a do-cent, "You know, the Manège was first built as a riding acad-emy for the nobility."

Not to be outdone, Fima jumped in again. "Yes, some crit-ics say that the paintings now here only fit for horses' stable! Hah, hah." His chest swelled with pride, and his eyes twin-kled as he congratulated himself on his natural sense of humor.

Philip, suddenly the center of attention, nodded, standing a little to the side, a thin smile on his face expressing some mild displeasure. "What's on a sober man's mind, the drunk-ard has it on his tongue," he quietly whispered to Susanna, showing off his knowledge of colloquial Russian as she nudged to silence him, realizing that he wasn't "getting" it again.

6

NUMBER 38 PETROVKA

THE HARPIST ON STAGE IN THE METROPOL HOTEL dining room played with languid, circular strokes, eyes closed, apparently oblivious of Susanna sitting alone at a front table, nursing a cognac in the morning before lunch. February felt like it would never end, but Lev was finally back in Moscow, and now she sat in this hotel dining room. At the entrance, the usual gaggle of pimps, drug-pushers, and currency dealers was hanging around, analyzing and assessing the guests entering.

Finally, she spotted him from the window as he hurried into the lobby, chin buried in the upturned collar of his coat. Shaking out his *ushanka*, he perfunctorily handed the hat and the coat to a solicitous young woman in the coat room, made his way past pink tablecloths and red banquettes, and sat down at Susanna's table. *"Privet, zolotaya,* Susanna, what a tragedy," he said empathetically. He reached over and, squeezed her hand. Lev, tall, blond, and slim, fit, with an open, Slavic face and probing eyes, was ingratiating and polite. Rearranging his chair, he sat down to watch the harpist.

"Isn't she an angel? Golden hair, white skin, white gown. All she needs is a pair of wings. Imagine what it's like for her, getting up at six in the morning, dressing, riding the metro from God knows where, to waste beautiful music on this crowd!" Finally making eye contact with Susanna, he stroked her hair, cupped her hand, and kissed it. He was studying her face—a reflection perhaps of his quaking heart, or a salute to her charms.

"I've been waiting for your return for weeks. How are you, and where were you?" Smiling, she removed the hand, tossing her hair.

"As the empire was crumbling, there were many changes for me as well," replied Lev, looking straight at her. "Dear Susanna. I feel such sorrow for your losses, at home and here. *Chyornyie polosa.* I'm so sorry for the black streaks in your life. I heard about Boris's murder and got to Moscow as quickly as I could."

"Impossible losses. My very center melted with Peter's death. I came back because, at home, my life had no shape, no sound. The heart is broken, and now Moscow is not even a Band-Aid—with Boris gone, I can't focus on business here, and I have no energy."

They shared another tense silence, broken only by, "My God, My God," whispered by Lev. He was overwhelmed with her grief and confused, sensing that hope for intimacy with her might not be reciprocated. "I understand. A tragedy, frightening *sudba.*"

With a shudder, she adjusted her chair and closed her eyes.

"For years, he was the reason I commuted here. I needed him and he was my anchor. I loved him and worked with him. He was my consultant, knew important people in Norilsk, and he was ready to introduce me to Mr. Bablidze. Now I'm just blowing in the wind and don't know where to turn." She gasped for air as if her feelings were strangling her, swallowed hard and felt safe enough with Lev to sob.

He listened in silence. "I am so sorry, Susanna." He reached for her hand again, looked into her eyes, determined to change the conversation. "Well, I have come out of retirement myself. I've formed my own, uh, 'analytical' company."

Susanna's sobs trailed to sniffles, and she smiled at the euphemism. "Your own business! Congratulations. What's your role in the firm?" she asked tentatively.

"Everything! We are registered in Kaliningrad. Same intelligence work here and abroad. Russian deals with foreign partners. Expatriates come for protection—people can't sleep at night and are frightened. I am the CEO—same business, in a new and pretty wrapper."

She shrugged and glanced around the room. The harpist's fingers had stopped for a while. The place was filling up, and waitresses were navigating the room at high speed.

"The Wild East," he said, "is coming too close to home. You know, Boris had some powerful friends." Lev observed her seriously. "I am insinuating foul play, definitely foul play—murder, to be exact. You don't need to be a detective to know that murder is often covered up with a heart attack or an electrical fire. Zhora and Sosa were in *Piter* with him on art business for their gallery in New York. Negotiating about two works from an unknown private collection, questionable provenance . . . the paintings were originally exhibited in Krasnoyarsk. Or perhaps the Georgian mafia business related to vouchers and shares, or the many friends he wined and dined for business, agents with and without diplomatic immunity. We know the guys returned to Moscow for the funeral, and vanished. St. Petersburg, Helsinki, New York—that was their route."

Susanna was not surprised. She sat up straight, and moved her chair a bit away from his. "I thought you would know about these logistics—and where are we going with that information, Lev?"

"I've been following the case, and have my own contacts. I've been in the security business for a long time—since Brezhnev. Important information bounces off my radar screen, especially anything related to you, Susanna." He formally handed her his *visitka*. She swallowed some cognac.

"My only interest is in finding the murderers. The local police say the case is not closed but languishing at police headquarters. Uncle Fima is too involved in his business. I know it's unfair, but I need you to fight for me! I can't get anywhere on this case without you!"

"Yes, scant and contradictory information. You're right, the case is not closed but merely left unattended. The process apparently quietly stalled. It will disappear for lack of attention, and join many other unsolved murders in oblivion," he said flatly. She studied his face for more, allowing him to construct an answer she could believe; but that was all he was willing to divulge.

"Yes," she mumbled at last, "the local police can never penetrate deep into the system. Boris was involved in many businesses. Important art was also stolen. Agafya Ivanovna, the housekeeper in his apartment house, is a suspect. What a joke—they know how to close ranks and remove evidence."

"It's still early in the day," he said abruptly. "Kalugin, the prosecutor, should be back in his office." Lev rose from the table, picked up a house phone at a credenza beneath the antique, well-preserved tsarist wall paper and quickly spoke with Kalugin.

MOSCOW BREEDS POWER. YOU CANNOT HELP feeling that you are trespassing in its path. Eight lanes of traffic raced in each direction through Kalinin Prospekt, bounded by five-story rectangles of concrete and glass and larger twenty-five-story buildings of the same design. Copies of the avenue could be found in every new city being erected, and it was a Moscow prototype of a march to the future. Their taxi sped along over a pedestrian underpass. Abutting the avenue stood the six-story complex that was the Moscow militia headquarters, regularly described in old newspapers as the "very brain center of Moscow, ready to respond within seconds to reports of accidents or crimes in the safest city in the world."

Number 38 Petrovka, a faded yellow mansion, looked shabby and in need of a good cleaning, its grime at once comforting and an affront. Leaving the taxi, Susanna and Lev hurried into the building, separately, as if hiding from each other.

Lev did not stop at the door but, flashing a card, went directly up the staircase to the second floor. Half a dozen people were sitting on chairs along the wall, all of them scrutinizing him and Susanna as they came in. Officers, like busy ants, coming in and out with papers and folders in their hands, shuttled between offices. "We're here to see the Chief, Mr. Kalugin, please," Lev announced.

"He is in his office, waiting," said the receptionist with an airy wave of her hands with its red-painted fingernails, finding it difficult to focus on the guests.

A uniformed police secretary ushered Susanna and Lev into the prosecutor's office, where a pile of dossiers sat on the desk. Kalugin gave Lev the faintest of nods, carefully studied Susanna, and continued reading a newspaper. The secretary promptly returned with tea and biscuits.

Diminutive and pot-bellied, the State Prosecutor seemed even thicker than he was. With brisk energy and a smiling pink face set off by wisps of white hair, Kalugin gave the impression of being someone's kindly uncle with a pugnacious, combustible side. He was a figure of unusual authority, however—as senior crime investigator of the Moscow militia, he oversaw all criminal investigations, representing both state and defendant. All arrests had to meet with the prosecutor's approval, court sentences came under his review, and he reviewed all appeals. No matter how great or small the case, everyone answered to him.

He answered only to the prosecutor general. His job was, thus, a balancing act: equal measures of aggressiveness and discretion. Since he was not an old party apparatchik, he had gone as far as he could in the system.

"Just returned from the Krasnaya Presnya district. Conference all morning. You see this enormous map of Moscow?" he grunted, pointing back. The map covered a rear wall and was divided into thirty borough divisions studded with lights. "And all the lights? One hundred thirty-five precinct stations, blinking day and night. No time to catch my breath. Now, what can I do for you, Lev Antonovich and the beautiful lady?" Kalugin's face had turned crimson with anger as he spoke.

"Sorry, Pyotr Pavlovich, this is Susanna Thompson."

Susanna rose and, with the erect carriage of a dancer, reached out her hand, which he ignored. "Vice-president of GMG, the Global Metal Group, recently promoted director of their office in Moscow. She has been working with us for many years, buying our platinum group metals for American industry. She is a longtime good friend of the murdered doctor and his family. Just returned to Moscow to find him murdered. As a specialist in homicides, I am sure you have studied the case."

The aging cherub pushed away the paper, shoved the dossiers forward, and said, "Yes, I am familiar with the case." He pointed to the file and examined the photograph affixed to the dossier. "The case is very delicate because of the politics involved. We have examined and photographed the body. Case number 2008 is classified as arson and art theft, not homicide." He folded the dossier, flipped it closed, and put it aside. "Fortunately, the officers on the case are at their desks. We can discuss the investigation in progress with them directly."

The first two officers to appear were members of the Moscow City Militia public security unit, the proletariat of the city's vast police and intelligence apparatus. They walked a delicate line between criminal and cop, could have gone either way in their career, and on occasion probably have. The ranking officer was a stubble-chinned sergeant who only spoke Russian. He wore jeans, a black leather jacket, and a pair of wraparound sunglasses up on his head. He read a brief statement on his findings from Agafya Ivanovna, the housekeeper and sometimes concierge on Tverskaya, and reported a few more facts, including some names and nationalities of Boris's friends. The assistant officer translated his report into illiterate, halting English.

"Georgian gangsters," the ranking officer declared in disgust. "Responsibility for the case has been transferred to another department," they announced in both languages, and excused themselves.

"Which department is that?" Susanna pleaded.

Kalugin did not respond. He was absentmindedly drumming his fingertips on the desktop, a habit he had never been able to break. He knew it was nerves and repressed energy. "We are questioning some hockey players, many friends, and

Agafya Ivanovna. The militia reported that two of his Georgian friends left the country. There is little chance of extradition, as your friend should know. I understand you are now in the international security business, my friend Lev Sergeevich."

For a moment, Lev was too startled to reply. He raised his eyes with a bitter smile on his lips as Kalugin ranted on. "We need a confession. Undetected or unproven crime is impossible to follow across oceans. Our militia does not work to combat art smuggled from museums or private collections in domestic dwellings. And this is Moscow, not the Hermitage in St. Petersburg."

Lev cleared his throat, sat up straighter in his chair, and declared in a voice ripe with puzzled indignation, "Murder is the aggravating circumstance here. You must change case number 2008 to homicide, first and foremost, Pyotr Pavlovich! The victim did not die of arson or an infarct. He died of asphyxiation, an inability to breathe. He was choked. Any rookie in your department knows that ligatures do not suggest accidental death. It was a *violent* crime. Murder is a *capital crime*. Why is the militia still investigating *arson* and *art theft*?"

The prosecutor sighed as an adult sighs to a child.

"These cases generally start with something extremely small, and then start unraveling—politically very difficult to prosecute. The local precinct analyzed the case and reported it would take months to know the results of that kind of an investigation. To convict, we need a confession."

"But Pyotr Pavlovich, we are very old friends, and you are the chief—a forensic specialist in homicides."

Kalugin leaned forward, knuckles on the table, and turned his belly toward him. "You know, Lev Sergeevich, revenge is a constant theme in Russian history: Man was not born a criminal but fell into error through unfortunate circumstances, or the influence of negative elements—egoism, sloth, parasitism, or drunkenness."

Disheartened and frustrated, Lev sneered, "Yes, I've also memorized the Soviet texts. Avarice and envy are merely vices that lead to the slothful belief that it is easier to steal than to work. But theft, arson, or murder are *personal choices.*"

Kalugin slammed his fist again on the desk. "But the statistics are more *serious* now—what we are seeing in Russia today are huge corrupt deals within state companies and foreign investors. And if you have big corrupt deals, then you have more private misunderstandings and contract murders. Now most crimes can be traced to our new 'democracy and market economy.'"

"Pyotr Pavlovich," Lev retorted, palms outspread,

"Boris was a Russian doctor. The prosecutor is responsible for overseeing and protecting the rights of a Russian citizen."

Susanna had meanwhile fallen into a resentful and sullen silence, only deepened by Kalugin's persistent monologue. There was no respite. "This case is not closed, it needs to be further investigated, yes, but remember what Stalin said: 'When you chop down a tree, splinters fly.' Your Boris Naumovich Rozenbaum is dead and buried. I cannot question dead people, and I can't arrest people who have left the country. A confession is the only evidence that counts."

"KALUGIN'S INVESTIGATION IS COMPLETELY INADEQUATE," Susanna whispered to Lev as they flagged a taxi. She remembered one of the grimmer remarks attributed to Stalin: "No man, no problem." Lev nodded. "Kalugin has no agenda here," Susanna went on. "This case didn't fall into his lap, and there are no relatives or officials paying a bribe. In the course of things, it will disappear for lack of attention and fall into oblivion—Russian justice."

"I must say," Lev replied dryly, "you've never been wrong, but you must understand—the MVD militia now is strictly limited to matters of national security. The investigation will come to a halt unless the KGB chooses to pursue it."

Susanna was taken aback again, too numbed to reply. "Why would the KGB pursue it?"

"The public prosecutor's office investigates all crimes except the political ones. If this case is of special interest to them, they have to define their jurisdiction here. This murder may turn into a political case of special interest to the KGB. Hundreds of our paintings are smuggled out of Russia, but this murder involved more than the art business. I am certain Boris was also involved in black market and business deals with foreigners—security issues, industrial espionage. Very provocative, outrageous actions for a doctor, some would say."

Susanna's eyes were wet with anger. "Yes, Lev, medicine was his profession, and many deals were protected under that umbrella. But this is Moscow! Would athletes, hockey stars, or his chess buddies confide to an American? I still haven't woken up from this nightmare. We must get our arms around the viciousness of this crime."

"We all know Kalugin, my old pal, is a bastard. Boris and his black market friends fell out over a division of profits. They killed him. It was planned, prepared, and executed. But choked to death is a little strange, even for them." Lev's voice was deliberate, bursting with contempt. "My friend Sergei Kotkov is a homicide investigator for the KGB." He avoided Susanna's startled expression as the taxi sped along to the KGB headquarters.

CHANGING NAMES AND ACRONYMS OF VARIOUS institutions was a holdover from the old Chekist days—secrets within secrets. But every breathing soul in Moscow knew the building

for exactly what it was: the old KGB headquarters, now the
FSB, overlooking the Khodynka airfield. Referred to as the
"Aquarium," it was an eyesore, a decrepit reminder of the
bloody purges of Stalin's day.

Sergei Kotkov didn't look like a homicide investigator but
an academic. He was about forty, of medium height, lean and
compact, with dark hair, not quite black, that he combed back
when it fell onto his forehead.

His strong face slightly hawkish but soft, with steel-
rimmed glasses and blue ball-bearing eyes, probably descended
from nobility, he appeared too genteel for the job. A smart,
engaging, and relaxed guy, he was calm and urbane, excellent
in gathering evidence, a skilled diplomat, and expert at his
work.

"Sorry, a conference at the Forensic Institute kept me
away," he said, adjusting his Coke-bottle glasses, when they
entered. "Close the doors, please," he ordered while shaking
hands peremptorily.

"Susanna Thompson, Sergei," said Lev.

"Consider it my privilege, Mrs. Thompson. Of course
I've heard of GMG. How can we help?" No secretaries, no
tea receptions here. "Lev Sergeevich, it's been a long time.
Where have you been?"

"Away from Moscow for a long time. Started my own security business for corporations. Due diligence, special assign-
ments, industrial espionage. I am staffed with good people
collecting information, eavesdropping on rival companies, and
stealing documents. Sometimes less sanitary services. Every
Russian corporation needs its own mini-KGB." Lev's voice
remained sonorous and direct, as he handed Kotkov his new a
business card. Kotkov fingered it. "Analytical Company, Director—offices in Kaliningrad and London, with a beautiful
bodyguard?" Kotkov quickly studied Susanna and smiled at

his egregious euphemism. "Personal security for high-level executives when they are traveling here and abroad."

"Excuse me," Lev countered, "fighting the *kryshas* is good business," making something less of the comment. "You must know that Susanna Thompson is the Moscow representative and director for GMG. Global Metals' Group offices are in the Slavyanskaya. They are one of the largest conglomerates dealing in precious metals, from mining to financial services, to supplying industry. The firm is capitalized in billions with offices in 130 countries."

"Yes, of course, Welcome to you both. What can I do for you, Lev Antonovich?"

"The unsolved Moscow murder of Boris Naumovich Rozenbaum, one of the city's best physicians, serving our sport teams in the international competitions of our New Democratic Russia."

"Petrovka is the place," Kotkov said flatly, "and you are wasting my time." He rolled his chair between the desk and the window.

"Sergey, Dr. Rozenbaum was Mrs. Thompson's very dear friend and worked as a consultant for her company. He was also associated with George Bablidze after the big sell-off in voucher auctions for privatization of Norilskmetal.

Mr. Bablidze practically supported sports when money ran out and funded many trips for our hockey team to Europe and America."

Kotkov's eyes registered approval. "Kalugin and his department in Petrovka," he emphasized.

"But Kalugin has diluted the case to theft and arson, and a collection of loose ends and dead ends. Some suspects have already fled the country, the process has been neglected and has quietly stalled."

Kotkov comfortably rolled his chair to his desk, brooding

over the pair, and reached for his cigarettes.

"This is obviously a case related to organized crime and contract killings, one of our most lucrative industries, as you know. Routine stuff, of course. Arson, theft, description of crime scene, injuries to victim. Mafia-type crime information. But national security?" He paused, looking at the pair. "You are the expert here, Lev Antonovich, but if you like I can get the file transferred to my office. Not to worry."

Feeling ill at ease, Kotkov rose, suggesting it was time for them to go.

On the street, Lev wrapped his arm around Susanna's shoulders. Another grim and gray day had ended in Moscow, and she was overcome with a feeling of emptiness.

7

ARAGVI RESTAURANT

N EITHER SUSANNA NOR PHILIP HAD EVER dined at the
Aragvi, a Georgian restaurant in Moscow well
known from Soviet times, a favorite dining spot for
Stalin, whose bodyguards, called "the back-room boys," invaded the kitchen and tasted all the food to be served to the
vozhd.

The place was less baroque and less gaudy than the newer
establishments, and maintained an old-world Soviet-Georgian
charm. It had dark green walls with scarlet velvet banquettes,
simple Russian Arts and Crafts chairs, square and round malachite tables, very high ceilings with gold modernist electrified-
gas chandeliers, and Gallé style table lamps. It was in a word,
impressive.

But the atmosphere was stuffy and morose, and there was

a faint scent of mold and must from the old maroon carpet and the intricately fringed curtains, both of which needed an airing.

Again, Uncle Fima had made the arrangements—a private corner room in the back, with scarlet velvet banquettes, chairs, and a round malachite table elaborately set with what looked like Kremlin silver. At a small square table outside the main dining room sat three aides-de camp, minders: Volodya, a gun unobtrusive in his jacket, and Bablidze's and Fima's drivers, Makarov pistols buttoned up in their suits, cradling their drinks, sucking on cigarettes.

Six people sat around the big table in the smaller dining room: Susanna and Philip Dunlop; William Burke, the former director of the USSR Division of the U.S. Department of Commerce, now retired and newly appointed president of the Russian American Investment Bank, owned by GMG; Uncle Fima with a perennial lady friend, Tanya, whom he confidently introduced as his Moscow cousin and whom Susanna remembered as Fima's mysterious escort in the white gown, and George Bablidze.

"Yes, of course you have met Tatyana Rubinshtein, at the exhibition at the Manège."

Susanna was energized. "So pleased to see you again. You looked beautiful there, but we had no chance to speak. Remember, I visited your splendid collection in your apartment in the Arbat last year. I love some of your paintings and really want to see them again! Especially the Daineka, a sensuous pose of the woman—such energy and color. So aesthetic and yet angular, brilliant Constructivism." Susanna was almost as eager to buy the early Daineka from Tanya as she was interested in success with Norilskmetal. "How are your beautiful daughters?"

"*Normalno*, thanks. Growing up very quickly. One, like

mother, studying art history, the younger in veterinary school." Tanya tentatively extended her hand to Susanna and the others.

"A great relative and friend, very interesting woman, a curator at the Tretyakovskaya, and a great artist in her own right," Uncle Fima announced as Tanya shook her head bashfully, overcome with the attention, apologetically rolled her eyes and squirmed back into her chair.

She somehow felt pressured to speak about the museum and avoid conversation about her private collection. "The Tretyakov Gallery, in Moscow, is one of the world's largest museums of fine art, and I am curator of non-conformist art— you must know, art not accepted by Stalin. The Russian avant-garde, Cubism, Futurism, Constructivism, Dadaism, and Surrealism. Rodchenko, Malevich, Goncharova, you know— artists created great art despite purges. Now of course, our museum also shows Picasso, Cezanne, Degas, Matisse, Gauguin. We invite you to visit, of course." Tanya was justifying her presence and did not know how to continue. She grinned and sank into a depressed silence, her emerald eyes shot through with apprehension. Uncle Fima saved the day again. The contrast between the two was too great to be ignored.

"You must know name of Tanyusha's father, Kuba Rubinshtein, best private avant-garde collection in Moscow, good friend of Boris's father, Naum Rozenbaum. Begun in NEP period—I've heard stories about both of them competing for the Malevich in Tanya's collection. Now, Tanyusha has a private museum in her apartment. We have all heard the sentimental nonsense about wives wanting to get rid of mistresses, hah hah. But we can't get rid of beautiful and intelligent relatives—hah hah!" He grinned wickedly at his own wit.

Tanya smiled timidly, hands clasping her chair, lips quivering.

A SET OF VODKA GLASSES AND elaborate dishes of Georgian appetizers arrived on the table. Uncle Fima explained the content of each; and when the waiter was gone, a guitarist strumming Georgian folksongs appeared at the table. Large, sumptuous plates materialized as if on a conveyor—marinated mutton, vegetables, sauces, all covered by immense silver domes. Tuxedoed waiters, two gorgeous young kids, unveiled course after course with remarkable flair, raising broad silver lids from big silver plates, making sweeping bows in unison to reveal brown food beneath. The dinner, in fact, was served Kremlin style: a waiter behind each chair, pouring, tidying, rearranging the silverware, making guests uncomfortable, and intently watching their every move and wish. Soon a small loaf of thick khachapuri, a homey flatbread with soft ricotta-like cheese, appeared on each bread plate. Again, new wine bottles on the table. Susanna was distracted, wondering why Boris's father hadn't bought the sensuous Daineka painting in Tanya's collection, one of the artist's best.

The group made sentimental toasts in rapid succession: first to Bablidze, then to exotic Georgia. Susanna began:

"To Georgia; I've only read Lermontov about the white peaks of the Caucasus range and the rugged landscapes of wild beauty."

Fima waxed poetic: "To our guest Georghi Bablidze—from the land of white-capped mountains glistening under an infinite sky where guerrillas ambushed czarist soldiers a century ago. Hah hah!—and of course, the land of black-eyed lasses!"

Bablidze nearly threw his arms around Susanna in embarrassment and gratitude for his beloved, now independent country. "You are invited, any time, and I personally will be your guide."

He was a small, energetic man with thick black hair and chocolate brown eyes, soft hands, and the elaborately courteous manners of his native country, now living at the edge of the world. The remoteness of the Arctic magnified his power, while foreign investment placed him in the eye of the hurricane for Norilsk tenders. Trained as a geologist in Moscow and Tbilisi, the ancient elegant city of cobblestoned streets and sidewalk cafes, a son of an NKVD officer, he had been a political prisoner, spent years in prison cells, and once had been stabbed by a political provocateur in prison. "I was locked up with the underclass—hereditary criminals, informers, socially hostile elements, fascists, enemies of the people. Violence, randomness, wildness." His face red and his feelings finally unbuttoned, he continued sweeping back his long fingers through his hair, lighting one cigarette from another. His face was surrounded by a haze of smoke, while Fima tried to cloak Bablidze's litany by coughing and chuckling.

"When I was released and back in Tbilisi with a wife and two children, I struggled to make ends meet."

More toasts followed—to Tanya, Russian culture and art, business, Susanna, Philip, William Burke, and America. Soon, when it was time to get down to work, glazed eyes and alcoholic stupor were interfering with the business agenda. Bablidze was besotted—in a surprisingly soft-spoken voice, with a slight stutter, and a smile so gentle it was almost wimpish, he began slowly and officially. "After all, Russia has vast mineral wealth and is the world's second-largest producer of non-ferrous metals," he declared. Every statement was punctuated by sharp exhalations of cigarette smoke and a leisurely stretch for the vodka bottle. "To realize our potential, your cooperation is of interest to us. We have already privatized the company, and systematized corporate restructuring, but as always in revolutions, mistakes have been made. We need our partner's investments to upgrade technology in Norilsk. We also need American drive, initiative, and adaptability," he added softly.

Fima, his face flushed with excitement, leaped in and rattled on nonstop. "Our *ukaz* is now profit motive. Our official ideology is to make Russia a great country again!"

"But this is not a place for business discussions, Fima Abramovich. We invite you, Mr. Dunlop, and Mr. Burke to Norilsk to structure a protocol agreement with Deputy Director and Industrial Manager of Norilskmetal, Aleksandr Kulichkov. I will study details of the financial investment tender very soon," Bablidze added calmly. He paused, pushed back his chair, and studied his spit-shined shoes.

"Yes, of course, whatever you suggest, Director Bablidze," Fima added, grinning obsequiously.

Susanna and Dunlop were encouraged by such authoritative and direct comments. Susanna, gripping the soothing velvet upholstery, sat up, breathed deeply, shot a glance at Burke, looking for support, who said, "Since we are a private investment bank, instructed to draw foreign direct investment for this project, I am on board."

Susanna paused and assessed Burke's statement. "Well, we will report to corporate headquarters and organize our plans for a preliminary visit to Norilskmetal. When my work is done, our chief will fly his new private airplane to Moscow, maybe to Norilsk!"

Bablidze couldn't resist. "A private plane?"

"Yes, a Gulfstream, I believe. Mr. Hanken uses his own plane to visit the firm's operations in countries worldwide."

"Understood, I hear your chief was very courageous, a great ally in our war, and now a great business leader."

Burke, sitting very quietly, officially interjected,

"We will be eager to study this important project with our bank and the American Chamber of Commerce in Russia, the Council for Trade and Economic Cooperation, and the State

Department, of course."

The deal was already happening. Uncle Fima grew cautious, shocked by so much cross-cultural information, and again resorted to humor. "We are all good friends, Susanna. You know the old Soviet *anekdot*. As friends, we agree on price and costs, and then we find metal in Siberian *oblasts*, especially Norilsk. With your investments and technical support, we will also build plant for refining and recycling in the Motherland, and ship our own bullion to Amsterdam, Zurich, and even Detroit!"

Susanna took a deep breath, twisted her napkin, and, scrutinizing Philip's face, thought about Boris. She needed him at this discussion. He would have known what to say, how to interpret, analyze the body language. Finally, making a rich sound in her throat, a complicated mixture of affection and authority, she replied, "As director of Norilskmetal, Mr. Bablidze must know we are speaking of very big business here. We are here because of Russia's natural resources. Trading in commodities, our technological expertise and financial strategies can give us the widest global scope, and will provide good growth opportunities for years ahead. Our company is financially very strong, our multinational sales force makes business happen all over the world, and I, as director of the Moscow office, hope to make it happen in Russia!"

It became apparent that Fima's objective was to collect as much information about the deal as his laughter and jokes would permit, and call it a day. "Yes, Susanna, you are the modern symbol of famous old Marxist and modern capitalist idea: The empowerment of women! Hah hah! And of course, negotiation and compromise. I remember my grandfather, long life to him in heaven! A true Bolshevik, he worked with Comrade Lenin in New Economic Policy. Now we just change name from 'NEP' to 'Privatization, Democracy and

Free Market' but now we will have success."

Bablidze lowered his head and muttered something in Georgian. Slavic despair and depression had swallowed him, his mood turned the color of the Aragvi's dark green walls and the malachite tables. He slowly made eye contact with Fima and exhaled. Fima, sensing his mood, gestured to ease the atmosphere. Looking up at the sparkling crystal chandelier and pushing back his chair, he rose, startling the waiter behind him. Everyone swallowed hard and waited. "After great food, economics is bad for the digestive system! Perfect time for Russian 'romansy' and more Georgian folksongs!" He snapped his fingers for the musician.

William Burke sensed a change in the mood and tried to impress the group with his knowledge of Russia. "Last year, I accompanied a group of engineers and geologists from Royal Dutch Shell to help negotiate pipeline permits. They had invested billions of dollars to develop the world's largest oil-and-gas field in the Russian Far East. They were harassed by government regulations for two years—including absurd threats that the company would not meet Russia's environmental standards. The moment Shell was forced to sell the controlling stake in the project to Russians and reduce its share to twenty-five percent, all environmental concerns vanished."

Bablidze silently looked up at Philip.

"You know, Mr. Bablidze, I've also been to Krasnoyarsk Krai and the city of Norilsk, the old center of gulag labor camps, the northernmost city in Siberia, built on permafrost," remarked Burke. "A desolate set of snowdrifts and snow in all colors—black, dirty yellow."

"Even pink," added Bablidze sadly.

The musician had already strolled to the table, and Fima shouted, "Davai, davai, Misha! Let's hear some romansy and ballads for our beautiful ladies, Tanichka and Suzanochka!"

Goodwill returned when the guitarist strummed some Georgian folksongs, and Tanya joined the singer in a wonderful Soviet war poem and ballad, "Zhdi Menya." Tears came to Tanya's eyes, Philip fidgeted uncomfortably with his hands, and when the music stopped, the happy group quietly applauded.

Bablidze sighed and slowly continued as if nothing had happened, "Yes, my friends! We have beautiful Soviet legacy of poetry, music, and art! This is a country of miracles! Forget the pink snow! We managed to change a Soviet penal colony into a multi-billion-dollar metal mining business! We have a people's capitalist revolution! We are well positioned globally for the future, especially Norilsk. The Soviet state gifted their patrimony directly to the Russian people."

"*Slava, and glory* to their chief, Mr. Bablidze!" Fima shouted.

Philip Dunlop, who had been diplomatically polite during the entire evening, quietly said, "Gentlemen, we appreciate Russia's cooperation with the World Bank and IMF. Russia has given up on nationalization and monopoly of employment, and America is inviting Western trading partners to encourage your democratic process."

Another shot of vodka, more music, and a wonderful warmth and numbness embraced Susanna's body. She was mellow enough to change the conversation. "Yes, here in Moscow or in St. Petersburg, it looks like flourishing neo-capitalism—immense blossoming of stores, flashy cars, Mercedes-Benzes, Aston-Martins, Bentleys, beautiful restaurants. All about money and power. But if you go to the *real* Russia, little has changed—you see poverty, conflict, misery, and criminal capital. The more life changes there, the more it remains the same, and our conglomerate is very socially aware, very concerned."

Bablidze slowly exhaled again, and scrutinized Susanna. "Gentlemen, there is a Russian saying, '*tishe budesh, dalshe yedesh.*' We need time. Norilsk offers our people all the sweeteners and rewards from Soviet *ancien regime:* Our workers in factories are our family, friends. We have five thousand, and Kulichkov knows most of them by name. They are happy there. I'm proud of what we provide them with: apartments, schools, kindergarten, day care center, orphanage, hospital, cultural center, sports complex, supplementary benefits, yes? We also offer workers apartments in cities in the south. They sell them and like to stay here."

"Ura!" exclaimed Uncle Fima again. "GMG can get richer here than anywhere else in the world. I already have name for your chief, Mr. Hanken. He will become the first American *Stakhanovite!* Hah hah! Another Victory Day for our Patriotic War! But I don't toss my hat in the parade, Susanna—we toast instead, and drink to America, GMG, General Motors, and our joint venture forever, in perpetuity!"

Susanna's eyes gleamed. She was relieved but confused. "Yes. As you must know, Mr. Bablidze, Mr. Burke, the new president of GMG's Russian-American Investment Bank in Moscow, already provides advisory and brokering services for clients from the West and the Russian Federation. We work with the largest commercial banks in the Russian Federation: Stolichny, Menatep, Rosbiznesbank, and Omega Bank. We have access to regional markets in Yekaterinburg, Novosibirsk, Vladivostok. At this point our bank is studying the Chubais loans-for-shares program."

"Of course—*bezuslovno.* Norilsk has completed the voucher auction and they are trading on the Moscow Bourse," Fima happily interjected.

Philip sensed that Susanna needed encouragement. He cleared his throat, shifted his weight from left to right, and commented, "Besides the International Monetary fund, the West has set up a new agency, as I'm sure you're aware—the European Bank for Reconstruction and Development, the EBRD, to help the old Soviet bloc shift to capitalism. Yeltsin's advisors have placed New Russia firmly on the road to democracy and free market economy. With Susanna's work and your cooperation, our State Department will study this project."

Bablidze joined his soft hands and looked around the table. "Russia, wedged between Asia and Europe, will be an economic *powerhouse*! Our natural resources, our native talent, and our desire for success will make our country the most dynamic marketplace in the world! Perhaps we can be first bridge for Russian, American, and international investors in many important commodity projects—our productive assets, under private ownership, are the most promising investment for you! Most remarkable transformation of the twentieth century!"

"Okay, we're on the same page." Susanna's tone was more serious. Philip's eyes met hers without meaning to, and he raised his eyebrows. He felt little sense of urgency, none of responsibility.

8

KULICHKOV IN MOSCOW

HAT WAS LEFT OF COMMUNIST PARTY headquarters fit into a two-story gray stucco building off Dzerzhinsky Square. The large vestibule smelled faintly of roast meat, boiled cabbage, and cheap tobacco.

On the first floor stood a security desk with a grim gray-haired security guard; nearby, two ancient babushkas with benign smiles were in charge of a pile of newly printed pamphlets titled *Marx: Frequently Asked Questions*. At the end of the hall were the offices of the Moscow Children's Shelter Charity, with a bulletin board announcing donations of a thousand dollars or more. The philanthropist of the month was the owner of the Casino of the Golden Khan. His photograph, and that of the casino, were proudly displayed.

Party headquarters occupied the second floor. On the wall

hung a portrait photograph of Lenin, a red Soviet flag, and a campaign banner that demanded, "Who Stole Russia?" The air reeked of cigarettes, sausages, and musty clothes. Beyond lay several offices, a secretarial pool, a large conference room with coats hung on two old coat trees, and boots piled helter-skelter into the corner. Walls were covered with photos of past Soviet glory: the Russian flag raised on the roof of the Reichstag, a cosmonaut in the space station Mir, a mountain climber celebrating victory on Everest.

A welcome party was in progress for their old comrade Aleksandr Kulichkov, whose visits to Moscow always included getting together with his army buddies. Party Chairman Artyom Kadrov, short, balding, with a round face and crimson cheeks, had ordered the conference table laden with wine, vodka, red caviar, platters stacked with sausage, silvery smoked fish, fatback sliced so fine it was translucent, and the best black Borodinsky bread.

Aleksandr Kulichkov, a born *Sibiryak*, entered and smiled— a cashmere coat worn impresario-style on his shoulders, and no galoshes—and wiped his highly polished shoes, which had clearly trod no Moscow streets that season.

The group was unchanged from the old days—dull eyes, arrogant frowns, bellies that had never missed a meal, none of the elderly who sometimes picketed Red Square in the bitter cold for their back salaries and pensions.

They evoked nostalgia for the good old Soviet days—once young soldiers fighting the Wehrmacht on their own soil, now doddering ancients. Badly made, too shiny Bulgarian or Finnish suits, lapels stitched with tiers of campaign medals: Gold Star Hero, Order of Lenin, Red Star, and Patriotic War Hero.

"Welcome, Aleksandr Evgenievich! A faithful servant to the Motherland! And welcome back from 'bolshaya zemlya!'

This is like the old days. You remember Tamara Vasilyevich, now Party Secretary? One of our most respected members. She tagged along with our regiment." The old lady smiled and blushed. "She will fix a plate for you. You are surrounded by the Party, old friends. We love humble martyrs! Stay and eat!"

Kulichkov, a crimson-cheeked bull of a man with a pointy white beard and the ability to smoke two cigarettes at once, formerly a heavy-drinking, fist-thumping prince of the Soviet Union's industrial nomenclatura, spoke in a military baritone. "Thank you, comrades—only drinks for me. The smart ones, my friends, left the Party years ago. Now we are all rats swilling wine on a sinking ship. I can only stay a short time. I'm meeting a colleague for dinner."

"All the way from Norilsk, and you cannot be our guest? I made a special trip for Borodinsky bread, your favorite," sighed Tamara.

Artyom was in charge. The man was an oddity, a hapless relic shuffling toward life's end. Flustered with an impish grin, dressed in a suit that was a little too shiny and a little too wide, he was to be sure a die-hard Communist who had fallen hard from the Soviet Olympus but found company and solace with millions who shared his views but had somehow missed the boat.

Ran'she bylo luchshe ("Things were better before") was his motto. A veteran of the Leningrad blockade, he was now living on sixty dollars a month. Looking for Kulichkov's attention, he quickly went into a soliloquy. "I march in the first line of the victory parade every year, I'm entitled to several war pensions. I'm a veteran and an invalid. And I received the Hero of Soviet Labor. Nothing now for me. Politburo privileges? What a joke! We have nothing. No dacha, no car, no privileges at all. Only the apartment."

Kulichkov empathized. "Relax, Artyom Ivanovich, life will improve."

"And why didn't *you* leave the Party, Aleksandr Evgenievich?" a younger man asked.

"My father was a son of he Revolution, but a prisoner who slaved in the gulag. He was 'rehabilitated' and slaved for the 'Motherland' in Lepzig. I am also a son of the Revolution, a friend of the oppressed. I am a Communist and proud of it. I wanted to save the world through Communism. When Hitler invaded, I was only sixteen when I volunteered. I was one of the two thousand men who fought a battle near Kursk. Only seventy-five survived. But we defeated the Fascist invaders and imperialist aggression, and Leonid Brezhnev honored me by the Norilsk posting!"

The group loved listening to his gospel.

"You are right to stay with the Party. Russia saved the world with her blood! Now we have to save Russia. Another victorious defense of the Motherland." He intoned piously.

"Yes my friends, through coup and counter-coup, democracy and privatization, the fall of the ruble and the rise of new millionaires—our country is in free fall now—run by thieves who are shipping countless billions offshore, bankrupting the Motherland. But the Party will go forward!"

Kulichkov sucked up his chest and bellowed, "As Marx predicted, the State has withered away! Not under Communism, but under Yeltsin. Comrades, we have witnessed the total collapse of our Russia. We have capitalist revolution! It's humiliating. Our country is weaker and smaller now than since before the days of Peter the Great." He was short of time, but armed himself as a visionary and historian. "Yes, yes, you must know, Artemy Ivanovich, your new place is right above the old Kirov Station, deep underground." Kulichkov rambled on about the metro's glories, the enormous chandeliers under the Kropotkinskaya Station—the former Chistye Prudy, with white marble hauled from the Urals, black marble from Georgia, pink marble from Siberia.

"When the Germans bombed Moscow, Stalin worked here for the victorious defense of the Motherland. He defeated the Fascist invaders. He slept on a cot deep underground, on the platform, and the general staff slept in a subway car. They didn't have a fancy war room like Churchill or Roosevelt, but they saved Moscow. This ground should be like Lourdes—crutches abandoned on the wall, vintage posters, plaster Stalins for sale."

"Of course, Aleksandr Evgenievich," said Artyom, "this is sacred ground. Stalin enlisted the Orthodox Church and all the saints to fight Fritz. Now we also fight—New Russians, mafia, reactionaries in Kremlin, and real estate developers. Mayor Yuri Luzhkov is cutting deals. He wants to level the building for an American-style apartment house, European kitchens, with a spa and a sushi bar for thieves and whores." The man was out of breath, yet continued persuasively. "Our State used to believe in culture, not real estate! *Yob tvoyu mat'*—Fuck your mother! But we have to move with the times. We're a completely different party these days, more stream-lined and flexible. We agree to 'the primitive accumulation of capital,' as Marx said. Open and willing to adjust, not only for our ideals but for our valuable property."

KULICHKOV WAS LATE FOR DINNER AT Serebryaniy Vek, a gastronomic palace decorated in *fin de siècle* splendor and a magnet for Moscow's nouveaux riches, a private reserve for the new plutocracy. Pre-Bolshevik bliss, artifice, and excess: They came for the mountains of caviar, the chandeliered ceilings, the obsequious waiters who handled customers like pampered aristocrats reliving the last days of the tsar. Gypsy dancers

performed impassioned dips, and a slender brunette in a se-
quined scarlet dress belted out Soviet love songs. Guests were
vetted and large mirrors announced your entrance, reassuring
you that you belonged, that you'd arrived. The *maitre d'* hurried him immediately to Ossipov's table. The tall, sandy-
haired, barrel-chested industrial apparatchik, now Deputy
Minister of the Interior, was well connected to the Kremlin
and Russia's new exuberant business class, a man who'd spent
his entire career operating in the shadows. Proximity to power
inside the Kremlin's walls had always been Ossipov's defining
political imperative. His face was curious; a bushy mustache
and gentle, dark eyes, heartless and indifferent, cold yet sen-
sual, the man was always lamenting that he was going bald.
Kulichkov ticked off all of Ossipov's talismans, which marked
the new Russian tribe—the full-length leather jacket and tasseled French loafers; the hundred-thousand-dollar wristwatch,
a brand new Hummer, the young wife and younger mistress,
holidays on the Riviera or at Courchevel.

Ossipov greeted his friend perfunctorily. He was brooding
and glanced at his watch as his guest was seated. With a malicious laugh, he suddenly clutched his hand. "So good to see
you, Sasha! How is Norilskmetal, and how is life away from
the Moscow grime and big-city politics?"

"I see feverish commerce here," Kulichkov observed dryly.
"Moscow has always been on the make. Luzhkov wants to be
the only pig at the trough, but with this new market economy,
all the other pigs are eating now. But we have our own grimy
capitalist revolution above the Arctic. Staking out a claim in
the post-socialist wilderness is hard work, but we are used to
hardships! We will persevere."

"You look well. Siberia and business agree with you."

Kulichkov, skipping all social formalities, lunged to the
heart of the matter. "You know, I've had my unpleasant issues

with Bablidze, but we have worked together and couldn't wait to privatize the plant. You know the drill: mass voucher privatization. We undervalued the plant's assets, made it easier to sell vouchers. Our workers were clueless about vouchers. For seventy years they hear that capitalism is bad, paper assets worthless. What were they going to do with their vouchers: sell them in kiosks for cigarettes or vodka? Our workers sold them, and we bought them, making sure we were in control, our stake of shares always increasing."

"So how did your misunderstanding with Ghiya arise?" asked Ossipov.

"Simple, Pasha. He wanted to be the boss and impress the Kremlin, but he was never there. Bablidze had an exuberant lifestyle in exotic and exclusive places all over Europe. Suddenly last year, he began spending more time in Norilsk and opened his eyes. My friend, the former deputy director, became the director—and my enemy. I was pushed aside. My local friends got wary and raised suspicions about this outsider Bablidze and his Georgian mafiosi friends. Suddenly, Bablidze and the Georgians are buying shares for their own account. They have very deep pockets, sometimes paying more than a hundred times initial price, at times buying *my workers'* shares for television sets, consumer goods, washing machines, and refrigerators. He and the Georgians wanted enough shares to wield effective control. We have fought for control over the company, in the boardroom, in shareholder meetings, in the courts from Siberia to Moscow."

Ossipov nodded and uttered a sympathetic-sounding grunt. "There's no order in the provinces. It's a mess."

"Imagine, what betrayal! Behind my back of Old Red Director, Hero of the Motherland! Hero of Socialist Labor! This is *my property*, my industrial establishment for thirty years! Why sell something you can own yourself? While I always controlled the trade of vouchers! Bablidze and those thugs were the interlopers! They continued buying and were putting up a powerful defense. They claimed they were buying for the state—deals to prop up Yeltsin's politics while entertaining in the Dorchester Hotel in London, or Bablidze's new chateau in Cap d'Antibes," Kulichkov snorted bitterly.

"Maybe they were. You should have been smarter, worked more carefully to maintain credibility for the Kremlin." Ossipov remained distracted and uncomfortable, but continued. "I understand you had another civil war in Norilsk."

Kulichkov was out of breath. "Yes, we were the Red Cavalry! With our locals, we took the siege into our own hands, commando style, like actors in a Western movie, and snatched the company from Bablidze and his mafia by force—a four-month stalemate—a boring military siege. Yes, he is still the chief, but in name only, and I run the show as always."

Ossipov suddenly turned pale, pushed his chair back, and inquired, "Were the legal problems ever resolved in regional courts?"

"Since Soviet times, you know better than anyone, Pasha, how corrupt the legal and security bureaucracy is. No! They still own the majority block of shares. You know, there is never any muscle on the ground for laws. The state is weak and the regional courts have no authority."

"How can I help, Alex?" Ossipov whispered sadly.

"I am counting on your power brokers, Pasha, to settle the deal with the federal court in Moscow. Bablidze can enjoy his exuberant lifestyle in Switzerland and drive his Mercedes 600S all over Europe." He refolded his napkin and revealed a grin.

Ossipov's voice darkened to a whisper. "Yes, Ghiya keeps his best Mercedes here. Garaged near Kotelnicheskaya Naberezhnaya, where he has an apartment. A grand apartment, too—rooms stretching almost twenty-five feet, nine-foot ceilings, molded cornices, ceilings with outsize crystal chandeliers, gold fixtures in the bathroom and a fountain with frolicking, scantily dressed nymphs in the foyer."

Kulichkov lit one cigarette off the butt end of another, a delicate operation. "In our country, a man can only brag about how much he steals. I don't give a damn about his apartment, or how many girls he screws. Bablidze is on his way to becoming a metals oligarch in the Arctic. I am still the commercial and industrial director, and I need your special help."

Ossipov was staring gloomily at the further end of the room, where a group of guests was just seated, studying menus. He glanced at Kulichkov and whispered, "Our friend was not tending to the Kremlin or his far-flung businesses. Besides a wife in Tbilisi, a house in Knightsbridge, and a son in Eton, he was juggling too many women."

Kulichkov was genuinely puzzled by Ossipov's statement. "But, Pasha," he countered self-righteously. "You know the one rule we have. Never go into each other's private lives, mistresses and so on."

The few tables in their corner of the restaurant reflected absolute elegance: Pink tablecloths, radiant under crystal and gold chandeliers, the heavy smell of Cuban cigars, French perfume and Armenian cognac. Gold seraphim danced on the walls, pudgy arms hoisting aloft tall, gilded candles, coddled by heavy silk drapes to keep the outside out.

"A new chef here, just imported from Switzerland," noted Ossipov as they ordered a dinner of snails and caviar, king prawns, and medallions of New Zealand lamb while Ossipov pressed on with information.

"Bablidze's father was KGB, but he was arrested and perished in the gulag. After the Khrushchev thaw, Bablidze went to university, became a geologist, and got work in Norilsk where he earned a fortune selling export licenses, investing wisely in metals, raw materials. Yes, Ghiya was a newcomer to capitalism, creating a financial empire, a newly minted millionaire."

Kulichkov sensed the tragic end to the story, crumpled his cigarette, and poured another drink.

"Neizvestnyi designed and sculpted two beautiful statues of his car, with the keys encrusted in rhodium. I saw one sculpture on his desk in the apartment. The other is in Norilsk. This car here was his most treasured possession in life—the Mercedes *shestsot*, the 600S. Early last evening came a powerful explosion just off Tverskaya. Police found the Benz destroyed by a remote-controlled bomb attached to the underside of the car. A charred corpse was pulled from the wreckage. It was Ghiya. Two bodyguards were badly wounded as well."

Kulichkov blanched and trembled, his face darkening with anxiety, rattled by the information. "Why, I just spoke with him yesterday, and we have a meeting with GMG at the Slavyanskaya this week to discuss the American project for Norilsk. Ghiya was my good friend, Pasha, and I was hoping to put our differences aside, reconcile our disputes, resolve our problems in Norilsk."

Ossipov sighed with nostalgia. "I would sit with Ghiya right here and go through stories about the struggle for majority control, Aleksandr. I was willing to work the legal process for the two of you. Hoping for a cozy relationship. You would have made a wonderful team."

With another malicious laugh, Ossipov continued, "His accident was not about money. These people operate by Stalin's creed. No man, no problem. He inveigled his way into the Kremlin. But to get leverage, you have to be smart, and Ghiya wasn't smart enough. The murder indicates a deep rift between structures and darker impulses of the Kremlin. Death solves all problems. But Georgian honor and revenge is forever. He was screwing his associates, and Yeltsin, the Chief Oligarch, and the Kremlin did not like it. Please, sit with me and drink," Ossipov begged. "It is not right to drink to the dead alone."

Ossipov took another sip, narrowed his eyes, and told Kulichkov a story he'd never told anyone. Bablidze's mother had served in the KGB her whole life. Worse than that, she'd worked with the Stasi, the East German secret police. She knew what she was doing, but did as she was told. Ghiya lived in Germany because of his mother's job.

"I was born in Leipzig and lived near him. I've also lived my entire life lying. I always had to lie about my father's work whenever I was asked why I was born there. I said he was stationed in Germany for the Russian army.

My mother was always traveling when I was a kid, and Ghiya's mother was an 'auntie' to me. You understand. Back home, she was arrested later as 'enemy of the people' by Stalin's henchmen. She was a good person, but this is what I've always have to live with."

Kulichkov looked hard into Ossipov's eyes. "They were criminals, weren't they? The KGB, the Stasi, their armies of informants. And how was your father involved?"

"He was rehabilitated by the Party. He was a clerk, a mathematician doing accounting work."

The other nodded. "After the Khrushchev thaw, Ghiya was freed, and they moved back to Georgia, then Moscow and Norilsk. He was murdered because he wanted to accumulate glory for himself instead of the state." Ossipov again nodded, and lapsed into a silence that haunted Kulichkov.

At last Ossipov lifted his glass. "To Bablidze and his Mercedes, and to finding a friend to tell one's 'lies' to."

Kulichkov continued, sluggishly. "Yes, we are men made cruel by life. But we are *Russians* first, and we must avoid tangling with the state's interests."

Ossipov, his voice thick with alcohol, was growing weary, and wanted to go home. He glanced at his watch.

"What about the Ministry for Non-Ferrous Metals and their restrictions? I understand the state also has a large share of vouchers. Perhaps Ghiya was matching wits, not only with you, but with the Kremlin? Undermining national wealth is a long jail sentence, or worse, Sasha."

Kulichkov said nothing and, pointing to the ceiling, dropped his voice—an old reflex, as if the KGB were listening to the conversation. "Why, Pasha, the old management in Norilsk always supports the Kremlin and Yeltsin. I pay taxes regularly. I've got the best record with my friends at the Norilsk tax police. I follow the laws, and I sleep very well at night. Bablidze tried to play games. He wanted to be an insider but used dummy companies to conceal profits abroad: more than two million dollars skimmed off for 'ofshornaya zonas'—Liechtenstein, Cyprus, the Isle of Man."

Ossipov had been paying attention too long. "Your story and this evening are endless," he lamented but felt the need to pacify his friend. He checked his watch again. "I must go—a big day tomorrow."

The cherub lights dimmed, adding warm pinkish hues for atmosphere. At the far side of the restaurant, a beautiful jazz singer, an exotic African American import recruited to entertain the local elite, was sitting at the grand piano.

Ossipov nodded for the waiter to order green tea and ask about the kitchen's choices of ice cream. Ossipov chose vanilla with chocolate sauce. Kulichkov was still not ready to leave. He raised his eyes meaningfully to the ceiling, still afraid. He lit another cigarette, filled the glasses again.

"Pity, I was ready to help," Ossipov interrupted, slowly and dispassionately from a darkened corner of his mind. "But lynch law is the order of the day—an eye for an eye, a tooth for a tooth! The Kremlin wants only stability, a monstrous stability, and nobody seeks justice in court."

Kulichkov imagined that there would be more conversation, explanation, expressions of regret, but Ossipov asked for the check and muttered, "They are dividing the bear skin before the bear is dead."

Kulichkov sighed and replied bitterly, "He who goes to the woods should not be afraid of wolves."

MOSCOW IS LIKE A BIG VILLAGE, with gossip and important news spreading like wildfire. By the time Susanna reached her office, the news of Bablidze's murder was all over the Interfax and the Slavyanskaya Hotel: Bablidze, Director and Chief Executive of Norilskmetal, brutally dies. Remote-controlled bomb under his Mercedes Shestsot, early last evening. Driver and bodyguard badly burned, taken to hospital, condition unknown. A commentator, following the government line on a Moscow radio station, reported that either the police or the Georgian mafia might have killed Bablidze as a result of his "business activities," while police sources speculated that Bablidze had been eliminated for other reasons. "We understand that law-enforcement structures, and their representatives, take part in criminal feuds. But that doesn't mean that the authorities ordered it." Another political analyst's press release, reading like a political obituary, suggested that "Kremlin-backed sources claim that Bablidze may have been killed by a serious cleavage between power structures of Georgian investors in Norilsk and the State, in a direct challenge to the State authority and the Ministry of Non-Ferrous Metals."

What did that media-babble mean? Susanna had difficulty

processing the news. "What the devil is happening?" She felt like an amateur who had misunderstood something that she'd read somewhere, maybe in some detective story. Still standing, she turned toward her desk and picked up the phone. "Uncle Fima, what's *happening* here? My God, I just saw Bablidze and Kulichkov at the art show in the Manège last week."

"This death was ordered. It was planned, prepared, and executed. Bablidze was dead on arrival at the hospital, and his body is on one plane, his wife on another flying in from London, both flying to Georgia as we speak."

"My God, Fima. Now what? My horrors from home are being repeated here again, with this project."

"Yes, Susanna, I was astounded. Our dear friend Bablidze—an explosion of his Mercedes, the car torn apart, glass and scraps of metal flying and clanging all over Tverskaya, with shock waves hurling pedestrians to the ground—can you imagine?"

"Hold it right there! Uncle Fima, Preliminary negotiations were scheduled for next week in our office, with Bablidze, Kulichkov, Zhukov from Omega Bank, and my associates from the State Department and GMG'S new bank in Moscow. I must speak with Kulichkov right away!"

"Anything else you want to ask?"

"What do I do now? How do I proceed?"

Fima was cool, sounding like a surgeon informing a patient's relative. "I suggest you proceed carefully; diplomatically and with discretion. Bablidze is not the first oligarch to be brutally eliminated. I will be there to support you and give you further information. You must negotiate as if nothing has happened. Kulichkov will certainly continue business discussions. I understand how upset you are, and how you feel the human side." Susanna felt like she was in the theater of the absurd. The real world was slipping away from under her feet.

"But how? Yes, pragmatically Kulichkov was in charge, but Bablidze was the new director, officially in charge of project financing for infrastructure, and loans for shares. He and the Georgians owned the majority of shares."

"We cannot get the toothpaste back in the tube. I know you can do it, you will do just fine!"

"I am chilled to the core, Uncle Fima. Perhaps I am on that same list. No *pominki* in Georgia for me. I feel like a surgeon scrubbing for an operation without the instruments and without Boris's help."

"You have me, Suzanochka. This is the curse of big business in Russia. I am here for you. Good luck!"

Susanna sat at her desk and, shifting her chair from side to side, muttering to herself. Watching the people in the street below her office window, she was alarmed. She felt that Bablidze's murder had started a wild-fire under the Norilsk project, and that there was no knowing how it would spread or whether it would be put out.

She sat back in her chair, for a moment distracted by the people in the street below her office window, then forced herself to go back to work. She arranged a meeting with Kulichkov the same evening in the Slavyanskaya, where she waited for him at the bar, a chrome affair that looked theatrical in a haze of cigarette smoke; a long, leather-topped counter finished in marble, steel, and hardwood, with subtle lighting on the bottles behind and racks of glasses above.

Distressed, Kulichkov hurried in. Spotting a stool, he sat and began speaking immediately, before Susanna had the opportunity to greet him. "This town is a nightmare. I've got to get out of this accursed place and cannot—at least in Norilsk only pollution and fumes kill you." He scowled, offered Susanna a cigarette, took one himself, and lit them. His worried eyes surveyed silent expatriates cradling drinks and reflecting about another wasted day.

"Deepest condolences and sympathies to you and Norilskmetal about Mr. Bablidze's accident," she said. "How can I find Bablidze's Tbilisi address, so I can send flowers to the family?"

He leaned on the counter and muttered, "We don't do that in Russia. Flowers belong only for happy occasions or in cemeteries. But my secretary will find the address, and I will bring it to our meeting next week, as we confirmed." He shrugged, his eyes slightly apprehensive. "Not to worry, Susanna. We have been in Norilsk forever. My grandfather was a victim of a swampy gulag. He was shipped to Siberia on a cattle barge. We know how to buy the Georgian interest and we will proceed meeting your group of investors as scheduled." His eyes didn't move from Susanna's face, and Kulichkov's expression remained unchanged. She stared at him, sneezed and twisted her tissue to shreds. She stared at the bartender, was distracted with thoughts of Boris, but tried to consciously rethink Norilsk. She was being manipulated by two men who were now dead, and sucked in by the joker Fima. Was there a message for her? She'd never imagined it would turn out that way. She was as solipsistic as Hanken. That was business in Russia—now *urgent* business to be resolved, and she was afraid.

9

BUSINESS TRIP

M ARCH IS A GRUESOME MONTH in Moscow. The early charms of the snow wear off in January, the consolation of the New Year holidays is long past, and there are still months of grimy slush to slog through before the relief of spring.

Back in the Slavyanskaya the following morning, Susanna's head ached and her reflexes were off. Mind racing, she drank cups of strong tea and wrote still another, more urgent descriptive memorandum for her CEO. She first concentrated on an attention-getting executive summary, which she didn't entirely believe:

Russia is a world leader in non-ferrous metal production, and Norilskmetal is its largest and most productive natural resource asset.

Norilskmetal requires capital investment and infrastructure upgrading to reverse a steady decline of production levels.

The plant was privatized, and vouchers for Norilskmetal first traded in the fall of 1992.

GMG must position itself as the only financial partner for the development of natural resources on the richest frontier of capitalism.

Continued global economic expansion will lead to high demand for metals and higher commodity prices.

GMG must account for, and calibrate, political risk.

She breathed deeply and stopped many times to look out the window at the bundled up, shuffling, silent mass of people, collars upturned, in the haze and steam belching from the Kiev station. She continued crunching numbers the entire day for investment strategies so GMG could realize maximum export potential in "the most promising investment opportunity of the twenty-first century," and finished the executive summary with a business mission and a poet's philosophy:

GMG's commitment to innovation for success in Russia is unlike that of any other multinational.

GMG's culture is characterized by a quest to be first in opening markets, developing and launching products, and growing earnings and assets.

GMG's prospective investment requires a fact-finding mission to Norilsk to evaluate capital requirements, guidelines for management, assets, production costs, labor requirements, and operating costs. It is urgent that GMG send Russian-speaking legal and accounting support immediately.

Just as America absorbed the ideas of the European Enlightenment, Russia will absorb and adapt to the new geopolitics and become an economic colossus.

This market is hot, hot, hot. Please review and reply ASAP!

This was the information Hanken needed in order to believe that Russia was his new frontier. After countless telexes, phone conferences, and memorandums, she convinced him that Russia was ready for GMG, and Hanken was ready for Russia. The boss wanted to eat the Russian bear, and approved a legal consultant and an accountant to travel to Norilsk. Susanna responded with an enthusiastic personal telex. "Many Congratulations! You don't realize how strong you are, and how powerful GMG's money is. You are the key to the business and it's your skill and power that will bring us success."

"Privet, Dima! How are you, and the family? Susanna here, calling from dinner, between the borscht and the Kievski cutlet!"

"And vodka—dining with my cousin Boris, of course—the younger Dr. Rozenbaum. How is life in the Motherland?"

"No, I'm dining alone. Boris is away on business. *Normalno*, as we say, but Moscow is very cold and full of snow. Good for cross-country skiing. I have good news for you. How would you like to add to your mileage and catch a Delta flight to Moscow next week?"

"Who is inviting me, your company or the KGB?"

"Our big chief has just okayed our new project in Norilsk. I will Fed-Ex our latest plan, and Norilsk's annual reports, so you can come prepared."

A graduate of NYU Law School and also a relative of Uncle Fima, Dima Frishkin had come to America with his parents at the age of ten, his mother a mechanical engineer, his father a doctor in one of Odessa's second-tier universities.

Dima, confused and ambivalent about his roots, had

dreamed of the yuppie lifestyle of a well-to-do American lawyer. He had begun an immigration law practice, married, and had a family, and as a relative of Boris's, Susanna had helped him with many Russian-speaking legal consultancies for her firm.

That process of acculturation had been long and hard. The parents had "escaped to freedom" with their son in the 1970s. With work and the help of "friends," they'd recently managed to buy a heavily mortgaged fixer-upper in a trendy neighborhood of Park Slope, Brooklyn, which served as professional space and residence for the two families.

"This is America, and it's all about money. Here, money is king," the doctor often said. "But the American way is the same as in Russia—we can only trust ourselves and our family. We understand America enough to figure out how to steal from the government and insurance companies."

Determined to live the American way, the doctor had established a Medicaid mill on the ground floor, an office full of elderly patients, where recruiters were generously compensated for new senior citizens, all arriving by free sponsored "Access-a-Rides." The good doctor examined all arrivals for heart and blood pressure while a nurse, just off the plane from Bukhara, tended twice weekly to their physical therapy treatments for aches and pains while they socialized with friends. But for the doctor and his family, the holy grail was the Medicare or Medicaid number.

Dima's Moscow-born wife, Nina, who had only recently acquired a license to teach disabled children, also worked as a receptionist and legal clerk for Dima in her spare time. They worked 24-7 for the "American dream"—no Russian spoken to the children; Russian literature and culture sent into exile while their expensive Irish nanny spoke very proper English to their three boys, all under the age of six! His parents, *bab-*

ulya and *dedulya*, struggled with the English language and practiced a codified system of Jewish-Russian parental anxieties, totally devoted to Dima and his family. Like an entire generation of Russian women, *babulya* signed over her life to her son. She did the shopping, cooking, and cleaning, and as well as being the concierge and janitor, she also sometimes filled in for Nina as the receptionist and bookkeeper.

About one o'clock, Dima's mother appeared, as always, and covered part of his desk with a proper linen cloth to serve lunch. "Lunch again, Mama? The place around the corner delivers very good food, and God knows you have enough to do!"

"How are you this morning, Dimochka, my sunshine? My whole life is worry for you," she said, smiled, and tidied his desk. "When I bring you lunch each day, I have such pleasure. You are my life. Such delight! Remember, like finding Cuban bananas for your breakfast in Odessa."

But Dima was unhappy. He was ambitious, constantly trolling for more lucrative projects, and business was slow. Guilt controlled all family relationships. Although he had tried to break free of this criminal closeness with his parents, and their unbounded insanities, they easily manipulated this filial bondage.

Susanna's phone call was the perfect parachute.

Two hours later, posture straighter, more self-assured, Dima sat importantly at his desk, proud as a peacock, lecturing a client about unexpected problems with a green card. Susanna's phone call had liberated him: his tone more confident, he no longer felt exclusively beholden to immigration business from wealthy New Russians. He was envious of their million-dollar condominiums overlooking the Atlantic Ocean in Brighton Beach, leased Mercedes-Benzes, children's chess clubs, music and ballet lessons, nannies, and tutors.

In a spirit of *shadenfreude*, he quietly continued, speaking to his client, "These issues need immediate attention. The NIS is not giving us much time. I am afraid you will need another immigration lawyer to help you."

"Why is that, Dima, my friend? We need to relax with dinner at Tatiana. Great atmosphere for us, and gourmet food, fish swimming under your feet, live mermaids and caviar buffet, great music for dancing. Bring your lovely wife—and also your dear parents, of course. My wife loves the good doctor and his advice about her stomach problems."

"It's impossible now, Nikolai Aksyonovich," Dima replied abruptly, putting on his best Moscow accent. His tone was harsh and arrogant. "I have important business in Russia. I have just been invited by a multinational for a legal consultancy to Moscow, and I must leave immediately. You know my colleague, Yefim Brook. He is familiar with all the NIS business and will help you." He rose and reached out for a pliant and noncommittal handshake. After twenty years in the American desert, Dima had stumbled upon a different kind of tragedy: He had finally found his way home, but with an American passport. A new place to be unhappy, back in the Motherland!

SNOW WAS FALLING THICK AS DOWN the day Volodya picked up Dima and Will Diller, one of the company's senior accountants at Sheremyetevo. It was Maslenitsa, the ringing of bells, a call to prayer and liberation from sins. Dima's uneasy gaze at the airport, as he remembered events: one happy, and one sad: being inducted into the Red Pioneers as a boy, and being patted down by a burly airport customs official when leaving Russia, many years before.

The city had been mellowed by knee-deep snow. Cars crawled behind snowplows. Thirty-six hours without sleep had made Dima more silent than usual when he finally settled in for a briefing at the Slavyanskaya. Diller felt as if he were on another planet, totally disoriented, his asthma out of control, the rush of adrenaline needed was simply not there. Susanna couldn't manage an enthusiastic welcome for one of Boris's young American relatives who still hadn't heard the news. "I'm glad you came," she said quietly, hugging him as she smiled apprehensively.

"I'm sure you've studied Norilskmetal's annual reports and the other disclosures," she rapidly began. She was upset and anxious. "Descriptive memorandums, and all the rest. Bablidze asked Kulichkov, the deputy director, to Moscow for preliminary discussions, but unfortunately there was a fatal car accident last weekend, and Bablidze is dead."

Dima's adrenaline shot up. Suddenly alert and dumbfounded, he stared at the walls and ceiling.

"We'd best be careful how we approach the preliminary discussions, set for Wednesday. All the other players will be here. Welcome to Moscow. This is a murderous world."

"I am just so happy to see you, Susanna." Dima sat down and opened his briefcase.

"As a native speaker and lawyer, your responsibility is due diligence for all legal issues for Norilsk and GMG, when debriefing our chief and our legal team on Wall Street. I need you to study the relevant corporate documents to ensure that everything is above board, and to arrange for any incomplete documents to be rewritten. Make sure that everyone understands, in writing, what's legal and what's not."

Dima was intimidated by her remarks. The same Russia, but different; an important time working for a real business with an American conglomerate in Moscow—no longer the assured body language and culturally understood innuendos with his Brighton Beach clients.

"Susanna, I studied all the documents at home and again

on the plane. The problem is, no one has a clue right now what the law *is* here. How can I decide what's legal and what's not? The old Soviet documents are like the Tower of Babel—no sense can be made of them! Have you ever seen these Soviet accounts? A zillion pointless, unintelligible, and contradictory laws. In a Russian court you can prove anything for the right fee."

"I sent Norilsk's last three translated annual reports, going back to 1990," she said, "and was hoping Mr. Diller could decipher them."

"Hopeless! My three-year-old can make more sense of the math than these 'official' reports, never mind accounts of assets, receivables, and dollars, and what falls between the chairs and into pocket banks in the Seychelles or Cyprus."

Diller sneezed, then started sneezing seriously. He buried his face in his handkerchief while raising his shoulders, and sneezed and shook again. "Why are we here? Yes, I am the senior accountant for GMG, but why am *I* here? Dima and Susanna, you need someone who understands Russian."

The accountant tried to explain his research and Dima's briefings. "The accounting system is a nightmare—a new puzzle system—several sets of books customized for various departments. A set for regional taxes, another one for the Russian Federation, still another real one for the management of Norilsk that awards privatized 'owners' with rights to fraudulently 'invest' and resell 'vouchers' inflated for earnings and market value. A system optimally customized to achieve favorable results for all government levels."

Dima sighed, stared at the ceiling, then at Diller, and said, "You forgot about still another set, Mr. Diller—one for the 'proletariat': the books with depressed asset values and reduced earnings to negotiate lower labor costs for the miners and refinery workers whose wages are constantly in arrears.

Norilsk, authorities, ministries, and oligarchs all generate income from fudging data. It's a jacking of vertically generated 'rents' with no value added; optimally customized to achieve the best results for the oligarchs and the Kremlin."

IT WAS ALREADY DARK BY LATE afternoon when Susanna stood up, arched her back, and looked out at the swirling snowflakes crossing the light of a street lamp. It was still coming down, but now lacy and weightless, and people looked as if they were gliding in narrowed paths. Finally able to block her grief, she relaxed, smiled, and began small talk with Dima about his flight, family, and children back in Brooklyn.

"*Po tikhon'ku*, everyone is working hard, the older two boys are geniuses in school. When do I see Borya, Susanna? I must call him right away."

She answered quietly, without enthusiasm but with hesitation. "He's away in Pskov on business, but knows you are coming and he'll be home in a few days." Her face was taut and pale. She lowered her eyes, her lips tense, and he noticed.

"Well, let's call *Tyotya* Polina, the aunt I love the most."

"She is resting in Peredelkino. The phone lines to the dacha are very erratic, especially in bad weather—the perils of communication—but we can try."

"Why is Polina at the dacha in the winter?"

There was no way of avoiding it. Realizing that more denial would only bring on further anguish, she bear-hugged Dima and whispered, tears flowing, "Our Boris is dead, murdered before I returned. The apartment on Tverskaya was burned and trashed—burglary and fire. Worst of all, they had already cremated Borya and were only waiting for me to attend the funeral and the *pominki*."

Dima, stunned into silence, his face leaden, twisted in fright. He was screaming inside, holding Susanna tightly. She felt electric rods down his back. "For God's sake, Susanna, why him?"

"We don't know. His work, theft of art—he was murdered, *suffocated*. The police are investigating arson and infarct. Murder, the real crime, has been dropped from their agenda."

"Medicine was his work, his life."

"I wanted to believe that, but perhaps he had another business life. As an expatriate, I am investigating but getting nowhere. Fima has connections, I know, but he's afraid of the police, and I cannot bribe him to 'help' the investigation." A protracted silence.

"Susanna, stay away from Fima. He is a Russian *vor*, a schemer and a snake who would kill his own mother if he had to—uneducated, thrown out of university, and *not* because he was Jewish!" Dima shouted in nervous anger. "He never applied for Jewish refugee status—he's a deracinated, self-loathing Soviet Jew. Never celebrated Jewish holidays. He sang Russian, ate Russian, drank Russian, and sucked in Russian culture. The only thing he liked about being Jewish were the top Jewish Russian crooks in Odessa and Moscow." He was still holding Susanna's wrist when she freed herself to pour more coffee.

"I must call him anyway, to let him know you are here, and confirm our Norilsk meeting." She picked up the phone and dialed. "Greetings!" she said when her call was put through. "What a nice time at the Aragvi with your wonderful guests. Great to be able to speak with Tatyana! Believe it or not, our corporate lawyer, your 'American relative' Dima Frishkin, and a senior accountant are already here. Our bank president, Mr. Burke, and Mr. Dunlop are ready for the meeting on Wednesday. No guitars this time!"

Fima, astounded by the fact that the lawyer and accountant

had materialized so quickly, joked, always on the defensive, "Yes, my dear Susanna, we now work with American speed, and America will supply the infrastructure for efficiency and maximum profit for everyone. You will get rich in Russia!"

"You were a real ladies' man at the restaurant, and saved the evening for us, Uncle Fima."

"Yes, and Kulichkov found you most intelligent and charming. He has been carefully studying the proposals, and we will be ready for discussions with your American and European counter-parties in your office." He forced a familiar chuckle that calmed her. "No Aragvi and no guitars this time, Susanna. I am convinced your professional approach and charm will overcome all obstacles, no doubt." He continued the conversation as if Bablidze had never existed. She sensed that Bablidze would have been supportive of the project and that Uncle Fima was nervous about the murder. She swiveled her chair to the window and stared at the kiosks.

"SORRY WE ARE SO LATE," SAID an excited Volodya when he opened the door and walked into the office. "Traffic was jammed and no cars allowed through. Militia lights were blocking the corner to the hotel, where a snowplow was operating. The machine traveled in a haze of headlights with snow spewing from the blade. Two others were lumbering and grinding, walling off the sidewalk with snow. It seemed like the plow was going back and forth over the same spot, but I didn't see any glass or metal in the street."

"What was the delay?" Susanna asked.

"An officer jumped out of the car and restrained us until I showed my ID. I can't say anything else."

"An accident with no cars or broken glass?" she asked. Volodya knew better.

"Idiots! *Duraki i dorogi*," muttered Valya.

"Just a drunk pedestrian. He was lying in the street when the plows came through. With snow falling and coming off the blades, the drivers don't see much. They just rolled over him. Rolled him flat. We just saw rosy snow."

Susanna, with a "*Poka*" to Volodya and apologies to the other members, joined the group.

William Burke, Philip Dunlop, Alexander Zhukov, and Fima were already sitting around the conference table in the office, waiting for Susanna's associates to arrive. Having previously studied the project, they were discussing strategy for Norilskmetal. Diller, still disoriented from jet-lag, stumbled in looking for his chair, while Dima remained standing, waiting for introductions. Burke winced as Philip awkwardly deflected the delay with talk about jet-lag and Moscow winters. News travels fast, and everyone was aware that Bablidze was dead.

Susanna struggled for her business tone, and Dima finally sat. Bland handshaking and assurances were exchanged with each gliding his hand across the other, and introductions were finished quickly. Dima and Diller were studying business cards, but Dima, observing Uncle Fima, was uneasy, his face tight. The same short, thick-set, grandfatherly man he remembered, who had slipped him two bananas at the airport on the way out of the country, was now a serious *perestroika apparatchik* . . . and a *vor*!

Susanna briefly discussed each person's agenda, and reached into a leather folder, bringing out five small dossiers. She pushed the top three over to Burke, Dunlop, and Zhukov. "Since you are familiar with the project please quickly review the necessary documents again. As already agreed, Mr. Dunlop will work with us on U.S. policy, and Mr. Burke and Mr. Zhukov, from Omega Bank, on financing procedures." The other two dossiers went to Dima and the accountant. "Dima and Mr. Diller, you are also already familiar, *v kurse*, as they say here. Your responsibility is due diligence, legal and financial vetting. We all know that, as a corporation headquartered in New York City, we abide by all the RICA, CFTC, and SEC standards. Our multinational must go through the Norilskmetal books with the finest-tooth comb: accounts, figures, prospects, viability, their strengths and weaknesses. Any questions?"

"Thousands." Dima smiled sarcastically.

"I'll hear them later. It is urgent that you study the documents carefully and tell us the viability of this *project*. The home office is impatient. It is important that GMG hears from everyone as soon as possible, certainly before our meeting with Mr. Kulichkov next week!"

Her enthusiasm was running ahead of herself, as she continued. Susanna had a deep psychological need to be liked and be the best, yet unconsciously her business work in Russia telegrammed signals of failure.

"First, we must have a division of labor. We need this group to head up procedures and staffing. Procedures involve devising a workable accounting system with as much detail as possible: investigating the Norilsk auctions, establishing communication links with EBRD in London and the IMF in Washington, and then, whenever our future partners say something we don't want to hear, pretending the links don't work." She tossed the last and thickest dossier in Dima's direction and looked around the table. There was a discouraging silence—another reputable multinational corporation about to have a Russian baptism by fire.

ONLY SUSANNA AND VALYA ESCORTED the group to the elevator, shaking hands and making small talk. When they returned to the office, Dima was already shouting, his breathing harsh and quick, "How is Fima involved with Norilsk? He must have spread his wings above the Arctic. I know him only for his kindnesses and charming sense of humor. Very supportive of women. They fall all over him."

"He's always been part of the Soviet *Mafya*, with a sinister grip on sports", Dima remembered. "In Soviet times, hockey was controlled by Russian organized crime. His Odessa mob controls Russia's rich reservoir of hockey talent—the guys who are still here, and the players who left for Canada and America. It's all about bribes, extortions, holding families hostage, killings."

Susanna hadn't heard about Boris and the hockey business before. She grasped for associations with Boris's sports team's run-of-the-mill criminal activities.

"Yes, Boris and Fima were invited many times to their sport's parties, and managers wined and dined them."

"I haven't told you everything I know, also racketeering, extortion, loan sharking, money laundering, gambling."

Susanna's suspicions about Fima were finally confirmed, and she became uneasy about Boris's business deals. "You know, Fima's children are studying in America, and he was very close to Boris, treated him like a son."

"Susanna, part of you is like someone from another planet, naïve and impressionable, because you need to be loved by Fima. He never wanted to emigrate. And the story, about the double homicide in a club over a spilled drink in a bar near Izmailovo is famous in our family. My parents never trusted him and were afraid. They also spoke about Fima's father, a master tailor in Odessa, who had no patience with his son's criminal activities, and used to beat the shit out of him."

Diller chose this moment to be assailed by another sneezing fit, the second of many. It began with a series of single rounds when his breathing accelerated and then slowly petered out. He apologized, and wiped his face with a handkerchief.

Eventually Dima relaxed. "What do you know exactly, Susanna?"

"Uncle Fima is a cash bull for women, and has far-reaching influence—car dealerships, state-of-the art refineries, minerals, and metals. But with Boris gone, Dima, I need him precisely because he is who he is. He knows all the players in Norilsk, and patronizes many officials in the Kremlin and Siberia. Remember, this meeting did not happen," she said cheerily, her face pale, her hands trembling.

IO

NORILSK

T HE WORD *SIBERIA* MAY EVOKE IMAGES of harsh conditions, wild country, remote outposts of isolated humanity, penal colonies, and the like. But the truth is that nothing except the wild countryside is visible in Russia when traveling across four time zones. Flying east from Moscow, the Aeroflot flight crossed thousands of miles of grassland and steppe before it reached the Ural Mountains. A few miles further east is one of the great demarcation lines on the planet, the continental divide separating Europe from Asia, blurred endings and indistinct beginnings, a greenbelt carpet of snow and birch spreading eastward toward the Pacific, to indicate where European Russia ends and Asia begins.

The plane was cold, and the flight attendant, wearing a parka over her blue-and-white Aeroflot jacket, emerged from her cabin with only the tips of her fingers protruding from her cuffs. Snow, blowing through the door and settling on swatches of the curling carpet of the plane, didn't melt. Passengers forced their bags down the narrow aisle as the flight attendant cast a predatory look at them, sniffled, considered all the passengers settling into their seats, about thirty out of a hundred: green bulging Chinese parkas, scraggly unkempt hair under *ushankas*, hands cracked and raw, faces dazed with resignation. The luxury of a smile was unaffordable. The passengers dispersed down the cabin and stretched out in the deserted rows, paying no attention to the seat designations on their tickets.

The attendant wasted no time. "This is not your seat! This is not your seat!" She moved down the aisle, scrutinizing tickets, snorting puffs of frosty air and drawing her parka tighter around her. "You'll have to move to your assigned seat!"

There was no sense in this. The plane would remain more than half-empty for six hours to Norilsk. But she went on badgering and bullying and, within a few minutes, had set most of the passengers in motion. The cabin buzzed with grumbling and grousing; bags rustled, feet were stepped on, the carpet was tripped over, but Aeroflot's seating plan was maintained. The passengers ended up in the first seven rows. Many discovered that their seats either reclined or were jammed upright, permanently. Susanna's seat was alright, except that it had a rod running crosswise, poking her tail bone. Finally, with the pilot's call to order, the plane took off into snow flurries and dull evening light.

As the craft gained altitude, leveled, and warmed up, the passengers again dispersed down the aisles, settling in the least bony, most comfortable seats.

Soon, the flight attendant appeared with dinner, trays of chicken gristle and grease. The man in front of Susanna and

Dima, cigarette clenched in his teeth, prodded the bones with his fork, tapped at the stale bread crust, and raised his eyes at the stewardess. "What is this?"

"I don't know. Don't complain to me about it. We are obliged to serve. You are not obliged to eat."

From her bag, Susanna fished out sandwiches for herself, Dima, and Diller, and Dima produced a small bottle of very cold vodka. She found it impossible to concentrate on a book, wrapped herself tighter into the warmth of her fur coat and scarf, and, curling up by the window, was again lost in thoughts of Boris: How clearly she remembered losing all sense of time and place.

The privacy of the plane gave her the opportunity to grieve again for Boris and her son. Behind the tears lay anger and fear for the future. Susanna's life had now become overwhelming and she was certain that she was doomed to live without love for the rest of her life.

Monotony and fatigue lulled her into interludes of slumber. Next to her, anxious and excited, Dima abruptly turned pages, studying his World *Bank Glossary on Enterprise Management for Reconstruction and Privatization—English-Russian/Russian-English.* They coursed east, far above the Arctic Circle, through a hurried night. The man in the seat in front of them hesitated a moment and awkwardly advised that, before landing, they rub vodka on their faces to prevent frostbite.

They coursed into an auroral half-light, dawn over Siberia in winter. The plane's altitude was low enough for the snowy void to be barely visible on a polar day in the Arctic. An imperceptible radiance rebounded off the whiteness, the featureless plain gray-veined with frozen waterways spread in oblique expanses of dull mist.

The plane descended over a strangely empty landscape. Not a car could be seen on the highways that cut through the forests of the taiga. In the final descent, as the craft neared ground, strong winds hammered it, so that the wings wobbled and the flaps trembled. The crowns of needle-less pines emerged from the snow, and a fury of side winds lashed at the long, low descent. No banks, no turns, a thud and a skid, and they were on the ice in Norilsk, the core of the smelting copper-nickel ore industry—and of their important by-products, platinum-group metals.

The plane taxied down the runway and finally lurched to a halt. Listening to the howling wind, passengers grabbed handbags and parcels and began pushing into the aisle. A gangway was driven up, and the attendant struggled to release the hatch lock. It sprang free, and the door flew open. It seemed as though the passengers were walking toward an open freezer door of blinding white.

Susanna and the others emerged onto the mobile stairs. Dima, loaded down with briefcases, led the descent. Sandwiched between Dima and Susanna, Diller panicked, his eyes unfocused in terror as he clutched at the rail, protecting his body from being blown away. Susanna followed. The sky was as steel-white as the ground. She was trying to protect her eyes against the glare when an icy blast hurled her against the railing and her reinforced plastic bags of presents shattered in the frigid air, scattering cosmetics, cologne, and Lady Godiva chocolates in front of her. She had nearly lost her footing on the steps when Dima firmly seized her arm, and they made their way to Arrivals. Suddenly, the day became still, and the wind stopped. Still northern days were the coldest, and the most beautiful: a silent and seductive landscape never seen before. She looked relieved, smiled at Diller and Dima. The cold bit her skin and stung her nostrils. Her eyelashes and nose were freezing. Dima helped her find her sunglasses, so she was able to read the thermometer on the building—minus forty.

THE AIRPORT WAS DESERTED—NO stranded passengers, no flight announcements, no cabbies waiting for business. Two high cheek boned blond Russian women sat behind the kiosk near the exit, their skin creamy apricot, exquisite porcelain, the fur on their hats lustrous.

Bablidze was no more. Aleksandr Evgenievich Kulichkov, now chief of Norilsk, and his minions were the only people waiting for the GMG delegation. They included four of Norilskmetal's staff: Valery Borisov, fist deputy general director: Oleg Elyseevich Smirnoff, Kulichkov's chief of external affairs: Dr. Vladimir Bobkov, chief engineer of the Kombinat: and a well-maintained woman in her fifties or sixties holding a large bouquet of birds of paradise flowers, tightly wrapped in cellophane, for Susanna—in such a place! Yevdokiya Lebedeva was a whirlwind of lipstick and rouge, in a tight bluish fur coat, stylish matching hat, and mystifyingly high-heeled open sandals. Kulichkov, red-faced, greeted them with a jovial and enthusiastic smile, kissed Susanna's cheeks three times, and shook Dima's and the accountant's hands, while a thin-faced young man, who appeared seemingly out of nowhere, stepped forward and presented the visitors with ceremonial bread in a beautifully embroidered cloth and a wooden bowl with salt.

"Welcome to the arctic tundra, to the higher slopes of the Urals, Norilsk, the world's northernmost city! In Norilsk we have winter for twelve months, and the rest is summer," Kulichkov joked. Susanna and Dima smiled, but Diller, still bewildered and disoriented, nodded and mumbled, "Two hundred miles above the Arctic Circle! The first gulag camp which grew into the city of Norilsk. The world's treasure of copper-nickel ores, the principal source of platinum and palladium." Dima translated the end of Diller's sentence only. Kulichkov, subdued and serious, shifted his weight and introduced the entourage, beginning with his administrative assistant, Yevdokiya Lebedeva. She stepped forward, smiling. "Mr. Kulichkov and our professionals are responsible for our revolution of the Kombinat." The man did not own the town but had become the primary force behind the metals complex. Before Bablidze appeared on the scene, he in essence had controlled the fate of everyone who lived and worked in the city, and now, after Bablidze, he did again. "Everything Marx told us about Communism was false, but everything he told us about capitalism was true." Kulichkov was joking again, sardonically. "This is Norilsk: no sushi bars or casinos; no paved-over world. When you come to places like this, you really see market reforms working."

Born of the gulag, Norilsk was the quintessential Soviet company town built on the bones of prisoners. The town is permanently poisoned with toxic yellow fumes in which no trees can grow. The air is, literally, the dirtiest on the globe. Lured by riches hidden deep beneath its permafrost, Stalin had ordered the city constructed in one of the most forbidding climates on the planet. So Norilsk: born in the first year of maximum Stalin horror, set up by the prisoners who arrived in 1935. Five arctic winters later, the first functioning nickel smelter, whose metal production was carried to the port of Dudinka, a hundred kilometers away on a railroad line, was up and running—an immense accomplishment. Kulichkov's father was one of those political prisoners who had arrived in boats intended to transport logs, not people.

By the end of World War II the Kombinat had grown to include factories for oxygen, coke, and machine repair, a power station, coal and ore mines, limestone quarries, and its own airport. Kulichkov grasped Susanna under the arm, and led the group to two customized 600 S Mercedeses for the trip to the hotel. It was already noon, a rare period of dark blue sky, and

Susanna's eyes were blinded by the tundra—a vast, nearly level treeless plain. She searched the white horizon for a sign of life—human, animal, or vegetable—and found only mine shafts visible from the surface of the bleak landscape. Dima looked spunky, while Diller, recovering from the wind and cold, was still shuddering. Observing Diller, the deputy director grinned, "Relax, gentlemen, this is Siberia, not Moscow! The air's lighter here, the people more open. You could still be honest here and survive."

"Make no mistake," Susanna whispered to Dima. "Norilsk is a mob town, and now, the 'native son' is the one running the mob."

"No, who said that?" Dima wisecracked.

Norilsk—named after *Noril'lag*, Norilsk lager, a corrective labor camp, the first of the gulags—had grown up around it, and was, in old Soviet parlance, "a closed city." It required all visitors, Russian or otherwise, to register with the authorities. Just who these "authorities" were was never explained.

As they approached from the outskirts, the entire city seemed tinged in gray. From close, the Orwellian, jaundiced skyline of belching smokestacks was barely visible from within the billowing clouds of their own emissions. The air slowly became enshrouded in a yellow fog as gases descended. Sulfur dioxide, nitrogen dioxide, and hydrogen sulfide made it difficult to breathe. Diller, an asthmatic, began gasping for air, his eyes tearing, darting left and right, panting and coughing as he reached for his inhaler. Kulichkov, relaxed and smiling, trying to divert attention from the man's difficult state, jokingly reassured him, "Don't worry, the way our winds blow, our bad air reaches all the way to Canada."

"Another clown, another Uncle Fima," Susanna murmured to Dima.

The town was High Stalinist, but a central planner's unblemished dream of the old Leningrad as well. Many buildings in the center were pastel colored, in neo-classical style. "Our little Venice of the North," explained Yevdokiya. A dozen avenues, equally spaced, cut lines into a grid of neatly filed eight-story blocks of cement apartment houses, a pastiche of industrial decay.

They drove along the center of town, past the old party headquarters, as Yevdokiya, bubbling, described the important buildings: "We have two palaces of culture for drama, theater, two palaces of sports, we have stadiums and twenty-two kindergartens." The most obvious icon, in a place of honor, was the tall white-stone headquarters of the Norilskmetal Complex. "The residential complexes are just ahead," she continued as they drove past decrepit housing blocks and a statue of Lenin. "Here, in the Far North, we take care of everything that is connected with everyday life of our people from cradle to grave—food, clothes, industrial goods."

"Yes," concurred Kulichkov, "our workers and their families are our social responsibility, especially here where conditions are extreme—long, cold winters and longer polar nights."

Everything aboveground had been designed to fend off the cold. The stores, with three-door threshold entrances, were the same Soviet shops of the 1950s. Courtyards, formed in the center of each apartment block, were treeless squares of broken cement littered with Snickers wrappers and broken bottles but kept out the freezing wind. The apartment blocks housed the working poor, trapped heirs of the gulag, still home to some hundred thousand who kept the plant furnaces stoked. The houses were built on foundations planted deep in the permafrost; the first floor, set high off the ground, allowed the cold air to circulate in the space below, while streets and buildings belched out clouds of steam from a network of heating pipes.

Cold, wind, snow, and blizzards have shaped the city. Massive snow drifts sit everywhere. Norilsk is divided between the world of "here"—above ground—and "there," everything that lies below ground, far below.

"The hotel is coming up," Kulichkov added. "You are lucky to have made it to our tiny airport, so often closed by fierce winds and snow this time of year. Lucky, no 'unanticipated descents!' Now you have time for rest and relaxation. We invite you for small reception later. Our car will come at seven."

The Hotel Norilsk—$14.00 a night—was waiting for the Americans. The manager, a pudgy, gray-haired bureaucrat, was anchored behind the counter. With a reserved smile broken by gold- and silver-capped teeth, he welcomed the group, took their documents, nodded, and disappeared into the back. Immediately, two muscled young "assistants" in track suits brought hot tea and cakes to the reception area and vanished into the long corridor. The hotel was nearly empty, with the restaurant closed for "remont" as long as anyone could remember.

Originally called Venezia, built as a joint venture with Italians in Gorbachev's time, the place still retained an Italianate ambience when Susanna turned on the lights in her room. Flora and fauna of the Adriatic, Venetian waterways, blue lagoons, puffy clouds, sailboats, smiling sailors in striped shirts ferrying boats, and a small white carved bed and bureau greeted her. Steam was spurting from the radiator, and the place was hot. She soon discovered that, in the bathroom, the hot water in the shower ran brown.

SEVERAL HOURS LATER, THE VISITORS WERE in the lobby again, watching news from Moscow, when four men in dark suits, officials from headquarters, emerged from a polished black

Mercedes. They welcomed them to Norilsk and whisked them to a nightclub, Sibir, an attractive place decorated with old Russian watercolors and modern photographs of tropical fruits. The bar had an intimidating display of fancy European liquor, from Johnnie Walker Black to French cognacs and English gins.

The club nevertheless had difficulty establishing its identity. It had tried several: a cozy Austrian spot boasting a large variety of draft beers and demure waitresses in petite *lederhosen*, a financial center for international companies tendering business services to Norilskmetal; a disco; and, at that moment, a sophisticated, cosmopolitan establishment in sync with the metal and mineral resources of the Arctic tundra.

The disco was playing a mélange of post-Soviet pop punctuated by Ricky Martin. They were escorted to a table where Kulichkov, his deputy assistant Borisov, and Yevdokiya Lebedeva were awaiting their guests. Their mood was festive and relaxed. "Welcome again to Norilsk! Please meet Oleg Elyseevich Smirnoff, graduate of Institute for Foreign languages, great businessman responsible for Protocol and External Affairs. He was a great *Pe Er* success presenting the Moscow Olympics to the world and is now working with us."

Smirnoff, a sturdy, compact man with dark curly hair and flashing eyes, dressed in a sports blazer with the Soviet Olympic logo of the Russian bear on his jacket, reached for Susanna's hand and kissed it. Susanna smiled haltingly.

"Yes, of course. We all watched the Soviet Olympics—a powerhouse of talent that beat everyone in sports. Congratulations! I think I once saw you on TV. Great publicity. Now, strenuous work in Norilsk, I'm sure," Susanna remarked.

Smirnoff, with no trace of sarcasm in his comments, comfortably replied, revealing a grin, "Well, with Mr. Kulichkov as chief of this great Kombinat, my job is nothing, but I make very good money. This is a country where you can be great businessman without doing anything." He recited a long pointless toast while Kulichkov's gray, watery eyes narrowed.

Susanna was chatting up Smirnoff but curiously studying Borisov, who was observing Susanna and smiling.

He was short and bald, dressed all in black, but, strangely, the only one carrying a leather briefcase. He seemed to be quite at home in the place. She recognized him immediately, the same Borisov, General Director of Almazyuvelirexport, the Soviet State metals organization she had worked with in Moscow in Soviet times! Uncomfortable, she reached for her glass and returned his smile. Over spoonfuls of black caviar, snails, and whiskey, many toasts were proposed while the guests surveyed their milieu. A harem of young girls, behaving like cosmopolitan beauties, sat at the next table drinking bitter Baltic liqueurs, eating tinned pineapple and studying the guests.

When the deejay returned to the turntable, the nightlife grew serious. The girls began to dance, sweating and moving harder and harder as the music grew faster and faster. As the fever swelled, they were joined by three others, who took to the bar top to dance. Before long they ripped off their blouses and bras, notably raising the sexual tension.

Yevdokiya Lebedeva batted her lashes. Her mascara was running. Diller began to produce fearsome wheezing grunts. Several tables away a woman rippled the fingers of her pudgy hand at him, misinterpreting his distress for a smile. "I feel a migraine coming on—it's the smoke and smell of perfume," he apologized and continued between breaths, making inappropriate comments out of nowhere which Smirnoff translated.

"Yes, Russia is unique," Diller said, attempting to impress the Russians. "It is categorically and absolutely not like anywhere else. Imagine, our industrial consumers have named Susanna as the Russian 'palladium queen!'"

Dima was perspiring, and Susanna was exhausted. "It's been a very long day for you," Kulichkov said empathetically as he rose. "After a good night's sleep, you will all feel more *normal'no* tomorrow."

"Tomorrow, with pleasure," Susanna replied.

"Then it's agreed for tomorrow morning."

Smirnoff escorted the group to the car, wishing all a peaceful night.

They drove back to the hotel in silence. Diller, suddenly recovering, uttered the only one word of Russian he learned: *normal'no*. His nerves were giving way.

"Normal," he said with a laugh, thinking of the girls on the bar. "No matter what I say, the answer's always *normal'no*. I just can't fathom it. Just what in this country would you call normal?"

THE HEADQUARTERS OF NORILSKMETAL STOOD APART from the surrounding decay. The building's white Siberian-stone walls glistened in the yellow haze. The interior also seemed luxurious: security men, cameras, computers, walkie-talkies, all cutting-edge technology. A stocky woman with chemically tangerine-colored hair, in a tight angora sweater, short skirt, and impossibly high heels, greeted Susanna, Dima, and Diller, and escorted them to the new financial and industrial fiefdom of Aleksandr Kulichkov. He had been the first to take advantage of a new law that allowed him to withdraw the company legally from its ministry, lease land from the government, and operate independently. The workers, in their first democratic election, had chosen him as company director.

Kulichkov was already seated at the conference table in his oak-paneled cocoon. The room was a little shrine of his successes to himself in Norilsk. Autographed photos, cups and sashes, many medals, the certificate confirming his status as Hero of Socialist Labor. Dr. Bobkov, his chief engineer, Mr. Borisov, and Yevdokiya Lebedeva, now bouffant-haired and in horn-rimmed glasses, were also waiting, and rose quickly to welcome the guests. Kulichkov did not rise but grinned broadly, radiating warmth and power. Tea was served, but he did not drink it. He sat on the edge of his high-backed chair and spoke in a neutral, condescending voice, "My friends, behold people's capitalism in our industrial complex! Our managers and workers are our shareholders, and they own about forty-one percent of the enterprise. Our miners are among the best-paid workers in Russia. We pay the highest salaries, about seven hundred dollars a month, a fortune by Siberian standards."

Smirnoff quietly continued the briefing, in perfect English, as if quoting a combination of the *Metals and Mining Journal* and *Business Week*. "Metal companies from the world have been here, explaining projects. Metallurgical engineers and CEOs from Europe, Japan, and North America travel to Norilsk, working to conclude deals. Tenders for very interesting projects from start-up assistance to design and supply of equipment, to supervision and construction of surface and downstream facilities."

Susanna turned her chair, smiled, and focused on Kulichkov. "As you must know, GMG is unique in the international world of metals in innovation and finance. We not only provide cutting-edge technology and metallurgy consultants, but also the most sophisticated financial services. We are active in one hundred and thirty countries. Our partners, Global Metals Group Bank in Moscow, World Bank, the State Department, and the European Bank for Reconstruction and Development, have expressed interest in participating in our project."

"Interesting," Kulichkov replied dryly. "The whole *world* is interested in investing in the natural wealth of Siberia. We produce the major share of palladium in the world, and are next to South Africa in gold production. We welcome help and investment from our foreign partners."

Susanna plowed ahead. "GMG will invest substantial sums of money, with large financial profits for Norilskmetal. Our company is ready to send start-up equipment and deploy engineers and mining consultants to Norilsk. Our cooperation will be strong, and both parties will be happy."

Her win-win business philosophy culturally mystified Kulichkov, so she was forced to explain. "Of course, Norilsk will be the locomotive, and GMG will be at the back of the train!"

"Yes," Smirnoff came to life again. "Siberia is the power of Russia, and Norilsk is the power of Siberia. Our managers improve the lives of Norilskmetal's family. They are productive, and we compensate! Group vacations to the tropics, stock options, bonuses linked to company performance, will soon make them wealthy men!"

The secretary adjusted her glasses, nodded, smiled, and continued emphatically, "Mr. Kulichkov is highly popular among his workers for his fairness and generosity.

He has re-engineered our company and our workers. Everyone is productive and everything is provided for! Our people can even buy European clothes!"

"Imagine!" Susanna was impressed. "Great social engineering! You are reaping rewards for all your hard work. Our congratulations! *Pozdravliayu! Zdorovo!*"

II

KOMBINAT

ABOUT FIVE MILES UP A LOW mountain away from the center of town, Susanna, Dima, Kulichkov, Smirnoff, and Dr. Bobkov reached the nickel smelter, Russia's largest platinum, palladium, and nickel complex in the Siberian Arctic, a grim and polluting site, the source of one-fifth of the world's nickel and half its palladium. Diller's asthma had forced him to stay behind in the hotel. The road was rutted and cut with rivulets of clay, fissures filled with toxic sediment. The colossal red-brick monster officially named *Nadezhda* (Hope), known affectionately among the workers as the Crematorium, had been built by the *Zeks* (inmates of Russian labor camps) on the eve of World War II with merciless speed.

The chief engineer, Dr. Bobkov, a man of lean stature with

a bushy mustache and dark gentle eyes, had visited an American palladium mine in Montana and was taken with Susanna's gender in a man's world. "A beautiful and intelligent American woman in our hazardous mining world, still with GMG—congratulations!"

"Thank you. I've been with GMG for many years. I was working with Almaz in Moscow for a long time, and I'm happy to find a familiar face, Mr. Borisov, here in the Arctic," Susanna replied.

"An important man, Mr. Borisov. Imagine—our chief metallurgist in charge of our financial affairs and international tenders," remarked Dr. Bobkov.

"I remember you and your company from Soviet days," Borisov announced. "You must, of course, be familiar with Fima Abramovich Tsypin, one of your consultants and facilitators. He was just here last week checking some of our documents for progress with GMG."

Susanna was out of breath. Hearing about Fima again, this time visiting Norilsk, she felt a bubble of nausea, like an air pocket filling her lower chest. "Oh?" She passed her tongue over her dry lips, confusion spreading across her face.

"Yes. Mr. Tsypin is very important in our Tyumen region, bringing arts and culture to the icebound miners—the most important man in an offshore company."

"Called what?" Susanna was confused.

"Well it's not a company, it's a foundation. The Tyumen Cultural Foundation. Arm's length, then another arm. Fima Abramovich is a titan of industry, supporting our ballet school and museum. In Soviet times, our finest dancers ran away to the West. Now they stay in the Bolshoi but dance everywhere in the world."

Smirnoff silenced Borisov with a glare, and Dr. Bobkov began lecturing on the geological history of the industrial complex. "Well, as you know, in the nineteenth and early twentieth century, this area was the world's principal and most primitive source of platinum and palladium. Our miners lived in plywood barracks deep in the taiga. Cruel and nonproductive. The higher slopes of the Urals were a place of terror and ravages, even under communism. You see, Hitler killed his enemies, but Stalin was smart enough to put them to work and he wanted to make Norilsk the most productive center for nonferrous metals. We smelt copper-nickel ores that have the highest concentration of palladium and platinum in Russia."

Smirnoff proudly added, "This nickel went into the tanks and armor that saved Russia, and perhaps saved the rest of Europe, from the Fascists. In August, after Yeltsin heaved himself onto the tank, the Kombinat passed from state to private hands, and was renamed Russian Joint-Stock Company Norilsk Nickel, but for us, it will always be the same old Kombinat."

Kulichkov was satisfied and noted smugly, "Our liberal economic environment is a magnet for Western investment! Western companies come like bees swarming around the honey pot. We need to improve production levels. We only use our own nickel mines for feed. We must refine all platinum, palladium, and rhodium in our homeland and process and store concentrates and residues in Russian cities. No more shipments of refining scrap to Brussels, New Jersey, or India! Russia's natural resources must never be wasted!"

Susanna was slow to react and, looking at the group cautiously, she replied, "I congratulate you, Mr. Bobkov. You have the opportunity to invest capital for cutting-edge technology and you will get a very large return on your investment." It seemed he truly believed what she was saying.

"This is so much more than I expected, and your timing is perfect. We have studied and read much about geology, history, and political prisoners north of the 69th parallel, and had successful business with Almazyuvelirexport. In Gorbachev's time, we were able to buy export licenses for platinum-group metals for our industrial consumers in America and Europe. During perestroika, we tried to develop a joint-venture project with the Ministry for Nonferrous Metals. Now we hope to work with you directly."

"Gorbachev years—the worst years Russia has suffered since the Tatar yoke!" Kulichkov grumbled. "But we learn very quickly. We have engineers with the expertise to achieve maximum return on our wealth, scientists with advanced degrees—members of *Akademia*, like Dr. Bobkov, from the St. Petersburg Academy of Sciences. The institution was established by Peter the Great in 1724, the best of the best. Just recently, the rector of their Mining Institute visited our plant and read us his dissertation on state control of resources. It is the authoritative work for the Ministry of Nonferrous Metals in Moscow." He smiled with an irritating air of superiority, dragging out the resonant syllables of *aaakaadeemeemiiiyaaa* to let the Americans know of Russia's erudition and power while Dr. Bobkov blushed.

Two of Smirnoff's external-relations men lurked on the sidelines while a well-scrubbed adjutant, the chief of operational security, announced, "You know our policy here. No photographs, and no conversation with our engineers or staff, please," looking directly at Susanna and Dima. "Our staff is supervised very closely."

They all put on plastic safety glasses, face protectors, and hard hats. Kulichkov accompanied them but stopped at the entrance, removing his gear and metal hat. "I know everything about this facility, but I'm uncomfortable with fire and heat, and stay as far away as possible." He smiled broadly and, pushing his safety goggles high up on his nose, remained behind.

The Kombinat reminded Susanna of a scene out of Dickens. The foundry was the underbelly of the world, the size of a football field, a space so big one couldn't see the end of it, filled with dark and forbidding spaces belching fire, steam, and thick smoke. She stared in utter amazement. Whichever way she turned, she was simply swallowed up by smoke and fire in the haze of the polar day. Susanna felt as if she were in the bowels of the earth.

Nature had been abolished. Not a tree, not a bird, was anywhere to be seen. It seemed chaotic, even diabolical, the way the landscape had disappeared under the hand of man. But there was also something extraordinarily beautiful in the intricacy of the plant, a vast mass of machinery and ovens stretching out in every direction.

Terrifying machines hissed and screamed. Clanking, thudding, scraping, and screeching noises came from different areas of the foundry. A new flash smelter from Finland pounded, its lights flashing. Vats of molten metal bubbled, churning and sparkling like a fiery roaring kaleidoscope while shadowy men in hard hats and goggles worked this treacherous scene and poured flashing lava as if they were pouring beer from vats. Tense, unsmiling men hurried about. The risk involved in this grueling work required great courage.

Dr. Bobkov, the guide, stayed as far away as possible. They were introduced to all the processes of the mining operation in different areas of the Kombinat: raw materials, sampling and assaying, refining, the purity of nonferrous metals, water temperature and ovens, British versus German technology, versus Russian, as well as safety procedures, security, and environmental protection. His briefing took on a poetic tone. "What you see is a controlled pattern of workers, machinery, raw material, and capital behaving in an efficient and effective way. But we need more foreign investment to retrofit and make this place the best in the world! Ask your questions, I'll answer them."

Susanna shouted above the din. "I see the latest Finnish technology here. Dr. Bobkov, please explain how the three stages of the leach and recovery process work?"

"Well, the engineer who manages this section is on a break, but he will explain later," he bellowed over the noise.

"And the dried filter cake for further refining, is it produced here as well?" The engineer ignored the question.

Smirnoff, who was closest to the action at all times, began shouting, "With GMG's capital investment, the United States of *Ameriiika* can become Russia's single biggest trading partner!"

Susanna's eyes were red and tearing and Dima's face was shining crimson. "But I think you have seen enough of our technical operation," Bobkov remarked. "Perhaps we can retrieve Mr. Diller and continue again tomorrow at headquarters where there is more air and less noise."

THE POLAR AFTERNOON HAD TURNED QUICKLY to night by the time they picked up Diller. Siberia seemed to have sunk into a never-ending silence. A desolate winter sky arched over them and the countryside lay stiff, as if laid low by a stroke. Susanna and Dima were quiet, bouncing on the ruts in the backseat. Diller's asthma was under control and one could barely hear his wheezing. "The Russians do what they want to do—a dog and pony show where we learned nothing about the Kombinat. From now on it's a blank wall."

Seeing Valery Borisov last night at the nightclub and the news about Fima hit Susanna with gale force again. She stared at Dima. "What the devil is happening here? Who are Fima's contacts in Norilsk?"

Dima hesitated and shook his head, smiling. "Remember

what we talked about in Moscow? He must know people at the very top—he is a political schemer, out to defraud our company, a facilitator not for GMG, but for the Kremlin." His voice trailed off, as if he had run out of information.

To lighten the mood, Susanna began speaking to the drivers, thanking them for their hard work and, reaching into her purse, handed each a carton of cigarettes and a high-tech cigarette lighter. "Am I hearing the howling of wolves?" she asked. "It's so desolate and still."

"Anything is possible here," the man behind the wheel remarked, staving off boredom with conversation. "Wolves, drunkards, dead on the road."

Dima grinned, and they introduced themselves as Vadim and Johnny. Why Johnny? Susanna wondered. Vadim explained. "It's just his nickname. We all call him that," he added with a belly laugh. "Just look at him. He's so pretty, he doesn't even look Russian."

Johnny was embarrassed. He was older and quieter, and sat in silence. He had only finished two years of university and served in the armed forces in Norilsk, helping man the secret missile sites that lined the low hills outside the city. "The missiles," he explained, "had been aimed directly over the North Pole,"at you," he said playfully. "You must all be hungry, and the restaurant in the hotel has been closed forever. If Okay, we take you to a warm and cozy local place," he suggested.

The place in the center of town had no name. It had stood across the street, until the melting permafrost leveled the building next door. Then it had been called The Taiga. So far, no one had come up with anything different.

It was dark inside, but the house singer, a velvety crooner from Kazakhstan with long black sideburns and flaring white trousers, was just warming up. Before long, the disco ball started to spin, and the tiny dance floor filled up. Everyone danced. A broad-busted grandmother twirled on the arms of a baby-faced teenage boy. Women danced with men, men with men, women with women, and boys with girls.

The place had remained Norilsk's hot spot, where families came to celebrate christenings, retirement, and jobs. Requests were shouted from the floor.

"This is for our friend Vanya, who just graduated and is heading south tomorrow to the *materik* from his loved one Valentina." A lanky, sandy-haired youth, pushing back his metal-framed glasses, stood up as everyone clapped.

"Vanya, we will miss you when you reach the mainland, but we know how much you have looked forward to this. We wish you the best of luck, we wish you safe journey and soft landings! You know, Vanya, your friends, we will be right here waiting for your return."

The group ordered *pelmeni*, which were served with tall glasses of vodka. The Russians and Dima downed their drinks and relaxed.

"These are the best *pelmeni* ever! Frozen in the ground, of course. Great! We don't get that in Brooklyn!"Dima called out.

"What brings you to this place, Johnny?" Susanna asked.

"I was born here and served in the army in Siberia," he said between more vodka and mouthfuls of dumplings. "I knew the salaries were good. Of course everyone is now trying to get ahead, and we do whatever it takes. Our great-great-grandparents were the tsar's serfs, our grandparents and parents were the Politburo's serfs, and we are their children, grateful descendants of communist terror, now in business." He smiled.

Johnny stopped to light a cigarette while Vadim listlessly continued, "Most people are too poor to leave, and there is nothing to do if they stay. Yes, many hereditary criminals, around for centuries, fugitives on the run, and socially hostile elements. People hunker down and drink for a night that lasts four months. They just drink, go wild, and steal their neighbors' chickens. A place built on the ravages of terror. Now *you* are here visiting our future showcase for capitalism—*Ura!*"

Swaying to the loud music, they drank and toasted, gulped *pelmeni* dripping with sour cream, and sank into the atmosphere of the place.

"Well, honestly, a day full of surprises, and I need to lose my edge," Susanna muttered, enjoying the feast. "Dima, you are all aglow and going home very happy. The prodigal son returns—and is running away, again. How is that?" Susanna smiled, glancing at Dima, while Mr. Diller, silent, observed the scene.

"I'm speechless and very happy, but it's more than just going home; the Arctic was surely very hot for me." Dima continued in Russian, so Diller would miss the conversation, telling the real story, not an *anekdot*.

"When we got to the hotel after yesterday's grueling flight and reception, I went to bed early. I had just dozed off when there was a rapping at the door. The knocking kept repeating softly. Perhaps some emergency, I thought. I draped a sheet around me, and cracked the door open ..."

"A Siberian surprise! Our nocturnal visitor!" Johnny laughed.

"A shapely woman in her twenties, red dyed hair, heavy makeup, crimson-painted lips, leather miniskirt advertising great legs!"

"Congratulations, Dima!" Susanna was enthusiastic.

"I make a mistake?" Dima giggled, imitating the visitor. "She saw my bewildered look, and suddenly I was awake. My sheet slipped off, and I was naked."

"You like me sometime?" she asked.

"I picked up my toga, and quietly shut the door behind her. Another Valya, Susanna! Another English teacher smelling of tobacco and heavy perfume, swept into the room, and found me wearing nothing but a grin."

Johnny and Vadim drank some more and roared with infectious laughter. Susanna was relaxed enough to suddenly giggle for the first time since she returned. Vadim shouted, "We salute you, Dima! First time here, and you've been already honored by our English schoolteacher! May the dick be hard, and may there be money! Surely, she will be waiting for you tonight."

Dima, drunk and nostalgic, muttered, "It was still night when she quickly and quietly shut the door and scurried away. Her perfume lingered behind her. I can still smell it..." To overcome melancholy Dima was drinking again and the outside world was forgotten.

"I am certain when she walks down the dark corridor again, the evil-eyed *dezhurnaya* won't question her in her way," Vadim muttered mockingly.

"No problem, Dima, *dezhurnayas* don't interfere with the hotel's 'intelligence' staff. But be careful about your briefcase, and the documents inside. Alla's fingers are sticky and she is paid for gathering information. She will be there, and the next time you come to Norilsk, and will even take a sabbatical for you! It's a worker's paradise now," Johnny muttered under his breath. They were all drinking too much.

Susanna, moving her shoulders to the music, looked to Dima and was ready to dance. "Yes, Johnny, for the first time here, we feel the real warmth of Siberia."

"This is home. Even recent arrivals have a sense of belonging. There is friendliness here. We are not going anywhere. We are proud of living in one of the world's most unlivable places." Johnny rose, took her hand, and smiled.

"Long live Norilsk's resurgent capitalism!" said Susanna, eager to dance.

"Surely the money has something to do with it!" Johnny grinned and led Susanna to the floor.

The music was loud and happy, and Susanna's dress sparkled under the strobe lights.

12

SLAVIC BAZAAR

SUSANNA, DIMA, AND DILLER REACHED MOSCOW on a quiet snowbound Sunday. Knee-deep winter snow had softened the city. Sheets of thick flakes, buoyant and motelike, fell steadily and kept avenues empty and white, resculpted statues, and transformed park paths into skiing trails. They stopped for lunch at a local restaurant, the Slavic Bazaar, a place of revelry and traditional specialties, a resurrected old-fashioned tavern unlikely to have listening devices. It had an old Russian atmosphere: wooden crossbeams, wooden pails, trays, lacquer utensils, peasant embroideries, stuffed birds that sang, and waiters dressed as serfs—a gastronomic Russian Disneyland where parents took their children for a treat. Since it was still early afternoon, it was a perfect place for a discussion about Norilsk before Volodya drove Diller and Dima to the airport.

The restaurant served a full six-course lunch: *zakuski*, both cold and hot, soups, pies, poultry dishes, a roast, and, finally, fruit and sweets.

The smell of sturgeon from the kitchen was nostalgically evocative to Dima. "This place smells like home! Out of Siberia and closer to Brighton Beach." He loved the place, fondly remembering his night visitor in Norilsk, and looked forward to going home to "Odessa by the Sea."

Susanna surveyed the patrons, the new Russian gentry. A round-faced grandmother was celebrating *Maslenitsa* (Butter Week), a festive holiday, with her granddaughter. The grandmother was explaining this pagan and earthy carnival that celebrated life. "Today the real Tsar of Moscow is *bliny*: a symbol of the sun, of beautiful days of good harvest, happy marriages and healthy children, like you! Moscow eats bliny hot as fire with sour cream, with fresh caviar, with herring, smelts, sprats, sardines, salmon, and sturgeon."

The little girl was charmed. Dressed in a flowery ruffled Chinese import, she gazed at her grandmother and other guests through big aquamarine eyes. The grandmother continued reading every line of the menu to her. "Have you understood all the variety of food they offer? You can have anything you like! Old Moscow was always the food capital of Russia, a feast for the gourmands, for sumptuous eating. Alexander Pushkin called our dinners 'a chain of meals!'" The girl's pigtails bounced, her eyes sparkled, and she grinned with pleasure.

Finally sitting comfortably at a table, and served vodka, *kvass*, and hot mead, the group relaxed. Susanna glanced at her watch and initiated the business discussion, reading her observations from handwritten notes. She asked Dima for a professional opinion about how Diller should handle the financial and accounting issues in a debriefing with the CEO. Diller said, "Here's what we know, people. Our fearless leader Jack Hanken, and GMG's board of directors, are planning to allocate $100 million for financial, technical, and advisory assistance to the Norilsk refinery. A drop in the bucket. They are ready to send engineers and mining consultants to the Arctic to evaluate the need for more efficient, high-capacity equipment. They will only see the tip of the iceberg. Susanna and I only saw that fires were burning, and we heard ear- deafening equipment clanking, but everything is under wraps! The Russians are well-paid professionals who are both the hedgehog and the fox!

Dima smiled, but Susanna interrupted. She was on a life-and-death mission. "We must get this solved! We can't have long complicated agreements. A simple one, and short horizons. Both parties will sign the contract for three tranches of the metal, to be countersigned and guaranteed by the Russian Central Bank. GMG delivers $100 million, and Norilsk delivers the first 25 percent of palladium ingots, priced by the London Palladium Fix, and hedged by GMG. We must price all three quantities, with agreed-upon future delivery dates. The first tranche delivery to KLM, Amsterdam, as soon as possible."

"When will that be, Susanna? We will be waiting for the Red Messiah," Diller uneasily commented, already sneezing.

Susanna stroked his hand. "A protocol agreement is in place. After the contract is signed, the first tranche is to be confirmed by KLM, for exactly the date stated in the contract. Payback from raw materials is pretty fast."

"Oh hell," Dima swore. "Susanna, you sound like you're on a combat mission. Let's all just calm down. Jack Hanken will encourage Mr. Diller to restore confidence of foreign investors in Russia," he said with a cynical edge.

Diller began to say one thing, then changed his mind and said another. *"Normal'no* for a Russian, but crazy for me." He paused and glanced at Dima.

"Norilsk is a *scam*. The Russians are clever, paranoid, and maximalist—only one winner and one loser. Win-win is for our Harvard consultants only."

Dima, a lawyer, remained calm and, like a lawyer, prevaricated, at times saying what Susanna wanted to hear, and at others not. This work in Russia was tempting, almost seductive. No more immigration law in Brooklyn but international corporate law, with great income potential. He would look out for himself and his family! Never mind the Russians in Brooklyn! Regularly traveling to the Motherland, inhaling the sights and sounds of his childhood, and visiting the Arctic! He began a "Brighton Beach" lecture.

"Russia has been plunged into capitalism. We need to be realistic. We've just witnessed a grand sell-off in Siberia, one of the greatest transfers of wealth in the world. In Brooklyn, they call it 'capitalism with a Russian face,' or corruption for the sake of democracy, *dermokratiya*." (Dima didn't need to translate the Russian word for "shit.") "Of course, also '*prichvatizatsia*,' Russian privatization, is simply grabbing or stealing from the Russian state—the murderous carve-up of the Soviet Union's vast resources of wealth."

"Yes." Susanna answered. "No country has ever shed an empire, reformed its economy, and developed a democracy at the same time. Yeltsin's democracy," she added, "has about five millionaires. Soon to be added are Kulichkov and Smirnoff."

Dima shook his head. "A project so huge and complex—it's very difficult for you to pull off. GMG and our investors could be *fleeced* in this new capitalist revolution—this is impossible. I don't mean to be insulting . . ."

Diller muttered quietly to himself, scribbling notes for his debriefing with Hanken. He took a sip of hot tea and Susanna, disturbed, focused on business.

She was undaunted. "Norilsk Nickel is Russia's largest integrated metals and mining company, and a global leader in the industry. The company boasts fifty percent of the world's palladium production. They need foreign investment to modernize infrastructure and continue to expand! I will telex a report about our trip tomorrow, before you get home, Mr. Diller. Jack Hanken is confident that Russia will become an economic powerhouse."

"Okay, yes," Diller replied. "A remarkable transformation after seventy years. But, Susanna, you never know who is ready to torpedo our work, and take the money and run."

"Sure, we must be very cautious," she agreed. "We cannot move without discipline and financial controls. That's why I am here, committed to this project. I have my own network of U.S. government and multilateral government organizations ready to contribute to our financing. We cannot let Norilsk go!"

"A *network*," Dima questioned, "or just some personal friends? And if they back out, what then?"

Norilsk's exotic deal was going to be Susanna's corporate focus, a personal trophy. She was obsessed with the project, and pressured to remain in Russia to uncover more information about Boris's life and death. She sank back in the chair in silence. This conversation was beginning to resemble a cockfight. Too much, too fast.

A wedding party had just left their shiny black Zhiguli and entered the restaurant. The happy bride, in an exquisite crocheted dress—a tiny waist, natural white rosebuds for the wreath in her flowing blond hair—had her arms wrapped around the arm of her red-faced, serious-looking husband, dressed in a black Finnish suit and inappropriate tie.

Although the waiters had been shuffling around their table many times, Susanna and the others were finally ready to order from the thick, beautifully bound book of gastronomic wonders. Susanna and Dima ordered for the table.

In the back of the room, the celebratory feast was soon in full swing, marked by singing, drinking, toasts, and loud music. It was difficult to continue the discussion. The wedding guests were transformed into a village for a replica of a peasant wedding. It was a dramatic performance. Joy and happiness glistened from the bride's eyes. A formal marriage contract was sealed by the drinking of many vodkas and chanting *gorko*, the bitter life to come. Women, dressed as *devitsas*, wailed plaintive ceremonial songs mourning the loss of maidenhood and lamenting a bitter life for the bride in her husband's home. This was followed by dancing the group ceremonial, the *khorovod*.

Diller, distracted by the music and gleeful noises from the wedding party, was enthralled by the performance. "This is not only a restaurant, but an ethnic museum—and a nightclub, Susanna!"

Finally, their table was served along with the wedding party's. Eating is serious business, and the place grew still. Diller was content, enjoying the tastiest *lapsha*, Russian chicken soup, and the most delicious fish in aspic ever, tastier than his grandmother's at Passover. "Yes, Russia is unique," he said. "It is categorically and absolutely not like anywhere else, super-*normal'no!*" He smiled for the first time.

The meal calmed him, and he remained cheerful between small bites of fish, while Dima and Susanna enjoyed their *zakuski* and vodka toasts, followed by tasty and aromatic borscht. No *maslenitsa* for them! Duck, stuffed with fruit and roasted to perfection, followed.

After finishing his gourmet feast, and savoring each bite, Diller happily continued. "So how do we handle the financial risk? Norilsk has no credit. The term 'hedge' is misleading. We buy metal for future delivery, pay them dollars, and hedge ourselves by selling paper contracts. What if they decide to cancel the contract? How do we protect ourselves against the Kremlin or nationalization? Very complex, and very risky."

"Russia," Susanna replied, "has always honored her contracts! They even shipped oil to Hitler after he attacked them in World War II! It's true, though, Mr. Diller—we must watch for irregularities and arctic storms."

She shrugged, turning her shoulders away from him, to watch the waiters' parade of dishes for the wedding party, but the accountant pushed on. "I live in order to untangle financial knots. I see embezzlement and botched-up accountancy procedures here, which make it impossible to execute my fiduciary duty for GMG or the company's clients. I see scandals for the corporation and our shareholders. I can't make sense of any of their ledgers." Wheezing again, he wiped his chin and shifted his weight around on the chair.

"Yes, Mr. Diller, but Russian industry and politics have been restructured. That's what we have to work with." She fidgeted, uncomfortable with her position, but these were her combat tactics. Mystified, Diller gave a noncommittal nod.

Dima poured a small vodka for Susanna. "I'm telling you again, Susanna—it's all a *fraud*."

Diller grinned. "I agree with you, Dima. I can't understand how any business works here."

Dima burst out in fresh exasperation, "Here's a list: guile, intimidation, violence, greed, personal connections, *razborkas*, *razelkas*, murder, lynchings." He was on a roll. "Not many Russians are lucky. Some still have their potato patch, and some, money in the mattress."

Susanna, with her usual intensity, sighed impatiently. "Look," she said mostly to Diller, "a small group of Russians has claimed ownership of some of the world's most valuable resources. Russian capitalism rests on the mass voucher privatization process. Workers bought shares in their companies, but they were clueless about what they represented. They had heard for seventy years that capitalism was bad, paper assets worthless. They need to relearn what property is and rebuild a middle class. With time, we will make it happen here, Mr. Diller. I've already worked with the mass voucher privatization process in Ukraine."

Dima raised a finger. "Well, you may not be wasting Hanken's time, Susanna. He was a marine, he likes danger and calculated risks, but Norilsk can hardly wait to grab GMG's cash fast enough."

"What if they don't deliver?" Diller demanded.

"Yes," she said under her breath. "How does the joke go? Talk is cheap until you hire a lawyer. The Russians are farther east, Mr. Diller, and more imaginative. The Russian hustlers and scalpers bought up those vouchers, and future oligarchs took control of the factories at ridiculous prices. But you must know, Dima, that historically, for Russians, contracts have always been like the Holy Grail."

The wedding party had finished dining, and the men were eager to get on the floor with serious Cossack dancing. It was a whirlwind of boots flying, shouting, hands clapping on knees, men dancing alone and bouncing with each other. Finally came the highlight—a man, with a full bottle of vodka balanced on his head, danced an intricate Cossack solo, his feet jumping precisely to the music.

Obstinately Dima shook his head.

"Russia will never converge on the American model of capitalism."

The music was loud, the show was amazing, but Dima remained unyielding and continued shouting. Susanna poked him to be quiet so she and Diller could enjoy the spectacle.

She was silent again while the accountant continued to support the attorney. "How can we invest millions in this place? I don't see many ways of skinning a bear that's already been skinned. You know, Susanna, I cannot come to Norilsk again. I'm an asthmatic, it's deadly for me."

"And I am Russian and live in Brooklyn, Mr. Diller," said Dima. "They remember all the capitalist tricks, seventy years after communism. It's in their DNA. They don't need a remedial course."

Susanna had grown weary of Dima's lecture. Waiters cleared the table and swept the tablecloth with birch twigs. For the next two minutes Dima thought of nothing but stared at the girls in the wedding party, and the girls stared back. Twice he cleared his throat and moistened his lips.

Susanna sighed, raised her eyes, ignoring Dima, and said testily, "Mr. Diller, you must make Hanken understand we have our government's support. Remember, their balance sheet reflects the old system. Assets were always added to the business sheet, inputs always exceeded outputs, and the economy had to operate in the red."

"*Normal'no*, for communism," Diller commented wryly.

She gazed at him, soldiering on. "You must stress the *bottom line*, Mr. Diller! Even *Russian* arithmetic leaves little doubt. Last year, Norilsk cleared over fourteen million dollars in profits. In the same year, it paid out little more than two million dollars in dividends. Our conglomerate has a short-term approach. Payback from raw materials is pretty fast. EBRD, IMF, and USAID will be on board. We must take the lead! This major business can be a first for investment banks in Europe and America. Even the *Financial Times* and the *Wall*

Street Journal have reported on our financing project. That's plenty of political capital for Jack. Be positive!"

The Slavic Bazaar did not turn out to be a good sell for Susanna. She lit another cigarette and paid with a thick wad of rubles, and then it was time for farewells. They exchanged handshakes and hugs, and she wished them a safe flight. There was a long silence before Volodya's car showed up for the drive to Sheremeytevo.

When and how will this project ever succeed? she wondered. How can I remain here? Susanna returned to the apartment alone, very tired and depressed, and watched the dim lights of the city from her window. She had nowhere to go. She was front and center in the Norilsk discussions, exhausted by her diplomatic and business work, simultaneously marketing for Norilsk and GMG. She knew that Hanken was a powerful man, and that she had no control over his reaction to Dima's and Diller's debriefings.

Disoriented and discouraged, and too tired for sleep, her mind obsessively replayed Norilsk scenes—the frozen tundra, the headquarters, the nightclub, the refinery, chemicals, the Hotel Norilsk. It was very late and the night dwindled away in ghostly silence.

13

RISK MANAGEMENT

A COMPLETE HUSH SURROUNDED JACK HANKEN'S suite on the twentieth floor of the GMG building, a land-mark historic art deco skyscraper. His offices suggested both imperial and low-profile executive power. He ruled the headquarters of one of the world's largest companies like a regent, having worked for thirty-five years to build this top multinational firm. Besides his many offshore companies, he was the largest stakeholder and common shareholder of GMG.

Here was majestic splendor, the complete opposite of the floors below, which were crowded with entrepreneurial chaos, a rough-and-tumble center of commercial buzz with money-making and risk-taking, like a casino without the alcohol.

Diller remembered that Susanna had once told him how

relieved she was to work in Moscow, rather than wake up each morning and think of Hanken "ready to bite the ass off each bear" on Wall Street.

Besides the receptionist and a pool of secretaries, Diller was greeted by an Asian butler straight as a broom, clad in a white jacket, who invited him into the reception room of the inner sanctum.

HANKEN, A HARDENED MARINE AWARDED A Bronze Star for storming the beach at Normandy, had created royal magic in his suite. His offices were another world—dappled light, entering the room though the open heavy drapes, streamed onto costly and elegant Persian carpets, enhancing a strange, reverent silence.

The walls were adorned with signed photographs of U.S. presidents from Eisenhower to Clinton. Also displayed on the grass cloth wallpaper was a portrait of his glamorous trophy wife hugging two Maltese terriers and a large sepia photograph of the Normandy invasion.

The room was decorated with exquisite antique Chinese vases and a miniature bonsai tree, garden, and waterfall—nostalgic echoes of the company's business origins in China. Diller looked out on the sweeping panoramic views of New York City, the tiny cars and people scurrying in every direction.

It was Diller's first meeting with the boss. Jack Hanken was a great bear of a man, with heavy jowls and thick eyebrows that met at the bridge of his nose.

Susanna had debriefed him after every trip to Moscow. She had been invited for tea many times and warned the accountant that the tycoon often combined disarming charm with a terrifying and intimidating management style. The staff compared it to a marine military style of command and control. He was a heavy hitter, fighting off threats and out-performing competitors in far-flung domains.

Considered a pioneer of one of the biggest and most strategic global corporations, he took great pleasure from the firm's aggressive, profit-driven culture that spawned commitment to innovation unlike any other company.

Diller was panicking and wheezing, his asthma acting up. He dropped his briefcase to greet the boss, but was still breathing into the inhaler for dear life.

"Your first trip to Russia, I understand. Tell me about it." Hanken always began with an inquiry, perhaps a throwback from his training with the Marines.

"Well, to use the Russian expression, it was *normal'no*, although there is nothing *normal'no* about Moscow, Norilsk, or the Kombinat, their ledgers, their infrastructure, or their finances."

Hanken listened carefully and was gracious while Diller, ill at ease, actually went pale and stared at his tasseled loafers.

"We support spontaneity in our management team, and know that Ms. Thompson has been working hard in Moscow and the Arctic on this project. Tell me, what did you learn?"

"Zaire with permafrost!" Diller replied. "The Norilsk project is completely opaque, a Byzantine business environment with connections to organized crime and the state. Corrupt bureaucrats are entrepreneurs at the mercy of oligarchs and the state. There's registration, re-registration, and certification with regional and state agencies. Twenty different entries show up on the books that can tax a company into bankruptcy."

"The blizzard of bad news about privatization is discouraging," Hanken admitted. "But Russia is our next most lucrative market. We will open Russia, not only for investments, but ideas about management, governance, and accounting standards."

Diller, surprised at these remarks, wheezed and declared, "As an accountant, sir, I cannot satisfy my professional responsibility, my fiduciary duty to the company or our clients." He sensed a return to statesmanlike calm. Hanken's mood was deliberate, the suite quiet.

"As we know here, we are not in an easy business. Metals or commodities are not macroeconomics, Mr. Diller. Success for us means not only proper pricing, but recognizing that we are in a risky business. We're not buying potatoes here."

"They don't understand the language of the market. The tax system, profit and loss, shareholders, corporate raiders, bankruptcy are all foreign concepts there. The Tax Inspectorate suffocates all business with contradictory laws. At least three types of books are kept at Norilskmetal—a secret black accounting book, showing real output in profits and losses, kept only for oligarchs amassing wealth. A white accounting book which shows low profits and high expenses, for bribing inspectors to avoid taxes. And a gray book, for oligarchs in collusion with the government, getting loans from banks in exchange for shares, and for the Russian state. They choose how much activity to conduct above ground, and how much below, and calculate each barter transaction."

"Mr. Diller, we are not relying on American accounting practices or standard risk-taking strategies. I've been studying the natural resource market in Russia for a long time. It presents tremendous opportunities, more promising than the old Shanghai business. We pioneered the Chinese market, and we have been famous and well respected by their leadership since the 1920s."

Diller's response was slow and steady. "This project is the most serious challenge of my career. I know our history in China, sir. We were the first foreign company permitted there, and the mayor of Beijing appointed you as the capital's first 'senior economic advisor.'"

The butler came around with more tea.

"Yes, I'm good friends with two former mayors of Shanghai," Hanken replied, "and, now, President Jiang Zemin and Premier Zhu Rongji. With my counsel, China initiated market socialism, rapid economic growth, and pulled hundreds of millions of peasants out of poverty. As the Chinese say, 'Getting rich is no crime'!" Hanken styled himself as the ultimate deal maker—a bit of hubris not terribly far from the truth.

"That's it! Soon you will be advising Yeltsin as well," Diller said meekly. "Russia needs your ideas and know-how."

Hammerin' Jack was swinging from home plate. "No Boxer rebellion there. GMG in Russia will be more productive than Commodore Perry, who opened Japan long ago. Our Financial Products group is ultimately under my control. We must be the first company on the block, we have vast opportunities to outperform our competitors to enter Russia ahead of our peers, and capitalize on our investments."

Diller, expressionless, was looking at the war photographs behind Hanken's desk. "I must nevertheless point out, sir, that any kind of audit and financial due diligence is impossible. Total nontransparency! And what about political risk? Should the palladium market move against us, the seller can stop delivery because he will get much higher prices in the open market than for our fixed-price contracts."

The chief leaned back in his chair and rested a shoe on an open desk drawer. "Your concerns are overblown. We know that Russia is a black hole for investors. But black holes offer opportunity. We will be working with a sovereign state. Norilsk, the largest commodity producer, needs to modernize their asset base and raise financing on international markets."

The butler returned, poured more tea for both, and bowed

out of the room again. Diller, his knees shaking, could barely keep the cup from spilling.

"GMG will help Norilsk become more efficient and productive in the global commodities market. Our best and brightest talent will work on pragmatic risk-management services for Norilskmetal, and we will trump Russia's opaque financial market. Our entrepreneurial history tells us there is no ownership of ideas. Put this into your head, you are a clever fellow."

"This is good news," Diller said, his voice grim.

"Look beyond their books, Diller, look outside the box! Plenty of intellectual-capital smarts here. Our boys in Financial Products have a proven track record, and our talent will provide international investors and banks as principals. They will strategize risk management solutions and sophisticated hedging products for metals."

Hanken wouldn't give up. His mind flew from one possibility to the next, around and around Russia's vast natural resources and dollar signs. "Norilskmetal wants their financial asset base modernized. The company has high cash flows, and we can raise financing. Don't you understand, our sovereign collateral will be Russia!"

Listening to Hanken's missionary enthusiasm, and imagining his salary increases, Diller's fiduciary responsibility was suddenly no longer so much at cross-purposes with his business conscience.

"Yes, and Ms. Thompson reports that EBRD and IMF support the Norilskmetal project. USAID is also ready to help with technical consulting on infrastructure. We will overcome the bureaucratic flimflam, raise financing with syndicated banks and on international markets in the form of Eurobonds, which GMG will trade as IPOs."

"I have deliberately studied all the data on the project, and as CEO, I will make the final call about risk-to-reward parameters after my trip to Moscow. Ms. Thompson and our boys, along with EBRD, and other international government entities, are handling this project. I will fly in for the signing. Russia is hot!"

So Hanken had tipped his hand about his plans for Norilsk. He loved challenges, and Russia was to be his new frontier. He wanted to buy Norilsk risk cheaply, sell it to another investor dearly, and make money without taking any risk himself. By wagering a large sum of money on it, creating a hedge, generating a demand for the metal, and selling it, he was convinced of success. The difference between what GMG paid for the metal and what GMG sold it for would represent the firm's profits on the deal. The idea was a dream. GMG, which sat in the middle of this transfer of risk, would take no risk whatever!

Diller had difficulty understanding the chief's ideas and inscrutable financial engineering. He swallowed hard again, and gave his views a final try.

"How can we use derivatives to hedge risk for the Russian commodity industry? What about information and dates, which must be disclosed under our federal securities regulations? Not revealing security requirements and lack of compliance is against the law. This deal can blow up big time with a tangle of lawsuits and accounting scandals, and wind up in international courts in The Hague."

"This isn't a question of legality. It's a pragmatic and convenient morality for GMG," Hanken stressed. "The strategy is being devised by our elite financial products people, and the contract will be countersigned by a sovereign state," he emphasized added again. "I will get the confidence of senior officials in the ministry, right up to the minister of nonferrous metals, minister of finance, and Yeltsin himself."

"Well, sir, so long as we have a contract, a legal vehicle under which rights and acts are exchanged for lawful consideration, with periodic underwritten payments and deliveries." Diller needed his pension, so he compromised.

Hanken's reach in the world of government and politics was wide-ranging and influential. He had achieved the desired effect and had enough. He rose from his chair, and the conversation was over.

When he was finished, Diller, one of the best professionals at GMG, was ready to thank his chief for the privilege of working for the firm.

14

BRIGHTON BEACH

N THE SHADOW OF THE ELEVATED subway tracks on Brighton Beach Avenue is a vista bustling with commerce. Even the Walgreen's sign, owned by third-wave Russian immigrants, is in Cyrillic. There are a multitude of Russian meat markets, vegetable stores, bakeries, delicatessens, restaurants, and boutiques with upscale designer clothes, exclusive furs, and jewelry.

In this neighborhood, generally inhospitable to outsiders, bordered on one side by the ocean and the other by enormous housing projects, the new Russians had erected a closed world often referred to as "Little Odessa."

People live in the well-kept art deco apartment buildings that face the Atlantic. The most prestigious and elegant of these Russian enclaves is the Atlantis.

Designed and constructed by international architects, the complex faces an endless horizon of ocean. The light pink condominiums, with a pool, landscaped gardens, huge protected balconies, and $2 million penthouses, dominate the eastern end of the neighborhood. A few blocks further are sprawling houses designed in the Roman Imperial style, with massive bronze crests, spiked gates, and enough marble to empty several Italian quarries.

It is home sweet home, or fiefdom, to Boris's friends Sosa and Zhora, who own the Nachalkin Art Gallery. Their friend, who manages the gallery, Ludmilla Sossin, not only has a green card but also a Ph.D. in art history from Harvard. The gallery is reputed to have the best and largest collection of Russian art in the world, from baroque to classical to avant-garde and contemporary. Ludmilla employs an émigré trickster, an older man who once worked at the Hermitage, who can detect and produce fakes and objects of impeccable provenance that collectors want to buy. He is also a professional art restorer and can clean and retouch any modern painting to make it look old. Truly a renaissance man, he is also a gofer, chauffeur, and bodyguard for Ludmilla, as well as a security guard for the gallery.

Ludmilla divides her time between Manhattan, St. Petersburg, and Europe. Originally from Kharkov, she claims to be a distant relative of an aged Russian countess with a villa on Long Island whose line can be traced to the deposed king of Yugoslavia. She is both an art history professional and the front for a gallery that pays no taxes. Another business group launders money, pays the gallery's rent, provides operating capital, and is responsible for all expenses, including the maintenance of her elegant Mercedes in Brighton Beach.

Ludmilla is well informed, and is a popular member of New York art world. She attends many important social events, where she is photographed gliding across dance floors with heirs to huge fortunes.

She is also part of the "New Russian" circuit, serious collectors who want to avoid burglaries and attention from unfriendly governments. Others buy decorative art to glamorize their lifestyle in their new *kottedzhes* and town *khauses*.

The Nachalkin gallery is the hub of an expanding market where Russians buy back the country's art legacy. When clients request a certain Somov or Aivazovsky "on order" she relies on the exclusive and shady business organized by owners of the gallery. She has worked her way up in the art auction world and often socializes with fine art dealers, auctioneers, and curators from Sotheby's and Christie's. This elite global club drinks far too much wine, gossips about bidders, and constantly bemoans the shifting fortunes of their trade. The lucky ones own Kandinskys, Shishkins, and Rodchenkos, and are always in the market for more. When something important appears in Russia or Europe, they buy quietly, and worry about the details later.

IT'S A BEAUTIFUL WINTRY AFTERNOON, AND the family is excited about Dima's return. Following the American custom, they welcome him at home, rather than the airport, in front of the doctor's Park Slope townhouse. Shivering from the cold, with flowers in hand, they are looking for the limo while the Irish nanny is getting the older boys from school.

The doctor's entrepreneurial spirit has filled his waiting room with people. A Medicaid patient from a no-fault insurance scam has just arrived by ambulette for physical therapy. Several more have made it to the office by Access-a-Ride. What a country! You can cheat on taxes, collect welfare benefits, pay with food stamps, and still enjoy a bit of Russian culture—newspapers, television, bookstores, and chess. These people came from a brutal society where the state and the government were as crooked as the crooks. The old xenophobia is still pervasive. Stealing from the government, and white-collar crime, are part of the Russian DNA. Blatant distrust of authority has carried over into the United States. While offering refuge and assistance, America is still the enemy.

Finally, the prodigal son arrives. Dima has landed tired and jet-lagged, and in a different mood than normal. His trip to Russia has transformed him from a run-of-the-mill immigration lawyer to an important metals law consultant, working for a stellar international commodities firm.

In brief telephone calls from Russia, he avoided any conversation or anecdotal evidence about the murder of cousin Boris. He only described the Arctic and the pollution in Norilsk. He discussed official government organizations and banks negotiating business in Moscow and boasted about the possibility of further "invitations" to London and Brussels.

BY EIGHT IN THE EVENING, THE NANNY had bathed the children and put them to bed, and by nine o'clock, the doctor finally made it upstairs for dinner. More crying, kissing, and hugging. He handed out special gifts, told stories about his sisters Polina and Bella, and poured special balsamic Russian vodka, unavailable in Brooklyn. Dima bluffed and stalled but, slowly, the tale of Boris emerged. "Boris was murdered," Dima told them, "suffocated in his apartment while Tyotya Polina and Bella were away at a sanatorium." He explained that Boris was greedy, involved in many businesses, and wore many hats, including helping Susanna with the Norilsk project. He bought Norilsk shares and vouchers, traded them on the MICEX, skimming cash. Boris also owed money to Zhora and Sosa. So the murder was made to look like arson—an electrical fire. Important paintings were stolen.

"Juggling too many businesses," Dima sighed. "We don't know the whole story—greed and lust for power. Vera believed that the keys to his apartment had been stolen in St. Petersburg. He had owed money, did not pay, and had been suffocated. The murder would make a good Russian detective story. *Mest*—revenge!" "*Gospodi*," Dima's father cried out.

"Susanna's friend, Lev Kartsev, is certain that the hit men were surely somewhere in Tbilisi, and Boris's trophy painting, the Aivazovsky *Sunset*, is living another life in Europe or New York."

THE FAMILY COULD NOT PROCESS THE DETAILS. Startled, the doctor trembled and turned pale; his wife was crying. "My brother's child. A near-saint. I loved him dearly. How can Polina survive without her son in that treacherous country?"

Babulya was wringing her hands, sobbing, and praying. "Our dear God, please listen to our prayers, our laments, without words. Please save our mothers from outliving our sons!"

"A horrible, crazy, bloody country! The evildoers must be punished." Outrage quickly crept into the doctor's voice.

"Revenge is the sweetest form of passion. His 'friends' came to the funeral and *pominki*, and gave Polina money for a *kapitalnyi remont*," Dima whispered uncomfortably. "We know that Zhora and Sosa, or their hit men, killed Boris. His friends chose to leave and are relaxing in the Atlantis as we are sitting here in Park Slope. You can either leave the country or get a bullet through your brain."

"What about the police? Boris was a prominent doctor working for the state."

"The police simply want to pretend they are doing an investigation. Remember, the empire has collapsed, Russia imploded. There are good grounds to believe that people in high official positions could be involved, and the police are not interested in identifying the killers, or the people behind his murder. The police are investigating a case of arson and art theft only. They have questioned his cleaning woman, Agafya Ivanovna, the building's superintendent, her husband, the concierge and other relatives. We know they are all part of the same 'underground mafia' servicing the building on Tverskaya. We have just heard that a court date has been set for the chief suspect, Agafya."

The doctor looked incredulous and confused. "You want to say that Boris was murdered, and a cleaning woman will be tried and sentenced for art theft? Impossible!"

"Yes. Agafya Ivanovna will be tried and incarcerated under Article 144 of the new Criminal Penal Code of the Russian Federation, her property confiscated, and she will sit in prison from two to seven years. I'm sure Boris's paintings left Russia months ago."

"You mean his Georgian friends are here and have been here since his *pominki?*"

"They have double passports, vanished from sight and will never be prosecuted."

Recovering some composure, the doctor nodded and muttered, "I don't have office hours tomorrow. *Babulya* and I will visit the Atlantis after my hospital calls."

THE EXTRAVAGANT, BLACK-AND-BROWN MARBLE entrance hall of the Atlantis is tastefully furnished. Brown velvet settees and end tables with malachite tops face a buffed mahogany monstrosity of a desk from Russia that was once stored in a Brighton Beach warehouse. Russians never seem to get it just right. They lurch from one extreme to the other. The concierge, looking like a runway model, sits there, busily sorting mail. The doctor flashes his business card, Soviet style, and says officiously, "We have an appointment in apartment

602."

"Of course." She smiled and quickly announced the visitors, pointing to banks of elevators behind a hand-painted mural of the St. Petersburg skyline.

The apartment was warm and huge, and unbelievably gaudy. At the entrance, golden nymphs pranced in a crystal fountain. Sosa was just stepping out of the bathroom—all gold-plated fixtures and imported marble. The place resembled a set of a grade-B movie.

He greeted Dima's parents enthusiastically, shaking the doctor's hand and kissing *babulya* like a long-lost relative. No amount of Western clothing and cologne could conceal his Russianness. It was etched in the sturdy forehead, almond-shaped eyes, and angular cheekbones. Pulling back his shirt sleeve, he displayed a chunky gold Rolex with diamonds encrusting the dial that glittered in the midmorning light streaming from the Atlantic. Outrageous gilded furniture and tables with glossy mirrored surfaces sparkled. To the right of the piano stood a small, silk-covered sofa and two armchairs on Persian carpets.

The couple sat on the sofa beneath a meter long painting of angels suspended over the Neva, playing harps. Sosa poured Georgian cognac, and they toasted Dima's safe return and Boris's tragic end.

"Our Boris was murdered in his own apartment. A good person, a respected doctor, a righteous man. Why? Murderers plunged my sister and our family into chaos and tragedy. There must be a motive, an explanation."

"A terrible shock to all of us, doctor, and Susanna, of course," Sosa murmured. "We are people of the Orient. What we don't know, we can sense. But we don't know everything. We just heard that Agafya Ivanovna is the prime suspect. She was known to the police for previous robberies, and will stand trial in Moscow soon, likely to get up to seven years for art theft and arson."

Babulya, still wailing, paid no attention. "Our poor Boris, and *zolotaya* Susanna! Lonely and lost. Boris was Susanna's life there," she whimpered. "Yes, as Dima's good friend, she had invited him for work in Moscow and Siberia. They were cooperating on an important project in Norilsk."

"And what about the Ministry of Sports?" the doctor asked. "A terrible, grievous personal loss to sports. I wonder what complications there might have been with the hockey team?"

"He was my boyhood friend, my mentor. We loved our intelligent and cultured Boris. We worked in the art business together. He had a good Jewish head and great social skills. We saw him last in St. Petersburg. He is reunited with his father now, buried very close to him. *Amin.*"

"The evildoers must be punished," the doctor shouted, raising a large fist. Hired killers can sometimes be found, but never the people who hired them."

"Such crimes are never fully investigated. In Russia the stakes are too high," Sosa adds quietly.

Babulya's body slowly sank into a religious rocking motion, deep in the thrall of God. For the first time, Sosa observed her with pity.

"*Ladno, ladno, babushka,*" he whispered as he reached for her hand and squeezed it. Russian depression descended upon the group as Sosa refilled cognac glasses.

"Don't worry yourself with ideas, Doctor. Why damage our beautiful friendship? There is nothing we can do about it. There is only one power structure in Moscow. The young Dr. Rozenbaum must have been part of it. Then one day, by his own choice, he was no longer. The consequences were predictable."

Sosa rose to his feet and ambled to the piano, sat down on the bench, and immediately began playing a piece of music that sounded as if it came from the angels in the painting on the wall.

BOOK TWO

15

LOVE AFTER DEATH

SLOWLY THE MUD AND SLUSH OF the last winter thaw receded, and it was spring in Moscow. The sun wiped out all memory of the cold. Spring is a waterfall; once it begins there is no slow growth of the buds. Suddenly, everything seemed to bloom at once—pussy willows, violets, anemones, and apple blossoms, all together. Days lengthened, and the race for early summer began.

Susanna was getting out of bed, but it was too early to dress for the office. She looked at herself, reveling in the shape of her breasts, her delicate limbs. She had always thought she could not go for more than a week without making love, yet she'd been living like a nun. After years of regular sex, her body had suddenly been obliged to cut itself off. It's been many months, she thought. Inevitably Lev Kartsev had become a desirable target, the man she hoped would satisfy her needs. And she was relying on him to solve Boris's murder. She couldn't love him and knew he was not Mr. Right, but he was Mr. Right for now, and she needed him to push the mystery forward. She also felt that he could not love her or be devoted to her, but she was vulnerable and needy and welcomed his affection.

One does not need to be told by a psychiatrist that it is bad to repress pain that one must let the mourning process take its course rather than bury oneself in work, or sleep with KGB men. These are the psychiatrist's stock-in-trade anodynes. She felt uncomfortable about the relationship, but Susanna always needed a man, and losses drove her to greater intimacy. How was she to mourn in Moscow? And how could she decipher the psychology of the Russian mind without Lev's help or his contacts? She was beginning to wonder if she had lost the ability to feel any kind of engagement, the need for familiarity and tenderness, the language that brings two people together. She had no craving for passion; probably better without feelings. Her friends would do anything for her to return to normal, to have good relationships with her, but her pain and work were obsessive, and she couldn't accommodate them. They tried to distract her, interest her in other subjects, but fell short. She could not throw her sorrow on people she was close to, and knew that she had to distance herself. The mourning process took time.

Fear, loneliness, and old demons controlled her private life. Weekly telephone conversations with her doctor in New York made her feel more together, more balanced and cheerful for an hour or two. But how to survive in Moscow with so many pressures?

After many office visits, occasional formal invitations to government events, dinners, and concerts, her relationship with Lev had grown more intimate. Now, in the spring, he would often bring a little bunch of violets for Susanna, bought at no small expense. Although her work with the Norilsk project was more challenging than ever, she was beginning to find life interesting out of the office. Since prices had been freed, the opportunities to buy Russian art were great. Pre-revolutionary antiques and paintings seemed to have crawled out of the woodwork in Moscow, and everything could be bought for dollars. On weekends, Lev often accompanied her to antique or art auctions, or drove to Moscow's outlying areas to visit decrepit but magnificent eighteenth-century estates. Elusive as he was, he remained ever present.

He was tall and well built, weighing a hundred and sixty pounds, with dark penetrating Eurasian eyes and an open Slavic face. He was neatly dressed and wore round wire-rimmed glasses, and always ingratiating, courteous, and mysterious.

Susanna had discussed the police investigation with Lev, who was empathetic and supportive. Moreover, she was never bored chatting about local politics and Russia's heady rush to capitalism, or the possibilities of getting art and antiques out of the country.

He visited her office regularly. She had become friendlier and more attached. Each time he appeared, she smiled gaily when greeting him. He was always cool, dispelling any intimacy. He stood awkwardly in his place, as if he had been trained never to sit down in the presence of a woman. Lev came in the late afternoon, waiting for her to finish the most painful part of her day, the telex and phone call with her CEO, which became more frustrating over time. She was exasperated with Lev, sensing that he knew more about the case with the KGB and the police, but was stonewalling. This time he kissed her lightly on the cheek, and she pecked him on the other.

"Another day, another dollar. I am grateful for the quiet

now," she whispered cynically, staring at Valya. When they were finally alone, Lev broke the silence, and touched her hand. "What is the matter? Are you afraid? You are lucky that I am a spy. That's the profession to be in now, especially here."

"So what have you discovered?"

"Just like Kalugin, I have been tracking the investigation of your Boris." He kept his eyes on Susanna.

"Dear God, you must think of saving yourself, having some fun! We have much more in common besides Boris's murder and business. So many mutual friends, so many interests—art, literature, antiques, nature."

"And, yes, you love beautiful women," Susanna added flirtatiously.

"You don't miss much, do you?"

"But you must have the pick of all the women you want, all younger and prettier than me."

"I've been waiting for you a long time," he said. "Even with Boris, I watched your face, eyes, smelled your fragrance. Are you lonely?"

Looking at Lev, she was not surprised. Her smile grew warmer. She had never been so aware of, and intrigued by, someone.

"I owe you an apology. I'm used to Russian women, and you're different in so many ways—well, but this is not conversation for the Slavyanskaya. Let's get out of here, have a bite at a local place in my neighborhood, and I'll show you the files on Boris and Norilsk. They're in the office at my flat on Herzen Street.

"You actually live there?"

"Part time, of course," he remarked casually.

She knew of his new business in Kaliningrad and his office in Moscow, but was not aware of his living arrangements.

Leaving the Slavyanskaya and the concrete avenues, they saw a grand magenta-hued dusk fall over the city and meandered down a poplar-lined boulevard where old women from the country were selling bouquets of pink peonies from plastic buckets. Susanna noticed the first dandelion leaves poke through the concrete sidewalks as they traversed smaller streets: a different Moscow—a city of many hidden charms, a mellower place of deserted courtyards and lanes in every hue of crumbling brick and stucco.

Soon they reached an older part of Moscow and walked along the side streets lined with elegant, fragile, and weathered mansions whose pastel-colored façades were now faded. Lev was taking her to his house on the corner of Herzen and Bryusov Streets, a time-worn two-story mansion said to have been built during the reign of Catherine the Great, resembling an unfinished film set.

Susanna noticed an ancient, elaborate, hand-worked iron fence encircling the front door as he unlocked the old gates. The building was elegant, with eighteenth-century windows set in narrow panes, circled by low-rounded balconies.

"Bewitching," she remarked, climbing the wide stone steps as Lev opened the door and led the way in.

"There's a tangled garden in back, and a lilac bush right under my window," he replied.

"My favorite perfume at the glorious peak of spring." She nostalgically remembered the lilacs in Peredelkino.

"Mine as well, especially this month when the fragrance of blooms invades the room."

"Yes, lilacs in Russia have a special scent, a heady perfume, both balmy and spicy."

Inside, the room, with its twelve-foot-high, plaster-decorated ceilings, resembled a museum. Tall windows were hung back with roped green velvet curtains. Old parquet floors were covered with antique carpets. A gold-framed mirror and flambeaus on either side with candles that had burned to the last inch hung over a simple marble fireplace.

The larger room was furnished with an assortment of pieces scoured from antique and *Komisionnyi* shops, including a well-worn down couch with an assortment of pillows. In front of the couch stood an ancient green leather chair, and against the wall an old bureau darkened and shiny with age. Books filled shelves, and paintings on walls, reflecting Lev's personal literary and aesthetic interests. Susanna was dazzled—her dreams had always been romantic. All magnificent. Impressed with Lev's lifestyle and fascinated by his interests, she began to see a person different from the smooth former KGB *apparatchik* she knew. Through half-open doors, she could see the office, more resembling a study. He held her hand and led her to a fine old wardrobe with a large filing cabinet inside.

Priding himself on his work, he pointed to hundreds of dossiers; some contained only a couple of sheets of paper, others bulged with material—classic KGB stuff associated with clients, and a special one on Boris and the murder inquiry. Pointing to a set of folders, he whispered,

"Bablidze's boys murdered Boris, before he himself was eliminated. The same reason, of course—Kremlin's vertical system. My dossier on Boris did not paint a pretty picture. KGB involvement, operations with shady oligarchs in privatization deals, UN diplomats and the art business. An unfortunate matter of timing for him, but serendipitous for me."

Susanna didn't know how to handle this information.

"Yes, Boris was a doctor, and professionally discreet about his work. Always very careful not to leave papers lying around, never taking chances—not that I would read them, anyway." Of all her evenings since she returned, this was Susanna's most uncomfortable.

Lyova didn't encourage her to continue the conversation. He'd seen the shock that followed trauma many times. Everyone handles tragedy in their own way, and there was nothing he could do about it except be there for her when she needed him, and he hoped the time was now.

He led her to a comfortable red velvet fauteuil in the bedroom and shut the door behind them. She sat dumbfounded, in a state of déjà vu. She glanced at the bed thinking, *What goes around comes around.* Her husband and his affairs in the New York apartment, Lyova and the number of women entertained in this bedroom. Those were her thoughts, but her eyes said something else. She was open to him—a universe of touches and looks that she did not understand, and that blotted out both reason and shame. Somehow, she felt safe. She searched for his hand and stroked the fine hairs on his wrist for comfort.

He hugged her by putting his hands on her breasts from behind, and took off her sweater while she helped with the rest. Lyova moved his lips to hers, and they made love. Susanna felt blurred and primitive, satiated and insatiable. It felt as if she had shed her skin, feeling with greater intensity, at once incredibly fragile, energized and strong. His distance melted as he pulled her closer, holding Susanna like a child after a nightmare. Discomfort, pain, and anxiety enveloped her—her life as she'd known it, in fact.

"I'd already tasted you before I kissed you. I didn't need to touch you to know how you felt. You were inside me for a long time."

"You're wonderful," she said simply. "It's you I want, Lyova, you I need."

He cradled her face with his hands, making her feel small, vulnerable, and alluring. He took her lower lip between his

and chewed gently on it, as though to eat her up one tiny, exquisite portion at a time. He was lying across her now as she
kissed him again, and they laughed.

16

SUMMER IN NORILSK

THE JOURNEY TO NORILSK WAS VERY different from the official one the previous winter. She was traveling with Volodya as security, minder, bodyguard, and driver, to a semi-barbarous hinterland to sort out the failure of delivery of the second tranche of palladium to KLM, critical to the contract. Only the day before, Susanna and GMG had suddenly been informed by telex of the "indefinite delay of the second tranche of palladium caused by critical metals delivery problems in Norilsk."

"This information will cause global chaos," she had said. "We've got to do something. We've got to get this delivery back on track. I feel like Don Quixote battling windmills, but I must fight, Volodya!"

"This isn't about Spain and windmills, and I am not Sancho Panza—how can you negotiate with the Kremlin? They just pulled a gun and fired bullets at you!"

"But the dates for discussions with Kulichkov and Norilskmetal had been confirmed with Smirnoff by telephone and telex." She was trembling.

Early the next morning, Volodya arrived for the Norilsk flight. They drove along her favorite Moscow embankment, where the river ran through the city like a silver snake.

As they got closer to Domodedovo Airport, the higher bank revealed a small forest. The smell of clover and other unique aromas rising from the grasses signaled the approach of the Russian countryside.

At least Volodya had bought the tickets at the right price. At black market rates, the tickets northeast from Moscow to Norilsk, equivalent to the distance from New York to Los Angeles, cost twenty dollars each.

Jostled by red-faced travelers dragging checkered vinyl sacks and plastic-wrapped suitcases for flights to Siberia, she and Volodya sat down near Security Control to follow the required Russian good luck custom: With hands clasped and eyes locked, they managed a few moments of silence before their flight was called. She was living on the edge, tempting fate, on a risky solo mission, her fears more than justified.

An airport policeman pointed to Volodya's knapsack and Susanna's briefcase, and asked that they be opened. He rifled through her case, but tossed everything out of the knapsack, pulling out personal items along with maps of Siberia.

"Why all these maps? Your destination is Norilsk. What are your plans for Norilsk?"

"What do you need to let us board?" Volodya sneered.

Susanna, shocked and embarrassed, reached into her bag, waved her visa and telexed confirmations at the policeman, and shouted in English, "I need your name, officer! Volodya, please call the American Embassy." Hearing her English, and the words *American Embassy*, authority relented.

THE BUS TOOK THEM ON A RATTLING ride over the heat-warped tarmac, and they jammed into a Soviet-era TU-164. The boarding was chaotic, some eighty passengers elbowing and pushing as if the plane door were about to slam, stranding them. Beads of sweat dripped from Susanna's forehead as she read the Aeroflot marketing blurb on her ticket: You have made a good choice. Aeroflot guarantees comfort and hospitality for our respected clients. The plane was half empty, the air inside muggy and rank, smelling of sweat and vodka. Volodya found their seats; they looked at each other and smiled tensely.

The flight attendants were surly, usual for domestic flights, and the restrooms reeked like outhouses. Down to basics. Neatly cut squares of *Kommersant* served as toilet paper. The headrests were greasy, the legroom sparse. On the other side of the aisle, a big Siberian woman was struggling to fit her bags of vegetables and a plucked chicken under the seat, and Volodya tried to help.

It seemed as if Susanna had known Volodya forever. He had been driving her around Moscow long before he entered university while she was still commuting for negotiations with Almaz. She had spotted his shiny yellow Lada, and had used him for taxi service when still living in the Hotel National. They liked each other, and their camaraderie opened the way to a respectful friendship. He was her Moscow Information resource about people, *komisionnys*, the ballet and theater. Volodya was always protective of her, while she treated him like a surrogate son.

A passenger, spotting a foreigner, glanced at Susanna. "Welcome!" He grinned from behind his toothbrush mustache. "Why Norilsk, for you?"

Susanna barely smiled, but he pointed to the attendant, gesticulating. "We need the best service here, we have a foreign tourist among us."

The flight to Norilsk lasted about five hours. Susanna gazed out the window and tried to sleep but couldn't, anxious about her mission to save the project and the commodities market. Endless summer daylight, swords of sunlight piercing her eyes, sky in shades of azure blue: she was staring out the window at the darkly verdant carpet of forest and undulating hills around Norilsk when the loudspeaker interrupted in Russian, "Ladies and gentlemen, we will be landing soon", and then in English, each word mispronounced, "It is not allowed to take photographs or use video equipment over territory of the Russian Federal Republic."

A handful of passengers nevertheless pointed cameras against the window and furiously snapped pictures. Old Soviet rules were not respected. Two drunk passengers danced a jig in the aisle before the plane came in to land while the passengers around them clapped. Susanna's insides churned with anticipation. Norilsk again. Volodya sensed her anxiety and tried to reassure her.

No welcoming committee from Norilskmetal, no flowers, no limousines this time—only a few beat-up Ladas. Modern Norilsk, the dirtiest city on the globe, surrounded by dead trees and poisoned by acid rain, is populated by descendants of prisoners who first built a railroad line to Dudinka in the 1930s. Five arctic winters later, a functioning nickel smelter had carried nickel upriver to the port.

The city remembers its horrific past, and its citizens are fiercely loyal patriots with a romantic sense of their own uniqueness. The taxi driver, immediately recognizing Susanna as a foreigner, couldn't wait to begin his story, unusual for Russia, where forgetting is easier. "My father was sent here in a boat intended to ship logs, not people. He was thrown down with others in the polar tundra and told to set up tents, build a bonfire, and begin building a fence surrounded by barbed wire. They couldn't even stretch out on the damp, naked boards. Many died beneath the open sky if they lost the battle to sleep near the fire. He survived because he was able to work very hard and get a better food ration. Only monsters could have planned something like this."

As they drove down Lenin Prospekt that August, the busy main thoroughfare, the past was remote and unreachable. Time blurs memory. It seemed impossible to imagine that there had ever been a Stalin, a gulag, or a country called the Soviet Union. Pretty women were on parade, and children chasing each other on bikes and roller skates, dripping melted ice cream.

They drove to Hotel Norilsk, which had recently undergone a *kapitalnyi remont* and returned to its original name, Hotel Venezia.

The hotel manager remembered Susanna and greeted her with a big smile. Glancing at Volodya, he immediately recognized his nationality and winced. "Welcome, madame. You are traveling alone, no Americans with you? Very brave, very modern."

"We have further discussions with Norilskmetal. Just two days this time."

"And the young man?"

"My assistant from the Moscow office. Also minder, driver, and bodyguard," Susanna said as she laid out passports, documents, her multiple-entry visa, and Kulichkov's invitation.

"All the way from Moscow. Welcome to the romance of Norilsk, and to our capitalist world. Norilsk is very special.

Our people are trusting, and our relationships intimate. It is summer vacation, and I'm sure our English teacher will be checking in for guests. Hospitality here much better than Moscow!" He smiled, winking at Volodya.

The hotel was the same, but in better shape; less struggle against nature, less crumbling concrete, rotten, bare wood mended. The restaurant was finally open and had been outfitted with a new Italian chef. Two fans were turning in the lobby, keeping the mosquitoes at bay, but helping the outside sulfur dioxide-laden air permeate the lobby. Volodya coughed; Susanna's eyes were inflamed and tearing.

The same Venetian canal murals greeted her in the hotel room, but the woodwork was repaired and repainted, and the water in the bathroom ran clear!

When they returned to the reception room, two guests sitting at a small table sipping cognac invited them over. One was a Swedish scientist, the other, his Russian colleague, introduced himself as an "environmental reporter." Susanna knew this was often a cover-up for members of the KGB.

The scientist stood and pulled out a chair for Susanna. The television, same as before, was blaring a Mexican serial, so it was difficult to hear him. "My Russian colleague is a local reporter for *Izvestya*. Anton and I are studying the ecological consequences of pollution. We have grants from Nordic countries and the UN Environmental Agency. President Clinton has also promised to provide financial help."

Anton added, "Welcome to our little Leningrad. You will love Norilsk. Many of our buildings are built in the neo-classical style constructed by the proud slave labor of gulag prisoners. Our smelters here produce more sulfur dioxide than the entire nation of France, and nowhere does it get colder." He grinned.

"Yes, the dirtiest place on Earth," remarked Susanna, "one

of the largest land masses on the globe ruined by air pollution, and destroyed air quality as far as Northern Norway, Sweden, Finland, and Denmark."

"Pollution traces are detected in Alaska and Canada as well," Volodya added.

Anton nodded, ready to regale them with stories of the dark history of the gulags, which he confided in a breathless torrent. "My father and uncle were *Zeks*, and I myself am a distinguished descendant of prisoners memorialized in the blue-and-white chapel near Mount Schmidt, up the hill. They were forced to work for a scrap of bread and a bowl of soup made out of dog meat. Yes, in the camps beyond the Arctic Circle, summer was no more bearable than winter. Temperatures rose above 30 degrees centigrade. Snow melted and the tundra turned to mud with gray clouds of mosquitoes filling up your eyes, nose, and throat. Today, the streams on the mountainside still throw up human bones."

"The world is grateful that the bastion of communism has finally fallen," Susanna softly replied.

Anton wanted to continue. "These men were heroes and made great sacrifices to provide the country with nickel. My father told stories of how their spirits were lifted and they worked harder, always ready for more sacrifice when praised by Party bosses, especially Beria's deputy. Reinstatement in the ranks of the Communist Party was the greatest happiness of his life."

"Can you imagine? Even as prisoners, they struggled and died for the Party," Volodya added bitterly.

"Many were idealists, Volodya! The gulags were sacrificial slaughter for the brave new world," Susanna said.

"But why not praise those who survived and their descendants?" Anton announced. "We are proud to have built our great city!" he exclaimed, looking closely at Susanna. "Are you also a scientist? I don't remember seeing you at our Norwegian symposium?"

"So sorry," she mumbled. "I forgot to make introductions! My name is Susanna Thompson. I represent the Global Metals Group conglomerate in Moscow. And this is Volodya Yudin, one of my Moscow assistants. My second time here, continuing negotiations with Norilskmetal, the mother lode of your pollution problems!" The pair rose to greet them, and they shook hands. Anton reached for a chair while the Swede poured cognac.

"How can you live where the sun doesn't rise for three months and temperatures stay forty degrees below zero?" Volodya asked Anton.

The reporter's eyes gleamed. "This is my Siberia, the source of Russia's copper and nickel for armaments and weapons, and Russia's wealth—the power of our Siberia is metals! Stalin was shrewder than Hitler."

"Yes, smart enough to have his prisoners work in the gulags," Susanna quipped. "But what about you, Anton?"

"One is privileged to live here. Good money, paid vacations for me and the family in Sochi, subsidized seminars to the south of France, even South America—Rio de Janeiro." He glimpsed at the guests, poured another cognac, and leisurely continued, "Ecology is of universal concern now. Politically correct, and getting more press than the commodities business. Our oligarchs are battling for total control of privatization in courts, and against investments from foreign companies like yours."

Susanna nervously looked around. "Yes, the zig-zags of privatization! Yeltsin is determined to forge ahead. His approach to economic reform is aggressive, and led by his economic dream team. The Norilsk regional court recently ruled for restructuring in favor of Norilskmetal's management. I'm sure you are *v kurse*, but who are they?"

"But you must know, Susanna" he said, "that the Georgian big shot was murdered in Moscow not long ago, and just yesterday, a judge was beaten up and a grenade was discovered outside the courthouse—everything is connected. Our local newspaper says that the ruling favoring management was unfair and that the Norilskmetal project will be tied up in court battles for a long time."

Susanna did not react: the Swede refilled their glasses again. "Really? I've been informed about disruptions here. But we have been in transit, and I don't have the latest facts."

"Well, for starters," Anton reported, "this morning, a man opposing the demonstrations threw a dead cat at one of the strikers, and a Moscow journalist from *Novaya Gazeta* was beaten up badly—his hands, jaw, and legs were broken. He is now crippled and unable to speak."

"Where are the state security agents in all this? Where's the KGB?"

"FSB now. The same can of worms, though. The reporter was trying to uncover official corruption by the police. Usually they're everywhere. The group responsible claim they were responding to a federal law outlawing extremist activity and disturbances. I have the newspapers right here," he said, opening his briefcase.

Ignoring the Swedish scientist, whose Russian was not fluent, he proceeded to read aloud about the local protests accusing foreign governments of spray painting FOREIGN AGENT across the Norilsk Memorial site.

"The regional newspapers also reported an explosion in one of the mines yesterday! Luckily it wasn't a major dig— only five people hurt and no fatalities. Our inspectors are investigating."

He grimaced, and went on reading from another article, titled "A Social Catastrophe for Our Citizens!": "Workers at the Norilsk smelting complex are striking, demanding the resignation of their deputy director Alexandr Kulichkov—wages haven't been paid since March! Also billions of rubles are owed since last winter! The oligarchs not only reduced the work force but also jettisoned their obligations to support other city services—families living in decaying housing. Another headline. 'Young people are departing for Moscow as if drawn by a giant magnet.'"

"But the Kombinat's issues, all related to privatization, are controlled by the Kremlin," Susanna observed.

"Yes, Volodya remarked sarcastically. "Conditions are deteriorating for miners. The well-connected businessmen and oligarchs fire miners and engineers. They call it Western productivity."

"You know, of course," Susanna added, that since last month another reporter from the *Wall Street Journal* is being held by Security and accused of espionage. His reports were syndicated and allegedly caused international outrage about strikes and other disturbances at Norilsk."

"Refresh my memory, Susanna—another foreign agent . . ." Volodya joked. "It's all 'normal'no,' as your accountant would say."

"That phrase evokes treachery and cold war espionage against Russians."

"Yes, but this reporter was an American,"

"You must be careful, Volodya. You will not be happy in prison, east of the Ural mountains."

Anton added with cocky assurance, "Foreign companies also want to be at the same trough as our own pigs. They are meddling in our national resources. Some are accused of industrial espionage. The Duma and the prosecutor general are investigating all tenders as we speak."

"How do you know this?" Susanna demanded.

"I am also an investigative journalist."

"GMG is here only to finance rebuilding Russia's social and economic infrastructure." She sighed. "Our interests are only commercial."

Anton shut his briefcase and smiled. "The Kremlin is in charge. These protests only consolidate the power of the current regime. On lower levels, managers are intimidated and coerced into corruption and conformity."

Susanna was upset, but she managed to smile back. "I have meetings with Kulichkov tomorrow, and since Bablidze is no more, I hope to get more specific information critical to our metal delivery problems."

The Swedish scientist rejoined the conversation. "We know that Gorbachev's *glasnost* and *perestroika* have made citizens aware of their rights."

"Fuck your mother's ass!" Anton barked. "Gorbachev was a piece of shit. His politics destroyed our Russia. We did just fine until Gorbachev!"

"What did he say?" the Swede asked.

"Oh, he was only complaining about Gorbachev's reforms," answered Susanna. "Nice chatting with you both, and thanks for the welcome!"

SUSANNA'S APPOINTMENT AT NORILSKMETAL'S headquarters was for noon the next day. She called to confirm, only to discover that Kulichkov was in Moscow, away on business, but that his deputy Mr. Smirnoff would welcome her.

They rose early to walk and have breakfast in town. "There's something terrible going on, Volodya. Looks like they're breaking the agreement, and no more palladium will be delivered. The market swings will be catastrophic—GMG and the entire securities industry is already losing fortunes."

She was agitated and stopped, clutching a wall for support.

Volodya didn't sympathize. He listened to her comments as if they were merely another swindle among many. "Susanna, get with it! The sun is shining. Is like *miracle* here in the far north!"

They made their way down Lenin Prospekt, the main street leading to the Kombinat's headquarters, but she was happier then, in the dark frigid days of last winter, with yellow or black snow in the streets.

"My first time in Norilsk, and I love it!" Volodya exclaimed.

"Remember, Volodya, I have to replace my lost camera today. Let's have some breakfast and look around for a shop."

It was late in the morning, and very hot. They spotted a restaurant with a free table at a window looking out, but found the inside more fascinating. A tall Russian woman in a toque was deftly flinging *pelmeni* into bowls, and ladling out volumes of vodka, two hundred grams each, into tall glasses—all before noon. She shot everything down the bar to customers, including the sour cream, never cracking a smile. Volodya walked up to the counter and ordered coffee, *pelmeni*, and *compote*. The waitress glanced at him as if he were an alien.

"No vodka?" she asked. "Where are you from?" Volodya, embarrassed, ordered two shots, which they finished with "breakfast." Susanna allowed herself to relax before they moved to their next stop, the House of Trade.

The three-story building was filled with lots of merchandise—tourism and sport hunting and fishing, Latvian men's clothing, Chinese televisions, tape recorders, cameras, Turkish leather jackets, Bulgarian women's underwear, Polish vodka, Serbian skirts, but alas, as always, no Russian products.

Finally, a short walk to the Kombinat's headquarters. At the entrance, three men who were talking stodgily among

themselves stopped to gaze at Susanna while, inside, two muscled hard-eyed boys in leather jackets vetted them. Behind, a
secretary with a mane of curly, henna-tinted hair welcomed
them in, shouting, "*Zdrasst'e, zdrasst'e*," not removing her eyes
from Susanna. Unfazed by their presence, more out of polite-
ness than duty, she asked absentmindedly: "What can I do
for you?"

"*Zdrasst'e*," Volodya said. "We are here for discussions
with Mr. Smirnoff."

Suddenly her eyes widened, and she smiled. "Oh! Oh, of
course! Why, welcome! He is expecting you in his office.
Please follow me."

Smirnoff was wearing the same Olympic Russian bear-
logo blazer he had sported the previous winter. He rose and
clasped Susanna's hand as she introduced Volodya.

"I have traveled again to Norilsk," she said, once they were
seated, "to meet with you *and* Mr. Kulichkov, specifically
about the failure of delivery of the second tranche of palladium
to KLM, guaranteed by Norilskmetal and the Central Bank,
the Russian Sovereign Bank. Our company's board of directors informs me that our investors and stockholders have lost
200 million dollars already."

Smirnoff grunted sympathetically, grimaced, and pulled
out the thick GMG folder. "Well, you must know that we had
to appoint a new chairman after Bablidze's accident, Dr.
Valentin Kotchetkov, former minister of energy and natural
resources. Kulichkov is now rarely here. He works mostly
with the Ministry of Nonferrous Metals in Moscow. He sends
his apologies."

Susanna was incensed, but not surprised.

"Management can only do so much. Regulatory and political issues are clarified in Moscow. It appears they have significant concerns about Norilsk and shareholder equity. Ms.

Thompson, frankly speaking, there are serious complications. Russia must control the natural resources of the Arctic."

He bluffed, stalled, denied. "The ministry is studying the shift from state control to privatization—our natural resources are Russia's sovereign wealth. Norilskmetal is obviously a government-related business. The Kremlin cannot be disobeyed. Our misunderstanding can only be resolved in Moscow."

She was intrepid. Russia was Hanken's new frontier, and Yeltsin's aggressive approach to economic reform justified GMG's foreign direct investment in Norilsk's infrastructure projects. Hanken's mission was clear. He had regularly called U.S. trade representatives, all of whom understood that the mission was in the national interest and supported the company's global reach. She was facing a life-and-death agenda for her and GMG. "I specifically flew to the Arctic to meet with Mr. Kulichkov. He personally confirmed our meeting here in Norilsk. As director and business manager, he is accountable." But it was clear that Kulichkov had suddenly become a non-person.

"That's not how things work here." Smirnoff smiled derisively. "We allowed commercial interests to get in the way of a strategic project. Government loans for commercial shares and collateral to upgrade and retrofit infrastructure are too complex! Only our banks and the government are in charge!"

Susanna kept calm, but her voice turned to steel.

"Norilskmetal, and GMG's investment, are our primary focus. The Kremlin's authority is a major threat to Russia's economic and social progress. They do not have a private license to break the law! *You* are the principals responsible for breach of contract. The contract was signed here. We will be taking this far-reaching issue all the way to the Internal Ministry of Affairs for the Norilsk region."

She was pretending to be certain and stood firmly, erect and alert. "The International Court in the Hague calls it 'legal nihilism,' a euphemism for judicial corruption." She looked at Smirnoff, expecting some explanation, but his eyes did not meet hers. For a moment, the dead silence was broken only by Smirnoff lighting a cigarette. No one spoke a word, and no one moved.

At last, the secretary abruptly opened the door and sauntered in, smiling. "We congratulate you and thank you for your support and cooperation in Russia's remarkable transformation to free-market economy. The Russian Federation and Norilskmetal value your work and wish you soft landings." With outstretched hands and a smiling face, the woman handed Susanna and Volodya handmade local souvenirs—two hand-hammered copper and nickel scenes—one of the taiga, a ravishing view of pines, wild plants and gigantic flowers, the other of the tundra, a vast, nearly level treeless plain, with stunted pine trees leading to a frozen lake.

"To hell with that idiot! A hundred and fifty million people here, scattered over nine time zones, and no one takes responsibility," Susanna whispered to Volodya as they left, and Volodya laughed, capturing a combination of despair and gallows humor that is particularly Russian.

"*Svoloch,*" she muttered under her breath, thinking about the impending global consequences of monstrous losses in the commodities market.

"Yes, that's Russia for you! State sabotage everywhere," Volodya echoed.

Susanna shrugged in resignation and despair, convinced that Dima had been correct, her face sallow and haggard. "I must get back to Moscow for discussions with the ministry, and get Dima to come and help with the legal issues."

Truth is not only stranger than fiction, it is more telling and more poignant. She understood that the talk with Smirnoff touched a chord of plain truth that fiction often misses. Hanken wanted to be omnipotent in Russia, and Susanna, his handmaiden, had been both obsessed with the mystery of Boris's murder and naïve about GMG's success in Norilsk. She had been living in two unreal worlds.

"Susanna, as the saying goes, 'Here we must ride fast in order to stand still!' Lucky for us it's already Friday in Moscow and Saturday in New York. You can telex GMG from our hotel and also telephone Dima, but you must relax and gather your energy. Hanken and his team will plan an international rescue mission. I insist that you take a rest and inhale the beauty of Lake Baikal for the weekend. It's difficult to exaggerate its beauty or its size. The blue eye of Siberia, its grand forests and mountains, will help you unwind. It's just a short flight from here, and you will feel more relaxed for the next *koshmar* with the ministry."

Gas clouds hung over the city as they boarded another Tupolev. They sat back, fastened their seat belts, and watched Norilsk gallop backward. Then, a delicious lurch upward through the orange-yellow curtain, to the sunlit blue above.

17

LAKE BAIKAL

N OLD RUSSIAN FOLKTALE SAYS that, when Christ looked at Lake Baikal, waved his hand and proclaimed, "Beyond this there is nothing." There are the Alps, the Caucasus, the Black Sea . . . but nothing like Baikal ("lake nature" in Mongolian). In the midst of the Siberian wilderness lies one of the most beautiful lakes in the world. It is not only abundant in wildlife, it's also the largest, deepest, and oldest freshwater lake on the planet. Particularly special is its sudden change of mood—it is silent and calm one moment, but when the wind rises, huge waves appear. It's like an old man grumbling.

Before long, Susanna and Volodya were standing in the dank Baikal terminal, still dazed by Smirnoff's attitude, waiting at a clanking luggage carousel with other passengers who had checked their bags.

Luggage at last retrieved, and swatting away mosquitoes, they were soon out in the sun, where Volodya was already haggling with a pug-nosed, paunchy Ukrainian in his late forties, with a crude face and scarred hands, whose head was shaved. He agreed to drive them to Baikal, shook hands with Volodya, and excused himself to make a phone call. Volodya was certain they were being followed—by another bandit, or a KGB contact, delivering bait from the U.S., this time, Susanna herself.

But driving was serious business in Siberia, and she found the driver's smile and pleasant openness reassuring. His taxi was a gray, listing Volga sedan of a model Susanna had only seen in old Soviet movies. "Where in Baikal?" he asked. "I take you to a great small hotel in village—Listvyanka—a fascinating place, three-hundred-year-old settlement, a hotel owned by my aunt with separate *banya* for lady, swimming pool, summer café with views of lake. We have had rain, and the road is all mucked up. . . Well, hop in." He introduced himself as Zhenya, and they drove off the rocky road onto a narrow, beat-up highway that ran like an alley through the forest, past stretches of mud and gravel. Across a looming taiga of scraggly larch and majestic spruce, bright light flooded the broadly spaced boughs. Logging settlements appeared on hillsides where rushing streams, blue with sky, glittered in the sun. The sky unfolded itself majestically.

"Look at this mud!" Zhenya said, wrestling with the wheel. A few more turns, and a large red, white, and blue sign declaring *All Power of Russia Comes from Siberia* appeared. "They dare to call it a federal highway. Just this winter wolves tore a woman to pieces out here. That is Siberia!"

And I may be torn apart by the commodities market for failure of delivery, she thought. Frantic, fighting anxiety and nausea, she forced herself to focus on the calm beauty around her.

"What brings you here, Zhenya?" Susanna asked.

"Back in the seventies I came to work on a power station. I'm too old to go home now, and anyway I like the peace and quiet. You can't leave Siberia once you learn to live here."

The airtime was filled with Elvis Presley music and Siberian talk radio. Zhenya and Volodya enjoyed listening to the host bantering about outlandish things, as well as call-ins and local events.

"You don't get news from Moscow?" Susanna asked.

"Hell, no. What do we care what they do in Moscow?" Zhenya said. "We don't need the *materik* here. Whatever they decide there, whatever changes they say are coming to us, here nothing changes. A fish rots from the head, we say. So far, no rotten smells here."

"*Slava Bogu*," Volodya replied. "Our multinational has been working with Moscow and Norilsk for twenty years, but this American has never been to Baikal. We are stopping here to see the pearl of Siberia."

"Tell me," Zhenya asked, looking at Susanna, "aren't you frightened of this hinterland, all forest and bog, peopled with drunks and thugs who would love to get their hands on you?"

A minor explosion interrupted his tirade. He and Volodya wrestled the spare tire free from the trunk. While they worked, Susanna ambled to a spot off the road on the edge of the taiga. Here was all birch, leaves so green they seemed to shine, and zebra-slashed trunks glowing from base to crown. Bumblebees buzzed around her ankles, and soon she was standing in a cloud of swirling fat bugs, as if drunk from the sun. "Hey, get away from the woods!" Zhenya shouted. "You can get a tick in the grass and be dead in a day—Siberia!"

Susanna ran back and jumped into the car.

The five-week Siberian summer was under way. It was as if nature had woken up in July, realized how badly she had neglected her guests, and completely overcompensated.

There was something gushing and hysterical in the show she put on: the sun with its dial turned up and staring in constant attendance; spongy vegetation; the carpet of wildflowers and lush colors, flashing dots of brilliant red, purple, and blue; and yellow poppies never to be forgotten, all overwhelming the eyes. She was thrilled and grateful to Volodya for taking her to Baikal to share the luminous light and haunting beauty of this land, but frightened by mosquitoes the size of hummingbirds, the swarms of midges, gnats, and small biting flies.

She closed her eyes in the backseat, disoriented and nervous about the prospective meetings in Moscow. Jolts made rest impossible. Volodya and Zhenya, in front, carried on a discussion about literature and politics.

"Are you relaxed already, Susanna?"

"This ride isn't very calming, Volodya, but rather than listen about Yeltsin, I'd love to hear about old political history here."

Zhenya took charge. "Our locals never warmed up to Lenin, Trotsky, or Stalin when they were in exile here."

"I know all the stories from university," Volodya added, interrupting the driver. "Can you imagine? Lenin was only exiled once, but he made another trip to Siberia posthumously in cold storage during the patriotic war!" They both chuckled. "But Stalin, as a young revolutionary, escaped from Siberia six times, you know!"

It was Zhenya's turn. "Yes, Stalin organized the swampy gulag-lands, but he also saved us from the Fascists. Not only us, but also the world. If not for him, what would have happened?"

Finally, they reached the fairy-tale Siberian countryside.

On a lakeside bluff at the foot of a steep, emerald green hill was the tiny fishing village of Listvyanka. The place was absurdly picturesque—a community of little gingerbread log cottages with elaborate wood trim on the eaves and around the windows; small, neat gardens; and chickens and geese strutting freely in backyards. The village had been one of the fanciest places in Siberia back when its merchants traded furs and gold by caravan between China and Western Russia. Much of it had been built over a century before, but life hadn't changed much, so you couldn't tell the difference from houses built recently.

Hotel Baikal, located on Ulitsa Kommunisticheskaya, faced a giant silver statue of Lenin striding forward into space. Its sculptor, a Politburo favorite, had said his conception was an Ilyich whom local people would want to approach for solitary contemplation, perhaps to ask advice.

"A real hotel, not a 'quaint' guesthouse with outhouse for toilet, and real shower," Zhenya assured Susanna. "Managed originally by Intourist, now privatized, owned by my auntie Kapitalina. The best *varenniki* in the world here, best boat excursion on the lake, to see freshwater seals, and best treks to see wolves, bear, and beaver. Our time is limited. Of course, we can't see it all."

Gray underbellies of clouds billowed above the fir-covered mountains as the sun and clouds of mosquitoes danced thick against the sky. Near the kiosk and off the hotel grounds, several loud young men, with dull expressions and pale faces, were socializing and sipping bottles of beer. They were sucking on cigarettes, cursing and laughing, and picking mosquitoes from their eyes, set in regal faces. Surely they were descendants of Polish gentry, Russian Decembrists, and the literary gulag Zeks.

Two pretty young women, their complexions creamy,

with slanted eyes set above high cheekbones, pushing baby carriages and drinking beer, navigated the buckled cement and joyfully greeted Zhenya's car.

Feeling better, Susanna climbed out of the Volga, and the pair strode happily into the lobby of the hotel where Zhenya's aunt Kapitalina was nervously waving, arms outstretched.

A short round woman with sparkling eyes, pink cheeks, and a funny grin, she greeted the guests. The broad Slavic planes of her face were neatly made up, with just enough rouge to complement her beautiful naturally rosy skin and blond, curly hair, done up for the occasion.

Zhenya put his arms around her and loudly kissed her many times. She had been living in Siberia since the forties, when exiled to the AlZhiR camp—for Wives of Traitors to the Motherland, near Akmolinsk. The reception table was set with cakes and coffee made by her husband, whose chestnut hair, the result of a bad dye job, did not match his gray mustache. "Welcome, Zhenya! Why have you been away so long?"

"Well, I returned with very important guests. This is

Volodya, and an American lady from Moscow, for rest and relaxation at your hotel, Auntie. I promised the best of nature and best *varenniki*!"

ARCTIC SUMMER TWILIGHT LASTED IN the evening until about eleven-thirty and returned in the morning about four.

The day dawned hot and humid, but strong breezes from the lake kept the mosquitoes away. Filled with a high sense of purpose, Zhenya was ready to introduce Susanna and Volodya to his old friend Mikhail Andreyevich Yefimov in a pre-arranged breakfast meeting with cognac and beer.

Delicate in appearance, Yefimov looked both at ease and imposing. A headful of graying black hair, blue eyes, and a thin nose and chiseled features revealed his Ukrainian ancestry. There was something sad about him; taciturn, a chain smoker in his fifties, with a phlegm-clogged voice, he was dressed in loose pants and sandals, with a long white T-shirt stretching over his tall, thin frame. He sat hunched forward on the edge of his chair, shifting his head nervously back and forth, next to a table of silent Japanese tourists with cameras and guidebooks. Yefimov jumped as they entered, kissed Susanna's hand, and held out a powerful grip to Zhenya and Volodya. He was thrilled to see new faces in the Siberian outback. They sat in the outdoor café, enchanted by the haunting beauty of the north, shielded from bugs by breezes and cigarette fumes.

Baikal, dappled in clouds and sun, shimmered in the wind and luminous light. Mikhail talked nonstop about how rotten life had been since the Soviet Union collapsed. "Greatest geopolitical catastrophe of the century—communism was banned after it had already died anyway. Everything here's breaking down, falling apart—there's no life," he insisted, and claimed he was fighting off insanity and bitterness. "Yeltsin is leading Russia into the future, but we don't know what kind and for how long. People want democratic reforms. We had hopes, and we were happy to look for changes ahead. Nothing has changed. We are more dissatisfied now because we are comparing ourselves to the West."

"The country's ideology has been ossified for seventy years," Susanna replied quietly. "Time to move on!"

"Personally, I still refer to Stalin positively. The Soviet Union could have been preserved. Stalin won the war and saved us from the Fascists. Gorbachev and Yeltsin—they've sent Russia down the drain. People in Western Siberia live in the world's richest region but can't buy anything!"

With bustling dignity Kapitalina served the guests cognac,

beer, large plates of sausage, salad Olivier, cucumber and tomato, pickled wild mushrooms, fried potatoes, fresh-baked bread, and finally Baikal's tastiest fish, *omul*. Zhenya, Volodya, and Susanna ate heartily while Mikhail Andreyevich drank and droned on.

"We welcome you here!" he said at last, and kissed her hand again.

"I am happy to be here on this wonderful summer day. This primitive beauty, this silence and peace of Sacred Baikal."

"Especially today, with not too many mosquitoes," Volodya added.

"Why don't you return to the mainland? How is it you settled here, Mr. Yefimov?" Susanna asked.

"I ended up here because, after university, the state sent me here for obligatory service. I wrote for the newspaper, married a local, and remained. This was my *sudba*, my fate, my destiny." That was his long Russian shadow. His life had turned out the way it had, and that was that.

"So you are part of the literary intelligentsia, Mikhail An-dreyevich," Susanna remarked seriously.

"There is no such thing anymore. I am proud to call my-self Siberian, to rely only on myself. They say Siberia is a hard place, especially hard after seven decades of repression and restricted freedoms. But I've got my potato patch. I've got cucumbers. I've got my cows and chickens, I've got bread and enough coal for the stove in winter. What more do I need? I have everything."

Winking at Susanna, Zhenya slapped Mikhail's back and laughed. "Yes, he is a true Siberian. Like myself, friendly and forthright."

"I go to Moscow on business, sometimes. Pressures of cap-italism and social upheaval have forced me to swap literary struggles for fur trading. Imagine, a journalist and literary scholar, selling Siberian furs!"

"Don't you find Moscow more interesting now?" Susanna asked.

"You are an American? And you think Moscow is interesting?" Mikhail snorted and smirked. "I don't know," he said. "I suppose everyone is allowed his quirks. I know your life. I watch *Santa Barbara* and hate Moscow. Why? They see people like me from the provinces, and don't give me the time of day. They're deceitful. All crooks and *zhuliki*."

He fingered the homemade aluminum cross that dangled from his neck. "The Jews sold our Russia and are, again, running the country. All Fagins, shylocks, all Judases. They want to steal Russia's wealth and resources. The Jews want to control the world again. They're dishonest."

"Unlike the people here?" Susanna asked.

"Well...maybe. We have a tragic history in Siberia, and too much drinking," he added as Kapitalina brought another round of delicacies. "This is a bad time here, and the country is in a mess. But it's all the Jews' fault. They stole Lenin's revolution and ran it, and they are behind all the trouble that followed: the murder of the tsar; civil war; famine; and more than seventy years of suffering at the hands of the central planners. They were Jewish as well, of course—a brotherhood of vampires. Tell me, do Jews control all the newspapers and banks in America?"

Susanna was uncomfortable and frightened by this tirade. "I don't know about you, Mr. Yefimov, but I get very nervous when people's minds are trained to hate. Your references to Hitler's work, and anti-Semitism, are heinous."

Volodya, concerned about a war of words, abruptly changed the subject. "Yes, we once believed that our country was the mightiest and the richest. We felt lucky to be Russian. We knew about the Ku Klux Klan, and how America was killing blacks, just as the Nazis killed the Jews. We gathered money in school to send to poor black children in America."

"What could they have done with our rubles? They could only continue to starve with them!" Mikhail added, and they all laughed while he politely, with knife and fork, dove into his plate and quickly finished his meal, but not his sermon.

"I believe in God now, and I want to raise a toast to God's ordinary, simple people. I was a Communist, but now I have a new religion—friendship and God. Man can't live if he doesn't have a soul, and neither Marx nor Engels, nor democracy, can inspire the spirit. Only God and love. Don't you agree?" He began to play with his crucifix.

The conversation was going nowhere, and Susanna was irritated. Pushing her sunglasses up on her forehead, she grimaced a tart smile. "Very interesting, Mr. Yefimov, but Volodya and I must see the churches and the old monastery. We must get going."

Yefimov gulped another cognac, sensed her discomfort, and again reached for her hand. "My dear Susanna, the market has always been in my blood. Like you, I'm a business person by nature. Even in university, in Soviet times, I managed to survive by trading anything—timber, coal, oil. Now something very interesting for you. My specialty, fur business! Russian mink, fox, sable."

Mikhail grunted and reached for the cardboard suitcase.

"I have absolutely the best quality sable pelts and the best furrier in Moscow to make a splendid coat for you. This furrier sews only for Kremlin wives. The Bargozin *shuba*, best in the world, will be glorious. Imported linings, your name in Latin letters. All you need to bring him is American label and wear it out through customs this winter." Zhenya had delivered Susanna for Mikhail's greatest deal, and perhaps Yefimov's and his own promotion in the KGB. "Five hundred American dollars! About two percent of the price for a sable coat in best New York store, *Berkdoff Gutman!*" He swished a pelt softly against Susanna's cheek. "You don't have to pay now. I will deliver to Moscow, and you can pay, how you say, 'C.O.D.'"

She smiled. "I don't know much about furs, but the pelts almost have an inward glow. They seem so light and so lustrous."

Zhenya, excited, smiled. "There once were sables, mink, and other fur animal pelts worth gold! But Siberia has been over-hunted. Now big fines for poachers but not enough control. Hunters earn more with each sable skin they can steal. This is a great chance for you!"

Deciding that this was a once-in-a-lifetime opportunity that she would have to miss, Susanna was diplomatic. "I must think about your offer tomorrow on our majestic lake expedition." Rather than worry about inbred anti-Semitism, she preferred to remain sensitive to Mikhail's words about kindness and love. She smiled brightly and held out her hand. "*Poka*, Mikhail Andreyevich. Huge thanks. It certainly looks like Volodya will be in touch with you after our trip to the monastery and Baikal."

Zhenya muttered something to Yefimov, and he mumbled to Zhenya that the deal would be a *bucksy* fiasco. Both were dismayed about the loss of a sale, and Zhenya would have no way to accuse Susanna of hard-currency speculation.

Volodya and Susanna waved another good-bye and took off through the winding streets, wandering through many lanes of the village on the way to the old church and monastery.

Surprised that she had reacted so sensitively to Mikhail's remarks about Jews, Volodya explained apologetically, "We have hundreds of years of Jew-hatred in Russia, and feel comfortable with it." He smiled.

"You don't understand, Volodya. The war against the Jews destroyed our lives. In Poland my parents were assimilated, a special class of Jews admitted to universities on a minuscule quota—doctors, lawyers, engineers. In America, they owned a grocery store. My father was clinically depressed, the ground beneath him always threatening to collapse."

On their right, the immense blue lake, legendary and mysterious, occupied the entire space clear to the horizon. On the left, exquisite woodcarving and microscopic embroidery on shutters and doors filled the town's houses, some sunk halfway to their eaves in permafrost.

Susanna asked Volodya to slow his pace. She was spellbound by the beauty of the walk, breathing in the air of the tall pines, scrub oak, and juniper. She sometimes held onto Volodya's arm for balance, feeling more upset and vulnerable. Suddenly, tears welled up in her eyes.

"I am sorry about your friend Boris," he said, "and the death of your little boy at home. *Chornye polosa*, black streaks from home, continue here with Boris." Volodya finally made eye contact, the smallest and most important gesture. They were walking slowly on a worn path that ran by a narrow river. In the distance, a rooster was strutting and crowing. They stopped for the sheep; the rams had bells around their necks and made a heavy clank as they walked, driven along by a scruffy sheepdog running ceaselessly around them—a serene scene out of a Dutch painting.

"Yes," she said, "Peter was a very special child, and I was open to giving and receiving love. He was gorgeous. Blond curly hair, aquiline nose, open smile, sparkling and mischievous eyes. Peter provided the tenderness and joy absent from my marriage, and his death was also the end of the marriage."

"Human sorrow is as great as the human heart," Volodya

murmured.

"I so hoped that the black streaks would somehow be lifted here."

Volodya returned her gaze.

"And the immense pressures of a divorce," she added. "My parents thought it was the end of the world. They had been professionals in Europe and here they owned a grocery store. I had to compensate for their greenhorn status. Ending my marriage to a doctor was devastating to them."

He was relieved that she had shifted the subject to ordinary divorce, and smiled. For a moment, he understood, took a tense breath, and responded, looking for more familiar ground, "Divorce—that's nothing so terrible. Here, we divorce many times for many reasons. For Russians, marriage, like all of life, is characterized by wild lurches from one extreme to the other. I have many friends, all with broken marriages. For ordinary Russians, life is stark, without pleasure. No theater, no music, no concerts, no books—the gap is filled with vodka and animal sexual release. Our life is destined for suffering. We marry only for a better apartment, a *propiska*, a job with better connections, opportunities.

Romance and romantic love, sexual advances, come only in courtship. Later, only envy, lust, and greed. Wife beatings follow."

"Well, at home it's very different. We have wealthy clients, shrewd divorce lawyers, bitter fights. The guilty party can be milked dry and left penniless. There are issues of adultery, betrayal, alimony, negligence, child support, financial assets and liabilities."

"For Christ's sake!" Volodya burst out in exasperation. "What was the problem? Doctors have a great life in America, lots of money—not like here."

"Well, Volodya, I knew about my husband's busy professional and business life in Manhattan, the parties and entertaining in the penthouse apartment, but I had only recently stumbled upon his double life—rumors and innuendos about his affair with his secretary, other entanglements, other women."

Volodya, sensing her urge to continue, took her hand again. She did not snatch it away. She leaned against him as they sat on a rock bench near a stream shimmering with sunlight. She breathed in the air warmed by the sun and scented by pine. "I've been maimed by lightning too many times. We were strangers living under the same roof. My separation and the discoveries, the deception—all devastating. I'm still trembling with rage."

"In real life, very bad things happen." Volodya clasped her hand tighter.

"You are my friend and my psychiatrist now, and I must go on." She glanced at him again and emptied her soul. It was easier with Volodya because she was not emotionally involved. He was a stranger but also a good friend. It was as if she had been writing her memoirs on this trek.

"Our marriage had long been over, but the death of our young child separated us permanently. We couldn't endure each other's pain. Death and grief replaced the boy and filled the house. The music stopped. His room, the garden, dogs, neighbors' children, a mirage of the past . . . a bad and frightening time that never ends." Tears flowed, and she was embarrassed, raising her hands to cover her face.

Volodya tried to distract her. "Look to the right! Birds flying toward the lake. The scent of pine and the warm sun— so peaceful here! Siberian miracles of nature."

"But Volodya, you don't understand. He stopped sleeping with me, blamed it on his arthritic hip. It was simple—other women, his place in New York! There were some good fights, but he talked about a 'European marriage,' '*liaisons dangereuses.*'" Suddenly she stopped in mid-conversation and fell silent and squeezed his hand again. "I was forty-six! In my prime! And Fred a womanizer and a manic-depressive. He committed a crime by withdrawing from me sexually, and the marriage was finished."

Volodya couldn't understand the issues she was struggling to explain. "Yes, he is rich, virile, and attractive, and brilliant, but his illness made his life crippling and suicidal. He could have done without such elaborate games and lies." Susanna shuddered.

"I can't believe the story. You are a beautiful woman! Men are always attracted to you. Even I find you desirable! A hot potato!" He looked into her eyes with an open smile. "Just here, divorce is *normal'no*—a *propiska* is just another piece of paper—but you married for a different '*propiska*'—for a luxurious life, country clubs, a house in the suburbs, like Hollywood movies."

"Friends advised I should look more desirable, sexier, use better makeup. My psychiatrist said that my anger and rage were emasculating him! Since the doctor rarely uttered a word, I believed him and was more confused than ever. Estrangement, no intimacy for a long time, only the logistics of business meetings, school conferences, dinner parties. I was always frustrated, always angry. We separated, and I partitioned my life into small compartments. I stayed across the Hudson and traveled to Moscow for 'love' with Boris and 'work' with GMG. Volodya, from the waist down, Fred was always limp for *me*."

And Volodya finally understood.

"GMG and Russia," she went on, "offered instantaneous glory. Commuting to Moscow, meeting interesting people, Russia was a dream come true. I was young and had no sense of self-worth. I was narcissistic and self-centered—my parents demanded that I be successful by marrying a doctor and I was forced to deliver. I wanted to be the center of every orbit that I entered."

"I don't understand. You really wanted to be here, when so many Russians are looking to leave?"

"Yes. I believed that I'd won the sweepstakes! My studies and my life were wrapped up in Russia, my love affair with Boris, Russia's history and culture, attending balls, concerts, theater, and diplomatic receptions, and finding antiques."

IN THE DISTANCE, THE WHITEWASHED WALLS of the monastery, the intense blue of its cupolas and golden crosses sparkling in the sun, beckoned.

A hallowed place, it was cut off from the modern world, a shrine to be reached only on foot. She sensed that she was distracted, traveling back in time, in the company of angels stroking her cheek. She remembered winters at home: Peter touching the sleeve of her jacket, playing with the soft and sensuous fur. She would forever miss this child, his laughing eyes, his gentle hands, and open smile. She often noticed and was arrested by blue-eyed Slavic boys his age. One would stand before her, resembling the child death had suddenly torn away. But looking a little closer, the aura of mystery would vanish, the hair still curly, but the blue eyes narrower, the lips thicker, the laugh different. But, never disillusioned, she was grateful for the chance to look at a boy who resembled him.

Soon they reached the very old church of St. Nicholas abutting the monastery, another masterpiece of ecclesiastical architecture evoking a hazy, half-mythical, ancient era where Moscow rose as Russia's unifier and despot. Reading the two tablets at the entrance, she realized that they were in the company of some of Russia's greatest writers, who had come to mysterious Lake Baikal in search for Russian consciousness, the Russian soul. Russia's spirit, and her best music, had been poured into her churches.

The service was very long, and the liturgy induced a trancelike, spiritual ecstasy. No pews, no order; a people's liturgy; people walking around stopping at icons, lighting candles and praying, searching for transcendence of suffering in this world. Beautiful chants and choral song followed. The singing became more energetic and joyful with lights, brightness, candles sputtering everywhere. Dense clouds of incense hung in the air around the worshipers.

She was there for spiritual rebirth, a clinic for the soul— they stood with the other faithful as priests emerged dramatically and disappeared behind the gilded iconostasis. Heavenly singing, bright candles burning, gold banners and icons everywhere, and an overwhelming scent of incense had created an atmosphere of intense religious emotion, while she prayed to a God she didn't believe in and lit many candles at the icon of Mary, who had also lost a son.

They lingered on the peaceful and silent grounds outside, and as they neared the monastery, men in monks' robes appeared in the courtyard and stared at them. She was relaxed and comfortable, as if she could stay there for a very long time. Volodya took her to a gnarled wooden bench. "I hear," he said, "clairvoyants are making a big comeback even in Moscow, and many of them are impostors, out just for the money. Not Brother Georgy! You must see him! He in fact does communicate with the spiritual world, and calls down spirits to dispel bad energies for you, your family, and your work. He sorts out problems with personality, sleep, and digestion. The best of the mediums and masters of the occult in Siberia, a holy man renowned, a hermit monk offering divine grace, an odd mix of Shamanism and Russian orthodoxy. He will intercede for you, even though you are not a *verushchaya*, one of us."

"I have no problems with sleep or digestion, but I am desperate for divine intervention with Norilskmetal."

Susanna tied the white embroidered kerchief on her head that she had just bought in a shop, and sat waiting on a low bench with other supplicants.

After some time, they entered. The simple hut, with a two-sided roof, teepee-like, covered with strips of birch bark, had log columns for walls also covered in bark, and a log foundation protruding to form a porch.

The inner sanctuary lay in darkness, with only candles sputtering at icons, and a small ground fire directly under the roof opening, keeping away mosquitoes and evil spirits. An assistant in the corner was softly beating a drum as the monk entered the sanctuary.

Brother Georgy was a specialist in the human soul and its destiny. Wearing a long white caftan, he resembled God himself. He seemed all authority, strength, and compassion. He was already in the far-beyond, in a trance, when he motioned to Susanna to sit opposite him, face to face. He crossed himself several times and took her hand, looking intently at her palm for lifelines, then sharply into her eyes, and he spoke a Russian difficult to understand. Volodya reworded the speech, imitating Brother Georgy's occult soliloquy and singing tone: "Child, there has been too much harshness in your life, but Christ will lead you through suffering and give the truth you seek." He looked up and crossed himself again. "You are a spirit divided between desire for peace and adventure, between ambition and tranquility. You cannot grasp God with the human mind," he chanted. "You have to absorb the external energy into your heart, the university of your soul, you know."

"But my heart is broken, and my work has been destroyed, Brother Georgy," she whispered plaintively.

"The majesty and mystery of Baikal, imparted by the presence of God, in revelations of nature, in prayer, in song, will give you energy, and you will live a long time." The room felt wobbly, the fire very hot, the candles spinning.

"Grief is given to all, but mourning leads us back to life and spiritual peace. Among the dark turmoil of this world, above which human souls swirl, I begin to understand you and your destiny. Pray with me again tomorrow, and the spirits will tell us more. You must be hopeful. May God hold you in the palm of his hand!"

"Interest in the occult is often an indication of an unstable personality," Susanna remarked jokingly as she and Volodya left.

"You know, I was just thinking the same thing myself."

On their way out he mentioned that the aboriginal clans of Siberia believed in many gods: for water, fire, fishing, and hunting. It was the ancient religion of his ancestors. "Brother Georgy is considered one of the best shamans in Russia. His people deify the universe and nature and punish crimes against her. He is both a Christian and a pantheist. The church and the Soviets outlawed these people as witch doctors. But they were physicians, priests, and prophets."

Susanna was moved, composed and calmer for the first time about Norilsk. Finally realizing that she had little control over future meetings with the ministry, she changed the subject. "You know, the brother's teepee is similar to indigenous Indian constructions. How do you know so much about the natives here?"

"We learned about them in university. I earned a 'five' in my social anthropology exam. Yes, more than a hundred years ago, Russian missionaries tried to destroy them. Later, Stalin killed many and sent them to the gulag, but somehow they survived and adjusted. Brother Georgy's religion is an odd mix of both faiths, using icons and nature worship side by side. Your eyes have already softened, Susanna. Remember what Brother Georgy said. You will see, good things will happen."

So Volodya had been right about Sacred Baikal. The village of Listvyanka, Kapitalina's hotel, and the lake itself had turned out to be a spectacular weekend stop.

When the airplane rose the next day they could see the sunset and evening twilight, and endless forests all around. Susanna focused on the beautiful and glorious lake below, all blue, blue, blue . . .

18

HEAVY METAL

A SLOW, STEADY SUMMER RAIN HAD fallen over the city—gray stone, gray sky. Returning to her office, Susanna glanced at Valya, the secretary, who gave her a certain look when she walked in. Susanna responded by raising both hands to her temples. She sat ramrod straight on the chair, sadness in her eyes, and watched people in the street below. She forced herself to go back to work but couldn't. She drank coffee at her desk and fiddled with the crossword puzzle in the *Moscow Times*.

Making little headway there, she found three of the five animals in the picture puzzle, then turned to the entertainment pages, consulted the theater announcements, and discovered a play she and Dima could see that evening. Thankfully, he had returned to Moscow to follow the crisis and confirm their scheduled meetings.

The first, at the Ministry of Trade, Committee of the Russian Federation on Nonferrous Metals, was strategically the most important for Susanna. All the major players supporting the GMG project were there.

The ministry itself was all old Soviet splendor. Men with briefcases were waiting nervously in the reception hall, occasionally getting up and circling the space, as Susanna and Dima hurried up an imposing marble staircase covered with miles of red carpet.

A clerk led them to Room 10, where the hush of state prevailed—magnificent high ceilings, chandeliers, windows looking down on the quiet, slate-colored Moscow River; a long, gleaming mahogany table and plush red armchairs—a lovely room spoiled by a hissing steam radiator covered by a grille, and the smell of stale cigarette smoke. William Burke, of the GMG Russian-American Bank in Moscow, Philip Dunlop, and another official of the Trade Council and State Department were already seated when Susanna and Dima entered.

Another twenty minutes went by before the Russians, in severe dark suits, showed up with dossiers in hand. They sat silently, stoically, holding their cards very close to their vests—a powerful presence.

Formal and correct, the parties introduced themselves. Business cards, Cyrillic on one side and Roman on the other, were exchanged and studied, as the Russians spread out the many dossiers. One unfamiliar business card identified an official from the economic secretariat in the Kremlin, another, Dr. Valentin Kotchetkov, former minister of energy and natural resources, now CEO of Norilskmetal. After sifting through all the particulars, dug from their briefcases, Dima introduced GMG, the company's multinational activities, the history of the Norilsk project, and their contractual agreements. Another folder of documents detailed GMG's invest-ment of $100 million, already spent on modernization and re-furbishing; a history of the company's negotiations; and contracts signed with Norilskmetal. These contracts were guaranteed by the Russian Central Bank in return for the No-rilskmetal sale of three tranches of palladium over three years, at agreed-upon fixed prices.

The first quantity had been delivered as agreed, Dima re-ported. GMG had hedged all three to offset the investment and price risk for future delivery. The contract was watertight and metal-proof, and dollars had been transferred, and con-sultants and engineers had arrived earlier to begin retrofitting the infrastructure. Already, higher-capacity, more efficient equipment had been installed. "When changes in emission standards for automobiles in developed countries were legis-lated causing an unprecedented spike in demand for the con-tracted metal, palladium, the second and third contracted quantities were not delivered. Vast capital outlays have caused losses of more than $200 million to Western banks, stockhold-ers, and our principals."

Silence followed, and more shuffling of dossiers. Susanna was anxious and distressed. This group was not the Russians she nostalgically remembered from Soviet times when there was camaraderie and laughter at restaurants, the Bolshoi, or Van Cliburn competitions. The president of the trade council continued, "Metal companies like Norilskmetal typically raise financing internationally and have always provided a good margin of safety on exposure to global financial markets and for institutions such as ours, EBRD and the IMF.

"Large commercial firms like GMG and European partners need to be assured of the price they will receive," he explained, "by hedging their positions in the futures market. This has been an established practice for commodities for centuries."

"Especially since Norilskmetal is a state-supported entity, their contracts are binding," added the director of the commercial section of the State Department, nodding to Susanna and the others with a pleasant smile. She made no attempt to disguise her mounting anger. She wasn't about to let this one go.

Dima went on, "The Central Bank, a sovereign entity, countersigned deliveries of palladium. Our engineers and consultants spent a week above the Arctic Circle in Norilsk. The construction team was ahead of schedule and on budget. Under the terms of our agreement any disputes are to be settled by an international arbitration panel!"

"Yes!" she angrily seconded.

Belayev, the minister, coughed, lit a cigarette, and retorted in halting English, "Duma has set up a commission to investigate voucher privatization and auctions of Norilskmetal, and the regional courts began their own investigation earlier in the year. There is a question whether the region should control the combine in which the government has a strategic interest. The commission needs clarification on the problem."

The deputy minister added in perfect English, "Foreigners are meddling in Russian internal affairs. Your consultants and reformers, including banks, are simply an elaborate plot, hatched especially by the U.S., to destroy Russia as a superpower."

Belayev put one dossier aside, opened another, and hunted around for what he wanted. Susanna saw a stony expression on his face that was more frightening than his words. She also noticed the impression of an official stamp, made with a red ink pad, at the upper corner of each page.

"Russia's strategic assets in Siberia's permafrost must be controlled by the state. All our natural resources, from gold to nonferrous metals, diamonds, uranium, as well as our fields of natural gas, are our *sovereign wealth*. Norilsk has been a source of power and profit, but none of its profits stay in this country! We have more gold than South Africa, and we can pump more oil than Saudi Arabia."

Suddenly, Dr. Bobkov, the chief engineer and the only face Susanna recognized from Norilsk, spoke up. "Of course, we must recover our sovereignty and control, and GMG may choose a supportive relationship with Norilsk, or be accused of embezzlement and industrial espionage against the Russian State—unexpected and disruptive events, flooding in shaft construction, and late delivery of equipment for surface installations."

"Our industrial and mining engineers," said Dima, glaring back, "produced the strategic information for retrofitting the ones who failed to deliver the metal."

"In any case, our regional courts cannot claim jurisdiction for the sovereign state," Belayev remarked in his dullest voice. He scooped up a sheaf of documents from another folder, which he passed to Dima, splattered with stamps like blotches across a modern work of art. Leafing through the pages to check the dates, Dima realized that large sums had been siphoned off to interested parties in other places, accounts unknown, not reported to GMG. Money was often funneled as loans to businesses controlled by unknown parties and laundered through banks and foundations to an orphanage in Norilsk, the arts cooperative in Chukotka, the Siberian Ballet in Krasnoyarsk, the Ethnic Museum Fund #3 in Kaluga. Terra Incognita!

Dima remained cool about the inside information discovered and looked up at Belayev with the mesmeric gaze of a cobra. "*Force majeure* is enforceable by any legal entity, in any international court, especially the Hague."

He casually closed the file and returned it.

"I think that's all for today," Belayev said.

As days progressed, more meetings followed with men in dark suits, but Kulichkov never reappeared. Both Dima and Lev predicted the failure of negotiations in Room 10. *Russia cannot compromise her sovereignty.* The intense and deliberate calm of the men in dark suits remained terrifying. Susanna's difficult and deliberate work on the project had done no more than suck her into a scam, and Hanken's "opening" of Russia was a delusion. *Russia's strategic industries are Russian.* Susanna's thoughts did not run consecutively, but rather swept over her in waves of experience and intuition. She understood that Belayev's administration was polarized, and that his ministry was a monolith, controlled by the Kremlin. She concentrated on meeting Belayev's gaze.

"We are not familiar with hedging strategies. Please draft a report about this problem which we will study. I don't understand," Dr. Kotchetkov deliberately remarked. "When we reach conclusions, we will issue a formal communiqué to Mr. Hanken and your board of directors." That was his only comment that day.

Susanna looked at him straight in the eyes, fiercely, with a sort of restrained fury. "We will sue and block your decision in international court."

"Of course we'll be speaking with you again soon," he remarked, smiling.

Dima preempted Susanna's sense of failure. "We know who you are," he said in a deathly calm, "and what you are doing, and you will be held legally accountable."

Again, she and Dima were the first to leave the ministry and Room 10, savaged and frustrated. She was earnest. She was intelligent. She was determined. She had that quality Volodya called *"klass"*, and fortitude, but was distraught. Her angry green eyes were lit with humor when she thought of what Boris would have said. *"They will do anything they want to do—you cannot stop them."*

"There is such intense pressure from within the system," she observed, *"criminals* working the ministries, that justice is almost impossible. The inquiry Belayev referred to will be carried out by the same officials responsible for the breach of contract."

"Yes, the Kremlin is mounting the guillotine, and GMG's will be the first head to roll. Everything has been said to you before, Susanna," Dima muttered. "I'm sorry your head has been a whirlpool of personal disasters. You have lost your sense of reality, and have been obsessed with success. Norilsk was your illusion; it would *never* happen. Not enough due diligence. Remember what our Siberian friend Johnny told us last winter. The fish rots from the head. Thanks, anyhow, for getting me back here to earn money. Remember. I have three kids. But I am as clueless as you are. Russia will never change. Communism has imploded, and comprehensive vertical embezzlement has filled the vacuum. There are no road maps here."

"Our huge investment has gone down a black hole of crime and corruption," Susanna barked. "There must be someresolution to this. Johnny also talked about Russia's need to be saved." She was still in denial. "He said, 'We have to hunt down the thugs, jail the bandits, and rule justly!'"

"When he was very drunk, remember," Dima pointed out with humor.

SEPTEMBER, AND MOSCOW'S POPLARS STOOD RED and gold in the fresh autumn air. A friendly September sun, a bright and brilliant yellow *babye' leto*, grandma's summer—a bittersweet lick of warmth that arrived after the peasant women brought in the harvests and the city savored the last gasp of outdoor comfort in squares around the Bul'var. The days were briefer, the weather often erratic, with showers during the day and false sunlight blazing in puddles and raising vapor from pavements. Susanna glanced at her watch as she sat uncomfortably at a low table in a café, waiting for Lyova again. She was drinking too much and had already ordered a scotch for him.

Yes, *ranshe bylo luchshe.* Earlier times were better. In the old days work had been bureaucratic and boring but stable. Her business in Moscow relied on her negotiations, contracts, pricing, and shipments. She had been treated like royalty, entertaining mandarins and *apparatchiks* in half-empty Soviet restaurants. They were her "friends." And there were concerts and recitals; festive and interesting evenings occupying the best parterre seats at the hallowed Bolshoi; intermissions with champagne and good caviar; and souvenir photographs while promenading around the white grand piano with important *nomenclatura.*

"Sorry I'm late again!" declared Lev as he rushed in. "More crises with expatriates and locals. Another civil war with *kryshas.* Russia has become a country of racketeers and extortionists, and the criminal underworld bears the stamp of the political system." He squeezed her hand. "One of my Russian clients in Saratov was just found in a pool of blood by a driver hired by my company. The Saratov police are investigating." He was sullen, his mouth twisted into a tight sneer. "Murderers and extortionists! A rival criminal syndicate gang wants the company's German business."

"The criminal underworld bears the stamp of the political system," Susanna flatly repeated, "the same system that murdered Boris and stole three hundred million from my company. Indirectly or directly, you are part of that—a gigantic mob family that rules this country."

Lyova was irritable. Scanning her face, he barked, "Moscow has alienated the masses both here and in the hinterland. The average Russians are left out of it. The small Western-oriented elite that pushed for liberal reforms, and *your* chief, have gotten us into this mess, bought into our new democracy, our 'free market potential.'"

"You are proof, Lev. Boris's murder and GMG's losses *are the same.* You must have been a fly on the wall during my many discussions in Room 10 of the Ministry. You just summed up their legal argument. Yes, Hanken wanted the Russian business, and I encouraged him. I didn't do enough due diligence. Between my chief and the need for success here, I consciously and conveniently compromised morality, and I helped him buy into this very costly game."

"You know history, Susanna. Moscow alienated the masses both here and in the hinterland long before Yeltsin.

Nothing has changed for centuries. Bribery and embezzlement have been traditional in Russian public life since the Tatar yoke and Peter the Great. Bribes were routinely accepted as a means for private profit. Officials have been paid little or no salary. The fact is, civil servants have always made their living by accepting bribes. They not only accepted them but actively solicited them. Certain sums will prevent problems. Yeltsin's cronies and 'American boys in shorts' lured your boss and GMG for badly needed foreign investment."

"Yes, the average Russians were always left out." She made a crying fool of herself whenever she saw Lev. "*Perestroika,* just a cosmetic change, and the new democracy a fabrication." The Norilsk project had become her personal fiasco as well as the financial tsunami that had already sent shock waves throughout the commodity markets.

She blamed herself, of course. Her eyes had always been open, but she was emotionally blinded. Unconscionable in her position in Russia.

"I think you have got to smile, dear. Someone is paying

attention here, and we must leave." Across the street, his eye caught two men sitting smoking in a gray Zhiguli. He quickly looked away, put a finger to his lips, helped Susanna out of her chair, and left dollars on the table.

IT WAS ALREADY MORNING IN NEW YORK, and an international financial storm had struck the likes of which the city had not seen for decades. The world of money was in upheaval. The brave new digital world was becoming global. Moscow's trading offices were spreading rumors and hedging their bets. News that GMG had been defrauded by the Russian State had lit up telephone boards across the globe like a clear starry night in the Rockies. Men in shirtsleeves were obsessed with screens and phones. In trading rooms across the world, numbers on screens changed with the speed of sound, driving platinum-group metals higher. Raging volatility reigned in equity markets as funds were rushed out of commodities and investors were forced to sell to meet margin calls.

The insiders reported that GMG was involved in a Wall Street takeover play. It was the first time the Street had turned and attacked its own. Customers were calling with questions about the storming and mutilation of GMG by heartless predators. The plain fact was that a combination of market forces, Russian failure of delivery, and gross mismanagement in GMG had driven the multinational to disaster.

19

NOVEMBER RAIN

BRUISED SKY WAS HANGING LOW and heavy over Moscow in the last days of autumn—blankets of yellow leaves everywhere, swept about by wind and a steady cold slanting rain. Early darkness, and twilight at noon, weighed heavily on houses, parks, squares, and streets. People with umbrellas hurried home down boulevards, past bare trees and gray stone.

The heavy rain was drumming steadily on the roof of Volodya's Lada as Susanna ran toward her apartment building, pulling her coat tighter against the chill and dripping trees. Near the building's entrance, a neighbor was being pulled along by a dachshund in a sweater. The dog sniffed Susanna and the pavement—but her neighbor simply looked through her as if she didn't exist. Rude, the Muscovites, she thought.

Moscow had become a city of shadows. Although the death itself was still being 'investigated,' the case of Boris's had 'de facto' been closed. Dima had been supportive and kind when he boarded the flight home. "Remember, it's not you, Susanna. You cannot take it personally. That is the way the justice system works in Russia. Byzantine bureaucracies, corrupt law enforcement, behind a government scheme to steal millions from one of their most prominent investors."

The week felt as if it would never end. The apartment, always a refuge, home away from home, had lost its charm and became a strange domicile in a foreign city. She was being squeezed to death by loneliness and often marooned in silence. Over the last days, a picture of Susanna's life at home had begun to form before it disappeared again. Her world was collapsing. She was in her apartment waiting to advise Hanken that she had broken the lease for the office in the Slavyanskaya and had safely removed and shredded important files, and was ready to board the Delta flight on Saturday. With a bad migraine, blood throbbing, she was again so afraid that she had to drive her fingernails into her palms to hold herself together.

She turned on the Culture Channel and watched an old version of *Giselle* while shuffling though a dated *New Yorker*. Thankfully, she found some relief in fantasy. She put the magazine down. Daydreaming about Boris, she imagined what it would have been like to be with him again— afternoons in hotel beds, their hours together always stimulating, exciting, passionate. "We were made for each other—you are the only man in the world I've loved," she would say, a melancholy sigh in her voice. "We must stay together." Stay together had meant, she supposed, a life of afternoons in her apartment, hotels, long weekends skiing in the Carpathians, summer getaways to beaches in the Adriatic, making love on a yacht in Trieste harbor, and occasional dinners in out-of-the-way restaurants in Moscow. She had never imagined it would turn out this way. The tables had turned. She had been made a fool. Used, manipulated, deceived, not for the first time, and not the last. The pulse of evil, and the unending flight from it, had turned her life on its side in a world gone wrong, struck by the deadliest of missiles at home, and again in Moscow. Lightning, three times! Her mission was over. The curtain had fallen. She'd stayed too long, was trapped and tired and eager to go home to America—free at last! She knew she must somehow find balance again and get back to normal, whatever that was. She was fighting the Russian State for GMG at great risk to herself.

And she was waiting for Lev, again. It was five o'clock and the lights were on already, one more day without a glimpse of sun. One wouldn't have suspected it was still there, behind a thick layer of angry-looking clouds. He was delivering plane tickets for Saturday. She had her American passport and was counting on his help to get out. She was impatient. She had hesitated, picked up and dropped the telephone, looking into the dark square for a sign of Lev, when finally she noticed a figure hurrying through the courtyard. She was already at the door when the elevator cage rumbled and the doorbell pealed. He kissed her and took a step back. She clasped his hands.

Curtains drawn, the room dimly lit, they sat comfortably with drinks and *zakuski*, with a salad she had managed to prepare already on the table. Large tears started rolling again. Her momentary weakness angered her, and she collapsed against the chair, agitated, ambivalent, but happy to see him.

"Ah . . . the ministry and the state are concerned with press releases. Disturbances in Norilsk are 'dangerous for your health' and 'inconvenient' for future foreign investment."

"I understand," she whispered anxiously.

"Calm down, Susanna. At this point, you are only under government surveillance, a 'person of interest' to the Kremlin, and not classified as a traitor or a 'foreign agent.'"

"Hold it right there, Lyova! What do they want?"
"Belayev and his ministry have become the very emblem of 'Russia Resurgent.' They just want to make sure your company is observing the rules that no other foreign company here is going to rock the boat. No more 'leaks' and syndicated publicity about Norilsk. You cannot win."

"Their games have worn me out. We can bring in more outside help." Her mouth was set hard, her look determined, close to defiant.

Lev's eyes narrowed in a parody of suspicion. "What do you mean, 'outside help?'"

"The FBI? Scotland Yard? They've said repeatedly they are ready to help if we need them."

"You must be joking," he sneered. "Your tickets are here, and you will get out."

"And you are only here to help with the logistics," she whispered sarcastically. She looked at him, expecting a glance of empathy, understanding. She was ravenous for affection, tenderness, but she had known all along that Russia was an escape from trauma at home, and that, with Boris dead, Lev was only a safety net. A fairy tale in reverse, again? She wanted Lev to make love to her, to spend the night. She had grown very fond of him, and he had given her a special place in his life. She couldn't go on without him now. She had long since crossed the wasteland of loss, betrayal, and misunderstanding, and survived.

Studying her face, he replied, "How can you say that, Susanna? You know how much I care for you, and how devoted I am to you. I cannot abandon you." He almost smiled, but she wasn't sure whether it was a smile of goodwill or derision.

"Remember Marshall and the Slavyanskaya joint venture? They are capable of violence. You have been commuting here for many years, you know the right people. If the Kremlin wanted to eliminate you, they would easily do so regardless of Volodya, GMG security, the State Department, Interfax News Agency, or brave reporters publicizing the Norilsk story."

"But I've been here for so many years. I've always liked it here. It's the loss of a return ticket to my youth—the Russia I love. Russian history, and the present, reveal themselves in glimpses—images of distant times flash into view, essences and illusions and people I shall never know.

"I believe in words, discourse, consensus, reason. This fiasco is a descent to the level of beasts. The schizophrenic Russian soul produces not only literary and musical geniuses, but people like Stalin."

"We are living," Lev whispered in a strangely calm voice, "on the underside of modern history. The old nomenclatura has deep pockets. They will always be in charge. The criminal underworld bears the stamp of the political system." He was terse and effective. His levity and mocking smile were never more than a façade for his demons. "And that's just the point. I don't think they care—never trust anyone, Susanna, especially the people you admire. Those are the ones who will make you suffer the worst blows."

"I'm afraid they've already tapped my office and home telephones, the office computer, and fitted an electronic limpet on Volodya's Lada. When he turns on the motor, he is afraid of an explosion."

"And they have also stuffed the car with ingeniously portable surveillance and audio equipment. Your comings and goings are being monitored at the Slavyanskaya—and here," Lev added, speaking softly.

Susanna reached gently for his hand, which was cold. She was asking for reassurance, which he provided by squeezing her shoulder. She seemed to draw courage from him, her smile dazed but grateful, irresistibly warm. He was worried that she might have a panic attack or break down, but when had he ever been able refuse a lady needing moral support. Much of her old forbearance was gone. He liked her and wanted to save her. Their affair had taken a turn mutually convenient for both and satisfying for her, especially now when she had to be kept, at any cost, from being arrested. Susanna needed to calm herself, and his only obligation was to seduce her. Moments of passion with him had become her only moments of escape, of revelation, of understanding life and herself.

"Susanna, watch your back. Think twice about what you are doing. Sometimes you behave like someone from another planet. You are causing too much trouble in Moscow and Norilsk. Too many business meetings with the EBRD, the IMF, and Philip Dunlop. Don't forget, your reporter friend Sveta is a recipient of the Human Rights Watch award, and is now filing reports on strikes, violence, and human rights abuses in Norilsk. Staying here, I sense a ticking bomb for you. They can still arrest you for tax evasion, or environmental violations, or worse. You may be involved in an explosion, or your car may be hit by a truck on the road, or drugs may have already been planted here, in your apartment, or in the office."

"I know," she replied, and silence fell between them.

"I was being followed from the airport when I returned from Norilsk, and tonight they tailed Volodya all he way to the Ukraina apartments."

His probing eyes suddenly looked into hers as she stroked his face. "No more conversations now. Forget Norilsk, your associates, and Boris. In this country, we are never surprised. No Russian is shocked by murder or dangerous business deals.

You are a great lady, trusting and impressionable. But if I may say so, you fight, and have the balls of a gorilla."

"Yes, that's me." She smiled graciously enough.

"I'm deadly serious. Look, I've explained to you, and you understand. I just cannot abandon you. Get out of Moscow. It's unsafe for you to be here. You are running great risks now. They want you out of Russia."

For a time, they were silent, and neither of them looked at a watch. Then she took off her sweater, her skirt, stockings, bra with lace trim, and soft-to-the touch ivory silk panties.

"As always, beautiful underwear," he said, a certain look in his eyes. "I like your panties, and in general, expensive women."

"Thank you."

Ashtray in hand, he was ingratiating and seductive. They lay in bed side by side in total silence. He only touched her face from time to time and he could feel the tension ebb from her body, as it did from his. Just being there filled her with happiness; suddenly she curled away and sat up, aware of the distance between them in that strange and hazardous world. His perceptive eyes met hers. "I will never leave you. I love you and will always protect you." He put his arm around her shoulder, pulled her close to him, but as dawn came, he slipped away.

No remorse. "Let them burn in hell for doing this." Only anger could stanch Susanna's fear. She was mumbling to herself as she crawled under the heavy quilts and tried to sleep.

20

CORPORATE CULTURE

SHEREMETYEVO LAY NORTH OF CENTRAL MOSCOW, some eighteen miles from the city—clogged during rush hour, but on Saturdays, when traffic was at its most reasonable, a journey of about forty-five minutes. Not that Saturday. A broken-down bus with a sports team heading to the airport had clogged the road with gridlocked cars, causing a huge traffic jam. "Between this bus and people still escaping to their dachas," said Lev, "we'll be sitting here for hours."

They were stuck in a line of cars, many honking their horns. Suddenly, two cars in front went into reverse, drivers gesticulating frantically for the car behind them to back up. A vast panorama of road rage followed, at times involving drawn weapons. A Russian *probka*, an enormous traffic jam. Since the flight was not for many hours, she was safe with time, and safer because of Lev.

The driver scowled and muttered, "As Gogol once said, Russia has two problems—fools and roads."

She was crying again. "Remember, lives of saints usually end in martyrdom," Lev said. She frowned and was still brooding when he gave her a complicit smile. You are in good company. Think of our geniuses—artists, writers, musicians— many forced into exile from their own country. There's no hope. The Russian State is a monstrosity, and Moscow a third-world megalopolis teetering on the edge of some spectacular extinction." Traffic still stopped, Lev climbed out to survey the gridlock and returned, slamming the door. "Hopeless," he sighed.

Two hours later, with a crowd of "volunteer specialists" working on the engine and others on the underside, the bus finally moved.

"Lev, I've been seeing the same car behind us from the time we got on this road. Somebody is following us, somebody you know, Lev?"

He tried to be discreet. "A friend, a CIA field agent. He is going to make sure you get to New Jersey safe and sound. Nothing else makes sense."

AT SHEREMETYEVO, THE DRIVER JUMPED OUT of the car, commandeered an empty baggage cart, and dropped Susanna and Lev at a long check-in and passport control line for the Delta flight.

"You are both angry and happy that I'm leaving."

"I care for you, Susanna, and you have become important for me. But you must hang up your traveling boots and settle for a less arduous life."

"Saying good-bye is breaking my heart."

Softly, he murmured, "Also for me, more. You are fortunate

enough to make it out of Russia alive. Don't even think about trying to make contact. We may never see each other again. I will take you as far as I can go." She thanked him as warmly as she knew how. He responded with a dignified nod. With what diffidence he could manage, he stepped forward and flashed his card, nodding humbly to the officers as they looked at Susanna for a moment and backed away. For further assurance regarding her safety, another wink and a nod, and Susanna passed through passport control. Fear began to lift from her chest.

"Many thanks," she said again in a strangled voice, and without a further glance she walked away toward to the dim lounge filled with silent expatriates waiting for the flight.

FINALLY SITTING UPRIGHT, STRAPPED IN, she watched Russia disappear as the plane lifted into the sky and clouds above. Dismal grayness was dropping away.

The Delta 767 was mostly filled with businesspeople going home after many ventures and challenges in Russia. The attendant in business class approached with a tray of champagne flutes, and Susanna raised one to herself, grateful that she was still alive, having survived the wasteland of murder and betrayal. When the attendant came around again, she ordered a double scotch to bring herself up to par.

Professional frequent fliers recognize each other by body language. She was sitting next to a drink-sodden expatriate and when she began speaking, realized that her voice was too high and needed to be brought down.

"Ah, hello!" Susanna said. "We're both going home!"

"There are thousands of us here, some hungry, others rich and idle expatriates, trust-fund babies looking for adventure. This is my last run! Stunning blondes, all English teachers, beautiful bars, *blinis* with caviar, but it's impossible to get anything going for my company. This country has no future! A business catastrophe!"

"Join the club," Susanna replied.

After more scotch and idle chitchat, her neighbor dozed off. Susanna began to evaluate her romance with Russia, the country she had been forced to leave, and the problems she was expecting in New York: past and present, indulgence and sobriety, joy and rigidity, narcissism and humility—her life a series of losses, betrayals, defeats, contradictions. *The heart believes in ideals, she told herself—in harmony, generosity, and you are passionate about the spirituality you discovered in Russia's churches, the lights of sputtering candles around icons, and you prayed to a God you didn't believe in.*

You loved Russia, where intellectual and philosophical discussions with friends and lovers were challenging and profound—a paper-thin stratum of frustrated intelligentsia, most of their families murdered by Stalin long ago.

Russia's internal contradictions fascinated and challenged. Maximalism, salvation and ruin, good and evil. Fascinating tales of heroic endurance that would make for engaging cocktail conversation with friends, regardless of one's ultimate compromises.

In the real world, her work was dangerously similar to Lev's. Their answer to Byzantine corruption was opportunistic compromise—to steal Russia blind—Lev for himself, Susanna for the fast track in GMG, bonuses, promotions, dangerous paths of love—amoral or worse—a concept confounding for a person trained in the humanities and the history of ideas. She remembered Siberia and Brother Georgy. Back to destiny and fate. Perhaps her life *was* in the palm of God's hand, and that was that.

CULTURE SHOCK AT JFK, BUT SHE was home. Again a dry run about her feelings of self-worth, her sense of kudos in GMG's master gamble for fortunes, and the huge fiasco of Norilsk.

By the time she made it back to the southern tip of Manhattan, she was aware that the conglomerate had fallen on hard times. The futures panic had reverberated through the markets, Norilsk's failure and gross mismanagement had catapulted GMG into trouble and thrown the world of money into upheaval. The firm was going through the most concentrated turmoil in its history. Hundreds of millions had been lost in commodities. The news was not completely unexpected to Susanna, since, before she left Moscow, the London office had wired a memo to Hanken and the board to conduct a review of businesses, and the CEO had wired back that "no decisions regarding personnel have been made." The opposite was true. The officers who peddled this line were either lying or ignorant. Susanna's instincts were confirmed when, on the weekend, an unnamed board member leaked a story to the *New York Times* that the firm was planning to fire a thousand people. For the first time, it was firing the smartest people, the best and the brightest for whom even yesterday did not exist, where the central code of behavior valued speed, risk, and cynicism over loyalty, responsibility, and commitment.

In a room about a third the size of a football field, traders sat elbow to elbow, forming a human chain. Between the rows of desks, there was not enough space for two people to pass each other without first turning sideways. This room was unusually silent, with anxious traders hunching forward in their chairs, trolling for press rumors about GMG and spikes in futures and derivatives.

She was jet-lagged and ill at ease when she found her chair in the long-assigned pecking order on the trading room floor. Hanken was doing his usual promenade when, suddenly, an internal memo flashed across the Quotron machines: "Failure of Russian palladium deliveries and events outside GMG's control have forced management to take quick action, cut back on staff, and prune intelligently."

Wall Street had turned and attacked its own "band of brothers." Susanna realized that she was a commodity herself and could be canned and sold like tomatoes. Senior management took the path of least resistance and fired the most recent additions to the office—a massacre of innocents, young people easy to sack. They had not yet built connections within the firm and had no voice. Once fired, they immediately lost the right to remain on the trading floor. A security guard would take their passes. Their arrogance and self-confidence was stripped, and they emerged shell-shocked. A few, when asked for their passes, told the security guard to "fuck off" and returned to the trading floor for a good deal of weeping and hugging—a most unusual sight, because no one ever cried on the trading room floor or showed any vulnerability or need for human kindness. In a rapid reign of terror, traders were banished from the building, escorted to the elevator dragging personal belongings, gym clothes, sneakers, and extra shoes.

Amid this turmoil, Hanken stopped by to personally welcome Susanna back. He waved his hand magisterially over the senior traders on her floor and smiled. "I don't understand what goes on inside their heads, so long as they create wealth for the firm." Good theater.

As always, he affected a statesmanlike calm, and since Susanna reported directly to the chairman, he invited her for tea and a debriefing the following day. His sangfroid was intense and deliberate. Susanna anticipated the worst because her sense of anxiety and panic were still raw.

The late autumn afternoon was fading when she appeared in Hanken's office at the appointed time. He was there alone, at his desk, jotting down notes on a yellow legal pad. He appeared empathetic when they sat down to tea. He started out with the usual remarks. "I've watched you closely since you joined us. I've been following your career. You may not have realized it, but I've taken a special interest in your development, and we have been satisfied with your challenging work in Moscow."

Wait a second, she thought. She knew that money was the absolute measure of one's value to the firm, that the Norilsk fiasco had cost the conglomerate, their stockholders, and official counterparts many hundreds of millions. It was a diplomatic waltz on Wall Street, this time.

He continued in a strained tone. "You acted very honorably. You were under tremendous duress, especially after the loss of a child. We're grateful for what you did for us, and we're aware of the cost to you, professionally and personally." Susanna lowered her eyes and trembled. She took a tense breath with an effort to maintain a brave front.

"You've done a good job for us. You've performed a valuable service. But even the little you know is too much. We can't let you wander around Russia and Europe with our intellectual property in your head. Much too dangerous, and too much liability for you and the firm."

His expression was glacial, his voice terse and effective. "If you honor your nondisclosure agreement, that should provide a full measure of compensation. On our terms, naturally—but the sum could be large."

It could have been worse. She was being forced to resign before she had the opportunity to quit, and float down the short distance to Earth.

Her severance payment was indeed generous, based on tenure. She could barely manage the closest thing to a smile when Hanken reached out to shake her hand.

EPILOGUE

A SHARP SCENT OF AUTUMN ON A SERENE and misty afternoon in New Jersey. She was exhilarated and grateful to be home. It was almost the peak of autumn leaves at their most beautiful—gold, deep russet, orange to pale lemon yellow—a riot of color on the hillside nearby, a kaleidoscope never visible in Russia.

She found dungarees and a plaid flannel shirt among her work clothes in a hall closet that still reeked of mothballs and emptiness, and walked to the dark wood shed abutting the garage. In a wooden crate, she came across the old gardening tools, many in disrepair, worn gloves and galoshes, and finally, her favorite bulb planter, trowel, and spade.

Rain had left the earth soft and moist, and the neglected garden, covered with weeds, dead leaves, and rubble was calling for help.

She worked the earth diligently and with her spade was able to split the soil with little effort. There was still enough time to dig in the tulip bulbs for spring that a neighbor had delivered as a welcome-home gift.

She had been at it for some time when she heard a noise and looked up to notice a familiar face, in a shiny red car with Virginia license plates rumbling into the driveway.

A smile came to her face, and she laughed. It was Philip Dunlop, in a black cashmere sweater. He walked toward Susanna. She stood back and gazed at him with approval. "Why, Philip, what a surprise! For heaven's sake, I knew you were back, but seeing you in my backyard—never!"

His face was flushed with excitement. "I missed you, so I am here to say hello."

With arms wide open, nodding like idiots in delight, they kissed and hugged tightly.

"Welcome back from the motherland," she declared. "I really didn't expect you to just drive in. I am only back a few days myself. How are you, and where are you?"

"Waiting for details about my new posting, and driving to see friends at Princeton tomorrow." He found the garden bench and asked Susanna to sit next to him. She beamed at him, and squeezed his shoulder again. "I've missed you! I was so overwhelmed with details, we never said proper good-byes in Moscow."

It was impossible to dislike Philip—that clear forehead surrounded by graying hair, those deep-set brown eyes, the straight nose and delicate, almost feminine mouth. She dismissed the thought of intimacy—which crossed her mind again—potentially good for his reputation.

"We must catch up on news," she said affectionately, but wanted another cuddle, so he provided it.

"But wait! Let me bring out some coffee, and a bottle of bison vodka, from the *pushcha* that I smuggled here."

"Remember, *Ya za rulyom*."

"Oh, I'm certain you'll be fine driving."

She emerged from the kitchen with an antique stenciled Russian tray with a coffee pot, mugs, a vodka bottle with bison grass floating inside, pretzels, and cookies. The mist lifted and, warmed by the afternoon sun, they sat close together.

"Your work in Moscow," he said at last, "was impossibly dangerous and trumped by the Kremlin from the get-go. We were afraid for your safety."

"Well, it's peaceful and quiet here, but I would go back in a heartbeat. Sadly, it's not going to happen. You must know that when all else failed, we opened a criminal investigation about Norilsk in Moscow. Here is how it went: We asked our detective to produce testimony about the charges. He flew to Norilsk but he was unable to question anyone. Our agent above the Arctic claimed to have lost the case materials. The regional judge overruled GMG and closed the case."

Philip munched on a poppyseed cookie and poured two half shots of vodka. Susanna noticed he was distracted. She clutched his upper arm and went on. "Dima returned to Moscow, and we appealed the case to the International Court in the Hague. The Kremlin ruled that giving broad access to shareholders is unconstitutional, and the case is still tied up with bureaucratic and legal issues that will go nowhere."

"Of course," he said. "Times changed. Yeltsin's so-called privatization is out of control. Your Norilsk project was the first test case. The Soviet empire morphed from our sworn enemy into a sordid kleptocracy with whom business can be done, but not the way GMG handled it."

She grimaced. "Right, a very successful lurch backward for us. In fact, the former minister of energy is now the chairman of Norilskmetal. He must be a man you know."

Philip nodded, made a sympathetic-sounding grunt, and reached out, pouring coffee into both mugs. "Russia behaves like Russia. Russia pursues its own hard-core national interests. That's realpolitik. Strategic enterprises are now off-limits. Natural resources are essentially owned by the state, and policies are in place to form huge state conglomerates that can compete with Western multinationals."

"Is there no light at the end of the tunnel?" she murmured. "No lesson for new democracies?" She was afraid to continue.

Philip raised his eyebrows, his eyes searching for hers. "Yes, our Russian friends only know how to feel depression, sadness, skepticism, and irony. Russia's unhappy fate is to show others how not to live. Susanna, stop carrying the weight of the world on your shoulders, always waiting for another ax to fall. You can talk to me. I won't hold anything against you."

"I've been fired, you know. But with an okay parachute."

She rose from the bench, kicking a pile of twigs she had gathered earlier. "Somehow, I'll sort out my life. No one lives happily ever after. What about you, Philip? Our life is as brief as autumn leaves. Get out there to the sun, get fit, savor life, live well."

"One more posting for me, Susanna. Looks like Nigeria next month."

"Congratulations!" she remarked sarcastically. "Russia without winter."

They reminisced about Siberia and Moscow, the artists and writers they both knew, museums, concerts, ballets, Spasso House receptions, Susanna's office and apartment. From time to time they lapsed into silences that spoke more intimately than words.

The Russian language has words for secrecy and loneliness, but none for privacy. Both needed someone to talk to, someone to listen, about the country that intrigued them. So they did both. Talked. Joked. Listened some more. He never mentioned his State Department work, and she made no further reference to Wall Street.

"How are my friends? Volodya, Valya? Last I heard, he was becoming a mogul in the customs business, and she is looking for another job. Ever run into Kulichkov or Lev, and what about Kalugin and the latest on Boris's murder?"

He hesitated and shook his head. "Kalugin, you know, wanted to get rid of the case. He ran through lists of suspects, pulling up mostly routine stuff—arson, theft, description of crime scene, injuries to victim. Mafia- type commercial crime. Finally, the housemaid Agafya's confession was the only evidence that counted, and the police closed the case. She was sentenced to a few months, or a year, for stealing paintings she didn't steal. She may be out already as we speak."

"A first-class display of law enforcement by Kalugin," Susanna sneered.

"But we have the information your friend Lev missed, and I wanted to see you immediately because ... because I knew you were still struggling with the loss—the murder, I mean."

"The pain is greater because of delusion—I realize that Boris was not the man he appeared to be."

"All off the record, of course, Susanna—our State Department is on the Garden Ring, and the walls of Spasso are magical and have their own electronic ears."

"I'm out of the loop, Philip."

"You know the joke—the Italian mafia plays cards, but the Russians play chess. Unfortunately, besides the art business, your Boris and Bablidze were both pawns in a serious Kremlin chess game, both on the same side, but the wrong one. Boris was skimming money manipulating Norilsk vouchers before selling them to Bablidze. Bablidze worked with the Kremlin to help plunder the spoils of post-Soviet Russia. He in turn fell out of favor because of greed and power. He refused to sell his shares back to the government and stay away from politics."

Susanna was surprised by the information.

"The . . . uh, the state is not used to people standing in its way. Bablidze and Boris were the kind of opposition the Kremlin needed to eliminate."

"This is monstrous," she muttered.

"I agree. Bablidze, on the other hand, already a billionaire, wanted *more* favors, *more* patronage, political leverage in the *Kremlin*. He was greedy and wanted *power*. He was the kind of opposition the state wants to annihilate. There was no other way out, for the government. And no amount of your energy, work, and tenacity would have changed it."

Susanna understood. "We may con ourselves into believing that Russia will change. It never will. Never, never, never."

The atmosphere had suddenly turned dark. Her features were burning with excitement. Philip's blue eyes fell on her now as she looked directly at him.

"No. Susanna, I've come to tell you something else as well. Our funny Uncle Fima, our court jester, not known as a bureaucrat, was very loyal to the state. A great scam artist, too— with no budget, no office. His *ukaz, his mission,* was to generate and facilitate your foreign investment in Norilsk, and keep the project moving forward with you, GMG, and his cronies. He started informing on you and GMG from the moment you returned. The dirty bastard is a master of the art of hiding large sums of money without Norilsk being able to trace them. He personally had, after all, to pay for all the information that was coming from a bunch of his friends, acquaintances, crooks, and misfits."

"No!" she shouted.

"Fima," he went on, "was in touch with Russia's security agents and intelligence officers across the country, constantly alert to the dangers and opportunities of the Norilsk project.

Remember, he was kept on a tight leash by them himself, and he supplied favors and requests to both sides."

She stiffened. Philip leaned across, took hold of her hands, and pulled her to her feet.

"The Kremlin wanted to force you out—not to eliminate you, but to prevent you from further meddling in the scam and their politics."

She sensed what was coming, and her stomach tightened. His eyes radiated purpose. "Uncle Fima was the spider in the middle of this web. Either he, or his contract killers, got rid of both Boris and Bablidze."

A tense silence followed. She couldn't process more and nodded faintly. Hardness invaded Philip's eyes. "Nothing good will ever come of Russia. When you were there, many thought that the new industrialist class would become a pillar of the state, replacing the Communist Party, the Red army, and the KGB. But Yeltsin is unable to maintain a reformist path. The security services have reemerged as always, a force to be reckoned with in society and business. The bosses must have order and stability before democracy."

"Shit."

"Yes," he went on. "In Russia, there are no business stories, no political stories, only crime stories. They laugh at Westerners who believe in progress, the rule of law, the goodness of men."

"Well, now what happens?"

"Nothing. The dogs bark, but the caravan moves on.

Democracy demands patience and a belief in the rule of law. The vertical structure of the Kremlin remains the same. Russia hopes to become a great empire again—an incomplete grandiosity, an authoritarian culture of judiciary corruption, lies, and deceit. That's what happens."

"I should be happy to be alive and home," Susanna replied.

A beautiful silence was settling between them, and he stroked her hand again. She needed that. Her passion was spent. She had no more ammunition, no more reserves. She was baffled; there was no redemptive value in suffering, and nothing happened by chance. But the world was full, and she was not ready to leave it.

About the Author

Author of the much-acclaimed memoir about the Holocaust, *The Eyes Are the Same,* Susan Gold received her B.A. in History from Brandeis University, and her M.A. in Russian Literature from the Russian Institute at Columbia University, where she later taught at the School for International Affairs, as well as at Fairleigh Dickinson University. She later served as a consultant for Russian business development for the Chase Manhattan Bank, rising to become Vice President of the American International Group (AIG), where she was chief representative of their trading office in Moscow. After retiring from AIG, she consulted for the International Agency for Development in Kiev, Ukraine.

As Churchill once said, "Russia is a riddle wrapped in a mystery inside an enigma." Russian history has always challenged and fascinated. This was especially true after the fall of communism, when Boris Yeltsin sought a future for a "democratic Russia." In this novel, Ms. Gold has written a tale of suspense in the time of the Oligarchs. She lives and writes in Englewood, New Jersey.

CPSIA information can be obtained at www.ICGtesting.com
Printed in the USA
BVOW07s1110060114

340916BV00001B/14/P